A TALE OF UN... OTHER
AND GOD'S ... US TIME

THE EVERLASTING FLAME

LINDA CHAIKIN

MOODY PRESS

CHICAGO

ISBN: 0-8024-2339-6

3 5 7 9 10 8 6 4

Printed in the United States of America

A TALE OF UNDYING LOVE FOR EACH OTHER
AND GOD'S WORD IN A DANGEROUS TIME

THE EVERLASTING FLAME

Matthew 7:7

In 1381 Wycliffe translated the Bible into English for the first time:

> "Axe ze and it schal be zoun to zou,
>   seke ze and ze schuln fynde."

In 1534 Tyndale hid from church authorities while risking his life to translate the New Testament from Latin into English:

> "Axe and it shal be given you;
>   Seke and ye shall fynd."

In 1611 King James authorized a new version:

> "Ask, and it shall be given you;
>   seek, and ye shall find."

WESTERN EUROPE IN THE 16th CENTURY

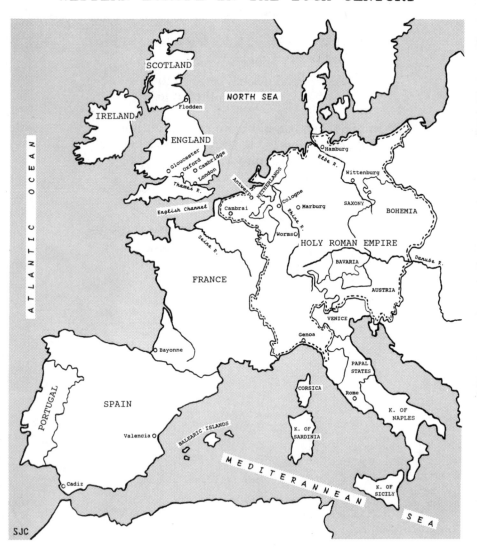

SCOTLAND

NORTH SEA

IRELAND

Flodden

ENGLAND

Hamburg

Elbe R.

Wittenburg

Gloucester

Oxford

Cambridge

London

Thames R.

Antwerp

NETHERLANDS

Cologne

Marburg

SAXONY

BOHEMIA

English Channel

Cambrai

Rhine R.

Worms

HOLY ROMAN EMPIRE

Seine R.

Danube R.

FRANCE

BAVARIA

AUSTRIA

VENICE

Genoa

Bayonne

PAPAL STATES

CORSICA

Rome

K. OF NAPLES

PORTUGAL

SPAIN

Valencia

BALEARIC ISLANDS

K. OF SARDINIA

Cadiz

MEDITERANNEAN

K. OF SICILY

SEA

ATLANTIC OCEAN

SJC

FICTIONAL CHARACTERS

Justin Brice, the hero
Lady Regina Redford, the heroine
Lord Marlon, Justin's close friend
Stewert, Justin's brother
Captain Ewan Brice, father of Justin and Stewert
Felix, a slave
Andrew, a pirate
Soleiman, baron on the Balearic Islands
The Nubian, bodyguard of the baron
The soothsayer, enemy of the Scriptures
Mirandola, Master of Arts in Rome
Marcus and John, fellow student-priests
The archbishop, relative of Marcus
The abbot at Saint Athenians
Lisbeth, a maid
Hicks, a stable boy
Bishop Constantine
Lord Simon Redford, father of Regina and Marlon

HISTORICAL CHARACTERS

William Tyndale, translator of the first printed English New Testament

John Wycliffe, translator of the handwritten English Bible in the fourteenth century; called "The Morning Star of the Reformation"

John Frith, able scholar and Tyndale's close friend

Dean John Colet, Oxford University, Reformer

Erasmus, Cambridge University, Reformer and translator of the Greek New Testament

Martin Luther, Wittenberg University, Reformer

Philipp Melancthon, Wittenberg, Reformer

Henry VIII, king of England

Catherine, queen of England

Lady Anne Boleyn, queen of England after Catherine; she owned a copy of Tyndale's New Testament signed "W. Tyndale."

Cardinal Thomas Wolsey, persecutor of the Reformers

Bishop Cuthbert Tunstall, who burned the English New Testaments at Saint Paul's Cross

Bishop Stokesley, bishop after Tunstall; bitter enemy of the Reformers; believed to have financed the man who betrayed Tyndale

Sir Thomas More, lord chancellor to King Henry; he wrote nine books against Tyndale and the English New Testament

Humphrey Monmouth, cloth merchant in London who aided Tyndale

Thomas Poynitz, close friend of Tyndale among the English merchants at Antwerp

Sir John and Lady Anne Walsh, Tyndale's friends and employers (While serving as tutor of their children, Tyndale made his famous statement to a priest, "If God grant me life, ere many years pass I will see that the boy behind his plow knows more of the Scripture than thou dost.")

Thomas Cromwell, chancellor to the king, successor to Sir Thomas More; a Protestant, he attempted to befriend Tyndale

Fredrick, elector of Saxony, who defended Martin Luther against the edict calling for his arrest on heresy charges

Miles Coverdale, friend of Tyndale and a fellow translator

Vaughan, friendly agent of King Henry VIII who tried to bring Tyndale back to England to serve in the palace

Henry Philipps, Tyndale's betrayer

Will (William) Roye, clerk to Tyndale during the first translation of the English New Testament at Cologne

Peter Quentel, printer in Cologne

Schoeffer, printer in Worms

Patrick Hamilton, young Scottish martyr

Mistress Margaret von Emmerson, friend to Tyndale in Hamburg

Thomas Garrett, London distributor for the English New Testaments

1

London, 1513

Windsor Castle stood in the distance, a sullen gray against the backdrop of a worsening winter sky, which threatened to overcome the weak sunlight before it had a chance to warm the frosty morning. The galloping hooves of several fine royal steeds broke the hush as a group of young squire knights raced down the road toward the stables of King Henry VIII.

To Justin Brice's left, the boundary of land was mostly marsh—the haunt of wildfowl. The headlong rush of his thoroughbred frightened a raven, which gave an irritated shriek and took off down a lane of trees, swooping among the low-hanging branches.

The faint patter of rain wetting his helmet swiftly turned into a steady downpour. His spirits, as well as his armor and the royal standard, were soon somewhat dampened.

But Justin felt generally good this morning. He had won the practice tournament with the squire knights, all sons of lords and earls.

He relished the victory, because he was not bred of English nobility. His father was from Scotland. The Brice castle, lands, and Scottish title—earl of Kendall—had been lost in the devastating battle at Flodden Field, when the Scottish king unwisely turned against his brother-in-law, King Henry VIII, and invaded England. Some of the best and most gallant Scottish fathers and sons had been cut down at Flodden. The king himself was left arrow-pierced and dying on the field.

Justin's father took to the sea then, where he became a famed privateer in search of ways to replenish his lost fortune. Captain Brice left young Justin and his two sisters in the care of an English friend, the head groom at King Henry's stables. Had it not been for Justin's close friendship with Marlon Redford, the son of an English lord, he would have found no acceptance among the sons of the English nobility. Now Justin anxiously awaited his father's return to the Port of London.

It was December. In the spring his father would be back, and Justin expected to begin his own career as a privateer, joining his older brother, Stewert, who was already on the Brice galleon, loading cargo at Genoa for King Henry. Justin dreamed of the sea, the sound of water lapping against the ship's hull and the freedom that sang with the tug of the salty wind against his tunic.

He glanced over his shoulder. He was still a length ahead of the others in the race to the stables. He also knew a shortcut through the dismal woods and turned his horse out of the road into the thicket where black branches interlaced overhead.

An angry shout reached his ears. The other squires admired his tenacity but dared not follow.

Superstition, mingled with erroneous religious beliefs, lurked in the hearts of many. Old tales declared the woods a habitation of "wicked things" or—even worse—"heretics." Some were not sure which was worse, a cloven-hoofed demon or a follower of John Wycliffe. The ecclesiastics said they were the same. To question the difference often meant a charge of heresy. Justin had heard of some Wycliffites being put in dungeons and, if they refused to recant, being burned at the stake.

But he had no time to worry about cloven hooves nor yet to concern himself with the definition of heresy. He was soon going to sea! He would draw swords with the other corsairs and one day join the ranks of the explorers who had discovered the New World. It was enough to attend the services at the village church, rush through his memorized prayers, and go to the school where a determined Dominican monk relentlessly tried to teach him Latin.

The marshy earth was soft beneath his stallion's hooves as the rain fell. Ahead, a field that in summer was overgrown with purple heather was now dark with winter gray.

Back on the road the young squire knights reined their steeds to a nervous but proud prance.

The son of the earl of Roxbury threw up his face shield. "The Scottish knave has won again."

Lord Marlon Redford was especially vexed. He already felt irritated at losing the tournament to his friend, but the race too?

He gave a disgruntled glance at the earl's son, while he adjusted the angle of his helm and chin strap. Then with determination he leaned over and grasped the royal standard with his gloved hand. The scarlet banner hung wet but refused to yield its dignity. With that, he dug his heels into his horse's side and galloped after Justin, intent to run him down whatever the cost.

Justin raced the king's black stallion through the field. Beyond him, a few remaining oaks stood, reaching their web of dark branches to mingle with fir, beech, and pine.

A stream ran dark and sullen in the cloud-shrouded land, and the merging clumps of dark woodland thickened. Justin turned in his saddle and saw Lord Marlon not far behind. He smiled, for Marlon, a superstitious lad, feared the marsh as much as the others.

Darkness deepened and lightning flashed and the mizzling rain whispered through the black trees. Suddenly Justin pulled on the reins, and the horse dug in its front legs. Lord Marlon was not far behind and apparently too cautious to drive his charger past, even if that would gain him distance in the race. Instead he drew up beside Justin.

Justin had heard the sound of a skirmish ahead, and the smell of a campfire hung on the moist air. The noise of distant alarm set the horses to prancing with nervous anticipation, and he held his steed with firm hands. "Easy, boy, easy," he whispered, leaning forward to stroke the sweating animal.

Marlon tugged apprehensively at his gauntlet and scowled. "Fighting here?" he asked softly. "We'd best turn back."

Justin shook his head, still poised to listen. What reached his ears over the wind was not the sounds of battle but voices—and the cries of women and children.

"Trouble," said Justin. "Let's see what it is."

"No. If it is trouble among the peasants, let it be their trouble, not ours." Marlon fretted. "Do you intend to involve yourself in a matter you know nothing about?"

"Shall we not see, at least? It is the cry of women."

His friend managed a stern look that boasted the superiority of position. "One day your inquisitive nature, surely born of ill Scottish blood, will get you into more trouble than even I can squelch."

Justin ignored him and nudged the stallion cautiously ahead.

Marlon followed, still clearly reluctant.

As son of Lord Simon, Marlon Redford had gained permission for Justin to joust with the noble squire knights, but in fact neither of them was yet considered a knight. Chivalric custom denied the knightly accolade to youths under eighteen, except in unusual circumstances. Meanwhile they remained in subordinate rank as squires. If they became involved in a skirmish, Lord Simon would ban them both from training for several months.

Their royal harness jingled as they threaded their way through the trees, and Justin began to see signs of the trouble ahead.

At a place where a number of trees had fallen in some past windstorm, a number of unarmed peasants—men, women, and children—clustered around a campfire. A shouting argument appeared to be under way with a Dominican cleric. The cleric too was unarmed, but several men of civil authority were equipped with weapons.

"Wycliffites," breathed Marlon. "Stay far afield if you wish to avoid wrath. Come, let us go back."

The Wycliffites were followers of the man who had dared to translate the Scriptures from Latin into English in 1381.

"*Do* something!" Justin demanded. "Use your authority as a lord's son."

Marlon looked at him sharply. "Are you completely out of your mind? Confront a Dominican?"

"Aren't you the son of Lord Simon? The king thinks highly of your father. Demand that the clerics release these people in the name of the king."

"And risk not only the wrath of my father but that of the bishop? The Wycliffites are heretics. Why else would the clerics arrest them?"

Justin knew nothing of the beliefs of these people who, after a century, still followed John Wycliffe, a theologian and philosopher at Oxford, Europe's most outstanding university.

He knew the church had issued edicts against Wycliffe for heresy. The man had questioned the doctrines of the church and criticized the corruption of the clergy, but his worst crime had been to translate the Scriptures. Even though Wycliffe had died peacefully in his home, the church exhumed his body years later, burned his bones, then scattered his heretical ashes on the River Swift.

Wycliffe's followers were persecuted and nearly disappeared from England, but the theologian's ideas still troubled the church. And groups still gathered in private cottages or in the woods to hear the Bible read in the English tongue or to hear sermons, translated from Wycliffe's Latin, taught by itinerant preachers. These gatherings were unauthorized and the literature strictly forbidden under the law of 1501, which ordered the burning of any writings questioning the church's authority.

And now here seemingly had been such a gathering.

"Look—they are about to be arrested. Who knows what ill fate they shall meet?" Justin kneed his horse forward as Marlon reached out to halt him.

"In the name of the king, *stop!*"

Surprised eyes turned upon the rider on the black stallion. He wore chain mail with a dark tunic over it and a helmet. They could not see his face, and they stared, amazed.

Seizing the moment, the Wycliffites broke and ran in all directions. Looking over his shoulder Justin saw one old man scurry through the trees. He clutched a scroll and, as Justin watched, secluded it swiftly under a fallen tree. Then he ran on, disappearing into the shadows.

Justin stared at the spot until the angry cleric demanded, "Who are you?"

Just then Lord Marlon grudgingly rode up, giving Justin an angry look. He bowed. "Forgive our interruption, my lord," he said soothingly. "My friend is a mite hasty when it

15

comes to the practice of chivalry. He mistook you for raiders against poor farmers and wished to prove himself worthy of knighthood."

"You dare interfere in the arrest of heretics?"

"We did not know, my lord, that you were arresting heretics," Marlon hastened to assure him.

The priest looked at him askance. "Don't I know you?"

Marlon cleared his throat, obviously reluctant to identify himself. "My father is Lord Simon Redford." He bowed again. "Your servant, my lord."

The Dominican acknowledged the esteemed name.

Marlon removed his helmet, showing his face. His dark eyes angrily met Justin's. The incident could mean trouble for both of them, Justin knew.

"Ah? Is his lordship aware that his son keeps company with an obvious Wycliffite?" the cleric challenged, pointing a finger at Justin.

Justin removed his helmet as well, pushed back the sweat-stained arming cap from damp brown hair tinged with auburn, and scooped back the tendrils from his forehead with a mailed gauntlet. The face was handsome, and the blue-gray eyes did not yield to the priest's glower. He had been called many things since coming to London, and he supposed that being called a "Wycliffite" was only one more insult added to the others.

"What is your name?" the cleric demanded.

"Brice. Justin Brice."

If the name meant nothing to the cleric, the brogue did. He looked at him more closely. "Are you Scottish?"

"Aye."

"Hmm, and your father?"

"Sir Ewan Brice." Justin hesitated and added, "The privateer. He is at sea. I now serve His Majesty in the service of the royal horses. And I could not be a Wycliffite, my lord, for I know not who, or what, they are."

"They are heretics. And you have stupidly intervened in their arrest. I say your intervention was planned."

"Not so," he said simply. "His lordship and I were returning from a joust. We decided—that is, I decided—to race to the stables. We came this way . . ."

16

The priest scanned the youth and appeared to relent somewhat. Nevertheless, he still glowered. A band of heretics had escaped, and his black brows furrowed.

"And what will you do about your transgression?"

Justin shifted uncomfortably in his saddle, trying to remember what he had been taught about transgression.

"You have just made it possible for a nest of heretical cockleburs to escape. I have been after them for months! Are you also a lad bent on heresy?"

Justin felt his heart pound. "I could hardly be that. I know not even what these fellows read in their forbidden books."

Marlon interrupted. "My lord, hearken unto me. The lad"—he spoke of Justin as though he himself were twice his senior—"is, as I explained, merely anxious to win his knighthood by deeds of merit. I confess, sir," he added hastily, "to filling his mind with dreams of knighthood."

Justin turned his head sharply toward Marlon, who totally ignored him and went on speaking to the priest. "Release the stable boy to my care. I vow to see that my father, Lord Simon, rebukes his guardian for not keeping tighter control of the lad. May his transgression be pardoned with an indulgence from the church, my lord."

The priest rubbed his chin thoughtfully. His eyes took in the royal black stallion.

"The horse belongs to His Majesty," Justin stated swiftly.

Marlon grew animated. Thus far his intercession was appearing successful. "Just let the lad pay twice his indulgence."

"Twice!" Justin turned on him indignantly. "With what, your lordship, do I pay twice, when but once is beyond my penury?"

"Silence!" the priest demanded with such awesome thunder that even Justin felt struck by the lightning of doom.

For the first time, he measured the weight of his error. He fell mute. *How am I going to explain all this to my guardian, Balin York? Twice the indulgence! Where can I get the price to pay?* He began to think of what he might bring to the blacksmith to sell. *My hunting bow, my sword, perhaps my boots—they* are made of fine cordovan leather. My father brought them from Cadiz. Still—it won't be enough.

In the silence nothing moved but the wind rustling dead leaves overhead and the light rain pelting his armor and running down his neck. The stallion snorted and restlessly pawed the mossy, sodden earth.

"Master Brice," said the cleric, "see that you are at Saint Catherine's in the morning. The set price of your indulgence shall then be decided."

Tiny beads of perspiration broke out on Justin's forehead, and he wiped them away with the back of his gauntlet. "I shall be there at dawn, my lord."

"Be on your way then."

Justin turned the stallion and rode off swiftly, and Lord Marlon followed. Some distance away at the stream bank, Justin pulled up his mount.

Marlon's face was flushed with exasperation. "Yeoman clod! You have blundered us both into trouble." His dark eyes flashed. "My father will surely hear of this venture."

Justin gave him a dour look, then turned his horse in the direction from which they had just come. He stood in his stirrups to peer back into the shadows.

"Now what are you doing?"

"I wonder if the peasants escaped?"

"Do you not know that the Dominican will go posthaste to Lord Simon about this? I doubt if I will be permitted even to see you again. And you concern yourself with rabble Wycliffites?"

"The old teacher hid his parchment in the logs."

"Let it rot! I ride to Windsor. Perchance I can head off the Dominican with a worthy gift."

"Go then. I would see the parchment for myself."

Marlon looked at him with incredulity. "If Wycliffite writing is found on your person, you could easily be put on trial. Your call to be at the church was anything but a light matter."

"Have you no curiosity to see for yourself what these heretics are preaching behind locked doors and in the darkness of the woods?"

"No," Marlon said dryly.

18

"You are too typically a lord's son."

"Come, Justin! Do not meddle. Let the viper sleep."

"Go then. I will have a look. What harm can one glimpse do? Surely it will change nothing."

"Why I involve myself with the poor likes of you, I can only guess. Go then, yeoman, but I will not beg my father this time to help you."

The young lord rode off.

Justin watched him disappear among the birches, then turned his stallion in the direction of the little clearing where the followers of Wycliffe had met.

Justin drew up, stopping well back under the trees. The rain had ceased, although a few last drops fell from the branches. He listened and heard no sound. The Dominican had gone.

The small campfire no longer smoldered for the rain had dampened it out, but the smell of smoke lingered. It was a mistake to have made the fire in the first place, he thought, and they should have gathered deeper into the forest.

The horse snorted and shook his mane as though bidding him to go, and Justin felt an inward tug-of-war. *Why this curiosity? What does it matter what these Wycliffites think? Let well enough alone,* he told himself. Perhaps Marlon was right. Why risk it? *In a few months my father will dock at the Port of London, and I will join him for a life at sea. If the Wycliffites are heretics, let them be. And if the church is disposed by God to destroy them, then let them do their work. What should any of it matter to me?*

Yet a strange prodding urged him forward to find the parchment and read it for himself, to understand the motivation that drove men to risk imprisonment and even death in order to read forbidden words. What words were these that wielded such compelling power? What manner of man was this devilish Wycliffe, who encouraged men, women, and children to endanger their lives to read his work?

Darting from the shadows to the cluster of fallen logs, Justin removed his glove, then ran his hand under the spot where he thought the old teacher had hidden the parchment.

The Wycliffites called their teachers "evangelical men" or "apostolic men," and they were both laymen and ordained.

They used Wycliffe's tracts, sermon skeletons, and translations of Scripture portions, all in the English vernacular.

Despite the chill wind, Justin perspired. He looked over his shoulder once, in fear of seeing the cleric with hands on hips, ready to shout, "Aha! So we have you now!" but nothing was in sight except the king's restless stallion.

His fingers found the parchment. He lifted it free and with trembling hands shoved it inside his tunic. At that point, from behind him he heard an approaching horse.

Wheeling about, Justin saw a feminine figure on horseback.

She wore a hooded cloak of dark blue velvet lined with marten fur. Lady Regina Redford, Marlon's younger sister, gave him a smile. "Marlon said you went back for it."

Justin was relieved, yet disturbed for her safety. Regina's adventurous spirit surpassed even that of her brother.

"Trouble surely awaits you at Saint Catherine's tomorrow. What will you do for money?"

"You too, my lady, will know trouble if found with me. For your sake, you had best go. Look—a thunderstorm may develop, and you will ruin your garment."

"I fear neither thunder nor lightning nor rain. Indeed, such storms remind me of heaven's power over men. I rather enjoy them."

"A worthy description, my lady, and your zeal for heavenly matters is noteworthy. Nevertheless, Lord Marlon has ridden back to the stables. And you should not be found alone with me."

Justin pressed the concealed parchment against his chest and backed toward his stallion.

Regina was calm but adamant. He was aware that for weeks she had been spying on the Wycliffites, curious to know their condemned beliefs. Her tutor in the palace, Master of Arts Whitfield, knew some of the leaders of the heretical group.

With the skill of a fine rider, Regina eased her mount around the treacherous logs and rode up next to him.

"I will not leave without a look at the forbidden writing."

"You should not have come, my lady. It is dangerous to involve yourself."

She smiled. "Yet *you* do not hesitate."

Regina played with the reins while she looked down at him. She was to marry the earl's son the following year. The marriage was political, and Marlon said she was trying every truthful way to avoid it.

"I know something of John Wycliffe," she said cautiously, glancing about. "My tutor is a friend of Erasmus at Cambridge and also of Master John Colet at Oxford. Do you know that Erasmus criticizes the abuses in the church?"

"You are brave to admit there are any. You know too much for your own safety."

As ever, her intellect, mingled with her feminine graces, impressed him. Lady Regina was not vain nor was she boastful. He had learned long ago that her interest in serious matters was bred from a sincere desire to know.

His own learning at the small Dominican school consisted of simple Latin grammar, reading, writing, and some calculation. "I confess, my lady, that the school I attend is not fortunate enough to have your tutor."

"I have asked my father that you might join my classes," she said, looking about indifferently and flapping the reins against her gloved palm, "but he thought your presence would cause talk. And now, let us share the forbidden parchment," she whispered. "If not, I could go directly to my father about your heresy." Her brown eyes teased and challenged him.

Her determination had him trapped. He looked about. Obviously they couldn't tarry here. "There is a stream a few miles from here. I go there to hunt coneys. We should be safe there—for a while."

Beside the quiet stream, convinced they were alone, Justin drew the parchment from his tunic, and they exchanged smiles of anticipation. Then Justin's eyes fell upon the writing, and his breath caught. He stared.

"What is it?" Regina pushed her head close to his to see his reason for surprise.

This was no paraphrased sermon of Wycliffe's but a translation of Scripture into English.

Their eyes met.

"Do you know the penalty for translating any portion of Scripture into the common language?" she whispered.

"Yes."

The church had decreed in 1408 that no one could translate Scripture into English. It must not even be spoken, except in the sacred tongue of Latin.

"Look! The very holy words are in our own language," she breathed, awed. Her brown eyes gleamed. "Doesn't it make you feel strange?"

"Yes—like walking into a holy place where you have not been invited."

She glanced about. "Nonetheless," she murmured, "read them."

They settled themselves against the trunk of a great oak, and Justin began to read, hardly above a whisper. The brightening light of noontide fell across the handwritten page like a light from heaven.

"'Holy Scripture is the preeminent authority for every Christian, and the rule of faith of all human perfection . . .'"

Justin paused to consider 'preeminent authority,' then went on.

"'Five Rules of Studying the Bible: Obtain a reliable text . . .'"

Now how do you go about doing that?

"'Understand the logic of Scripture," he began again. "Compare the parts of Scripture with one another . . . maintain an attitude of humble seeking, and receive the instruction of the Spirit.'"

His eyes dropped further down the page. In clear handwriting the words *The Gospel of Matthew* stared boldly up at him.

"Now the birth of Jesus Christ was on this wise . . ."

As Justin read through the gospel of Matthew and Regina listened, the sun crept lower. A squirrel braved their quiet presence and sat close by among the fallen leaves.

But thou, when thou prayest, enter into thy closet, and when thou hast shut thy door, pray to thy Father which is in secret; and thy Father which seeth in secret shall reward thee openly. . . . Your Father knoweth what things ye have need of, before ye ask him. After this manner therefore pray ye: Our Father which art in heaven, Hallowed be thy name. Thy kingdom come. Thy will be done in earth, as it is in heaven . . . .

The afternoon wore on, but in Justin's heart time had ceased. There was nothing devilish or rebellious to be found in this writing. He had never heard such wondrous words, and his soul burned as he read of the crucifixion and the resurrection of Jesus Christ.

Regina wiped the tears from her cheeks with the back of her velvet glove.

And Jesus came and spake unto them, saying, All power is given unto me in heaven and in earth. Go ye therefore, and teach all nations. . . . and, lo, I am with you alway, even unto the end of the world. Amen.

They sat for several minutes, unable to break the spell. Neither spoke. Justin wondered at the new tenderness for Christ that burned like hot coals within his heart. He would know more of this wondrous Person—yea, much more.

Finally Regina stirred and rose to her feet. The sun was low in the west. If her maid Lisbeth were not waiting to sneak her into the castle, she said, she would be in trouble.

She wrapped her damp cloak more snugly about her, for it grew colder. Her dark eyes were dimmed with moisture. She turned her back to Justin and walked slowly to her horse. She stroked its auburn mane, then mounted without his assistance.

"Truly," breathed Justin, staring down at the parchment, "I do not know what to think." He placed it carefully in his tunic again and walked to the stallion. "I cannot see why the Wycliffites are persecuted or why they cannot meet to read such fine words without being hounded."

"You do know why," she warned quietly. "It is heresy to translate the Scripture into the vernacular, and no less a crime to read it." She shuddered.

His response arose out of sudden conviction. "It is considered to be so," he corrected. *But is it? Why should it be?*

"It was awesome to hear the words in English," Regina whispered. "And to hear so much at one time."

"And to read it," marveled Justin. "I tasted the words with my tongue, and they were like honey! I confess to being deeply moved."

His eyes sought hers. For the moment they shared the miraculous experience in the oneness of profound silence, his heart knit to hers, and he loved her.

"John Wycliffe is certainly no devil," he said.

"Yet to possess his work is strictly forbidden."

They turned their horses to ride, Regina to Windsor Castle, Justin to the humble cottage of his guardian near the stables.

"I will send word to your guardian tomorrow. You are invited to dine," she said. Regina often invited him to their table. "But Justin—will you not put the parchment back where the teacher hid it? If they find it on you . . ."

Justin shook his head. "Nay, I must surely read it again. There was so much to comprehend. I would go back over the story of the cross and the tomb, for I have never heard it so plain before."

"If you keep it or make a copy, and they discover it, you will be arrested," she whispered.

"I will memorize it, and then return it. It is better than the other things I am commanded to memorize in school."

She turned again to ride on, then looked over her shoulder. Her eyes were grave. "Do your best to please the cleric tomorrow. How will you pay?"

He glanced at the sun. It was late, but he must still ride over and see the blacksmith. "I will sell my sword." He smiled ruefully. "I shall ride with you to the road. It will be dusk before you reach Windsor."

Justin's guardian, Balin York, paced the flagstone floor. The herbs crunched under his boots, his sun-bronzed forehead was furrowed. His large hands, rough with work, the nails hopelessly blackened, dangled at his sides clenching and unclenching as his dark mood seethed with the gathering thunderstorm that threatened the night.

He was a great hulk of a man with little patience for the errors of others. Had the lad no wit? Must he forever meddle in the plight of others? Only the week before he had intervened to stop a farmer from using a tree branch on the donkey pulling his cart to market. Now, saints forbid, he had intervened to save heretics!

The Dominican had left their cottage, and Balin York was frightened. *Wait until the wretched lad shows up! Where is he at this hour? Supper's late!*

Mistress York stirred the blackened pot slung from a winch above the fireplace. Signs of weariness were etched upon her prematurely aging skin.

Justin's two sisters sat in wide-eyed silence at the scrubbed table.

"I tell you I'm at my wits' end with the lad," Master York growled. "He will have us all burned." He was sorry now that they had agreed to take Justin and the two girls into their cottage. Captain Brice would pay them well on his return from sea, but it was another thing to have a cleric come and question them about their "heretical beliefs."

"His will is strong," his wife said. "He is much like his father."

"Yes, and like Ewan Brice he will have a heavy price on his head one day."

"Was it not you who helped Ewan to escape?"

"To save his neck from hanging!"

"Hush!" She jerked her head in the direction of Justin's sisters.

Catherine played with the rim of her empty bowl, her eyes downcast, but Mary, only five, stared at them with her mouth open, her eyelids heavy with sleep. She glanced toward the pot simmering in the fireplace, perhaps wondering how much longer it would be until she could eat, then climb into her blanket in the loft.

"Husband, give him time to explain. The lad will have a worthy reason for his actions. Justin is no troublemaker."

"Bah, and where is he? He deigns to confront a priest, then keeps me from me supper!"

"Captain Brice will return for him this spring," she soothed. "Our days with him will be over. Has the captain not promised a worthy pay? Let the lad find a little peace here. He serves you well in the stables. You said so yourself only this morning."

"Aye, but we all might be burned before spring."

"Silence, I pray! You will scare us all into bad dreams."

Mistress York made no further comment but vigorously stirred the pot. Perhaps to relieve her rising emotion she cried, "You, Catherine, don't sit there gawking. Lend a hand. Bring your uncle's plate. Mary! Wake up for prayers."

Justin opened the cottage door and stepped into the room that served as both hall and kitchen, bringing a violent gust of wind and rain with him. He tried to enter quietly, but the blast caught the door from his hand and slammed it.

The room went silent as every eye fixed upon him. He had left the helmet and chain mail in the care of the captain at the armory and was dressed now in a dark tunic, a cloak, and a wide-brimmed hat.

"Well, lad?" Balin York boomed. "It's about time you showed your face. The priest was here. Tomorrow your wicked debt must be paid!"

So Justin's hope that the news would not reach them had proved vain.

"You have aided the accursed Wycliffites, and do you think that it means no harm? Know that the priest accused us of being followers of John Wycliffe. They searched the cottage for his writings—what have you in your tunic?"

His bright blue eyes seemed to bore a hole through Justin.

Mistress York, showing alarm, drew his two sisters away from the table.

"Nothing that will bring harm to your soul."

Balin stepped toward him and held out his hand. "Hand it over," he whispered. "If you refuse to show me respect . . ."

Justin, tense but with calm dignity, slowly produced the parchment. "It is a month's work by hand, at least. Treat it carefully, I beg you."

Apparently seeing his worst fears realized, Balin York broke into a sweat. He turned at once to his wife. "Take the girls and put them to bed."

"But, husband, our supper . . ." But one look at Balin and the parchment, and her face turned pale. She took hold of the startled girls and ushered them away, promising that they would eat later, and, if they were good, a sweetbread sprinkled with sugar and seeds would follow.

"This—" Balin choked. "Are you altogether mad? Will you have us all burned with you?" His eyes blazed. He whirled and in one giant stride was at the door, bolting it. In another stride he was before the hearth. He began ripping the parchment and throwing the pieces into the flames.

Justin stood stunned. Then he sprang at him, grasping for the scroll. "Will you burn the words of God?"

"I burn the work of the devil's agent!"

Balin's fist struck like thunder, sending Justin backward, and his head struck hard against the stone floor. He was dazed, and it took a moment to get on his feet. A trickle of blood ran from his lip.

Pieces of parchment smoldered within the flames.

A sense of horror engulfed him. He stumbled to the hearth and on his knees snatched wildly to retrieve the burning Scriptures. Pain seared his fingers.

With fierce determination Balin held the rest of the parchment to the flame as sweat dripped from his furrowed brow. The sparks flew upward, and helplessly Justin watched the last portion of Scripture turn into feathery ash.

Gone! Dear God, what have I done? I should have left it where it was. Now the old teacher will have nothing. And I? What have I now? A momentary vision of light, forever gone.

"Confess your sin that God might take pity on you!" Balin said hoarsely.

Justin stared at the burning coals.

At dawn, the spiritual dilemma of his soul continued. In a downpour, as lightning flashed across the still-darkened sky, Justin rode to the monastery, far from houses and farms. He reached the steps of the cloister, his heart weighted down with burden. In a small bag he carried the coins from the sale of his sword and boots. It would hardly be enough.

The Dominican was waiting behind his desk. A candle burned. The rain beat like small pebbles against the windowpane. There were dark circles under the priest's eyes, as though he had been up all night in a prayer vigil. For the first time Justin noticed how weary the man looked, how his brow was knitted.

The cash box sat on the desk, and a list of standard fees for indulgences lay before him.

Justin wrestled with the dilemma. *Why is it a transgression to be responsible for the escape of the Wycliffites, when the words they had met to read are only Scripture? Why are these words forbidden in the common tongue?*

He laid the small bag of coins on the desk.

The cleric ignored it. "Go in peace. Your debt has already been paid."

Surprised, Justin stood there.

The Dominican said, "A worthy sum arrived last night by the servant of Lady Regina Redford. She has been most generous. A brilliant damsel. One day she will stun the royal palace with her wit and learning. Whereas you had best watch the waywardness of your feet, before they turn you to the gates of hell."

The message of his father's arrival came on a fine June morning, and it was with difficulty that Justin restrained his excitement as he walked the London wharf. The clammy chill of dawn soaked through his cloak, and the mist hung heavily on the dock.

The harbor was rich with the masts of ships from East and West. The poignant aroma of the sea and the crisp wind that tugged at his cloak called of freedom. He took the steps down to the quay, walking among the bronzed and often barefoot sailors and dock hands, who carried bundles and baskets on their backs.

His hungry eyes took in everything, including the swarthy faces and boldly dangling earrings. His ears rang with voices shouting in unknown tongues. Along with the salt air, Justin inhaled the pungent odors of everything from fish to spoiling fruit, tar, and human bodies. In the eerie whitish-gray mist came the lulling slap-slap of water against hulls and the creaking of wood. Sea gulls screamed and wheeled in search of their breakfast.

Ahead, Justin caught sight of the ship he sought. The familiar gonfalon of his father's clan appeared, boasting the lion of Scotland.

As he neared the Brice ship, a crew member on watch saw him and scowled down. "What are you looking for, lad?"

"My father," Justin called up proudly. "Captain Ewan Brice."

The reddish brows under the blue cap rushed together, and he raked Justin's figure from head to toe.

The lad stood poised and waiting for the rope ladder to be tossed. It dropped toward him, hitting the ship's side on the way. He grabbed hold and climbed up and over.

The seaman stood staring at him. In startling ways the boy looked every inch a Brice, but the blue-gray eyes that met his were unlike the captain's, he decided. They lacked the brittleness of a man who had often drawn sword on an opponent and struck with deadly accuracy. There was a disarming quiet to the young face, with no spark of the Scottish ferocity that often drove his restless, moody captain to fits of emotional despair. And since a storm at sea and his fear of God's wrath, Captain Brice had grown worse, declaring that demons were after his soul. His moods were enough to downright spook a man!

"Is my brother on board?"

"No. He is on leave."

Justin flung his bag over his shoulder and followed the sailor across the deck. And all at once he felt at home. Dreams of exploration surged through his blood. Someday he would sail as Columbus had done!

"Captain Brice waits in his cabin." The man gestured ahead but made no attempt to escort him. "Careful, lad, he's a mite troubled tonight."

The captain's cabin was small. A lantern hanging above the rough wooden table cast its glow on the bowed, dark head of the massive man who sat there, poring over a chart.

Justin's heart pounded. His father . . .

For a moment he couldn't move, then he drew in a breath and ducked through the small arched doorway.

Captain Ewan Brice looked up with shrewd blue eyes that scanned him with slow recognition. He seemed taken aback, as though expecting the boy he had left.

Then a smile spread over his bronzed face. He stood, and his broad shoulders swelled under the dark woolen tunic. He seemed pleased with his son until his eyes fell on the sword at his side. Ewan Brice gestured abruptly. "Where'd you get that, lad?"

Justin was thunderstruck. After two years, was this his welcome? Hurt, he answered stiffly. "From his lordship Marlon."

"'His lordship,' he says. Do you not know that you yourself be a lord in Scotland? Am not I an earl? Hanging around with English blood!"

Words of defense rushed to Justin's lips, but he held them back. He owed much to Marlon, but before he could explain his father again gestured at the sword. "Off with it, me lad. 'Tis no mark of a scholar, nor yet a holy man."

Scholar? Holy man? Justin ignored the order and reached an arm toward him. "My father, I . . ."

"Dinna you hear me, lad?" His eyes sparked. "Off with it!"

Justin stared. The determination in his father's face was too clear to ignore, but he rebelled. "On board ship I will need a sword, and I use it well." He indicated his father's own scabbard resting on the small cot. "My father bears a sword. Why not his son?"

"Why, indeed, lad! Because you will not follow your father's steps. God forbid! Now do as your father bids. D'you think you be man enough to withstand a good whipping?"

"Father!" His eyes burned with exasperation at the thought of being treated like a child.

Ewan Brice started up from behind his desk.

Angry, embarrassed, Justin loosed the sheath and flung it aside with a clatter. Their eyes met evenly.

Then Captain Brice smiled. "'Tis better. Now come here." He gripped Justin firmly about the shoulders, looking him over proudly. "You look like your mother, may she rest in peace. You will not bear a sword while I yet live to stop you, and you will not take one step within my footprints. I have got your good future all settled, me lad, and proud I am of it."

He nodded toward the desk where a letter lay. He beamed. "From the good bishop in London, no less."

Justin tensed. "The bishop?"

"Who else is good enough to guide you while I take again to the sea? No more of wretched yeomen like Balin. And your sisters too shall be sent to a better place. You are too good for such waste. 'Twas a mistake I dinna see to this sooner. But me mind is made up now, lad. Your destiny lies not with me but in the church."

Justin did not want to believe what he was hearing. His father had surely gone mad. The *church!* He remembered the dank, stifling monastery. He wanted no part of it. He wanted the sea, the ship, his father, cantankerous though he be.

"A monastery, no less," said Ewan Brice with satisfaction. "My son shall be a saint. And shall make me proud."

"A *monastery!*" Justin stepped back as though his father had struck him across the face. He was stunned at this turn of events, and his frustration poured forth. "I will choose my own path, even as you did choose yours as a lad. I have done what you asked! I have excelled with the sword, the horse . . ."

"And nearly broke your neck in a reckless race in the marsh, so Balin sent word. And nearly mixed with heretics!"

Justin stiffened. So his father had already been in touch with Balin York!

"It will not happen again because you will be safe in the robe of scholar and priest."

"A fate worse than death. No! Never!"

"Silence!"

Justin could not be silent. "I learned to read and write as you wished. Is that not enough to demand of me? I will not accept the life of celibacy. I want the sea! A ship of my own!" His eyes flamed with a surge of rebellion. "What of my training as a knight? I handle the sword and great horse even better than Lord Marlon."

Ewan Brice was adamant. "That is what I fear. As my younger son it is your right—yea, your responsibility—to serve the church."

"Then it is time for custom to change. If my heart is not in it . . ."

"Tsk, tsk, me lad. A man's heart has nothing to do with it. 'Tis your duty. I have delayed your journey to Rome long enough."

Rome! "I have no wish to enter the cloister! Father! Be reasonable, I would even become a barrister, if it is education that will make you proud of me. I could go to Magdalen College, then to Oxford University, if I must. But a *monastery!*"

"'Tis not a barrister I want but a holy son, a priest, one to intercede for me."

Justin was so overwrought that he nearly laughed—which would have been a fatal mistake. *He,* Justin Brice, to intercede for his father? His desperation mounted. "And if I refuse?"

"'Refuse,' says he! You have no choice. You are my gift to God. Surely the Almighty will be pleased and my transgressions lessened in His sight by this act. I vowed you in a storm, my lad, only months ago. I cannot go back on it, nay." He shook his large head vigorously. "Not if it means me very life. I have already pledged you, my son."

"Pledged me? When?"

"At sea, as I said. In a storm. And this morning I visited Saint Catherine's and made it official. This letter" —he indicated a missive on his desk— "is yours to bring to the abbot in Rome. 'Tis a good monastery, the best, and full of wealthy and religious sons. 'Tis called Saint Athenians."

Justin tried to hold back his anger by clenching his jaw. His voice became cold and brittle. "Then you have consigned me to a living death. A dungeon of darkness is no better. Why not simply thrust me through with your sword? I would show that much mercy for a wounded animal."

"Hold your wicked tongue! God wills it!"

His father, a huge man with fierce Scottish blood, now grinned as his mood swung. The smile was broad and affable, and he threw an arm about Justin's shoulder. "Try to understand, Justin. Should death strike me, my soul will know rest for this worthy deed. Know you not my head is hunted this very moment by corsairs on Crete? They wait like vultures for a moment of weakness."

"All the more reason why I should return with you to the sea. I am good with a sword, Father. As good as Stewert."

"Nay. 'Tis your father's sin to wield a sword. 'Tis your fortune to seek a better road." He sloshed his goblet full of brew and drank deeply, then wiped his beard on the back of his arm. His eyes scanned the young man with obvious pride.

"'Twas no mistake of your dear mother to name you 'Justin.' A wise dove she was, gentle, praying." He drank again. "You have always enjoyed mingling with the booksellers and philosophers. The knowledge of a scholar will do you far more good than a sword ever will."

He scowled. "Aye, lad, you are like your mother," he said wistfully. "When she was alive, she had eyes as blue as yours, yet as stormy as the sea when she blustered at me. Yea, just like you. She will know peace in her grave now that I have vowed you to the church. I will go where she is buried on the cliff overlooking the sea and tell her so. She will rest in peace as you give yourself to prayers for us both."

"I will not do it—no, not even if I take to a stranger's ship to man the galley oars!"

His father smashed his goblet against the desk. "The words of a rebel! A mere lad born of my loins who dares contest the will of his father? D'you not know I could have you beaten to within an inch of your life?"

"It is not you I reject but—"

"Obedience is demanded. I am your father," he bellowed, "and 'tis your duty to obey. D'you think it a light thing to contest me authority?" He grabbed Justin roughly by the shoulder and slammed him backward against the bulkhead. "You are my *son,* have you forgotten?"

"No, I have not forgotten, but no man should vow for another. Not the king, not even a father. I have a right to my own vows, my own life."

"Who told you so? Speak! Who told you so? You have no rights but those I give you! It so happens I now give you none. Hear?" He leaned toward him. "None. If you wish to contest me—" he stopped and stepped back "—then draw your sword now." He swept up the scabbard Justin had thrown aside and tossed it to him.

Justin automatically caught it.

"We will see who is master and who is servant!" The great Scotsman drew his own prized blade from its sheath. He had drawn it often. His temper was known to be as unmastered as the race from which he had come. He lurched toward Justin, who remained leaning against the cabin wall, completely frustrated.

With a fillip of his blade Captain Brice flicked open the doublet Justin wore.

Justin threw down his scabbard in disgust. "Reason, Father, reason. Would I raise a sword against you?"

No. His father knew he would not. Never. So he pressed his son further.

"What good a son who brings me shame?" The tip of his sword sent a vessel flying across the small cabin. "He wishes battle and scorns the garb of a holy man!"

"Holy? Do you think I am fit for the priesthood?" He made a pleading motion toward his towering father. "Give me time, training at sea, then a merchant ship. Give me the navigation chart found on the Persian captain, and I shall bring back to London such treasures and fame as the merchants have never seen. You speak of shame? I shall make you proud."

"If merchant ships sail, it will be left to me to fight the sea. You shall fight the devil. Would you see my soul burn in hell, lad? Know you not the devil has me by the scruff of the neck? Yea! At night in my dreams I see the cavernous pit with leaping fire."

Justin stared, wondering at the stark fear on his father's rugged face.

"If I give you to the church, I shall be pardoned. Do you understand?"

The man's reasoning so frustrated Justin that he turned his back, leaning his shoulder to the cabin wall. The monastery . . .

His father, Justin knew, had anticipated gaining the upper hand in their debate. Had he also expected his son to react as he was now reacting, bridling his anger? Probably. He would know he could always depend on Justin's respect, even when he disagreed with his rantings.

Captain Brice's bellowing slowly ebbed. He sheathed his sword and sloshed another goblet to overflowing. "Do you not see? I have done you well, my son. Dinna you know you mean more to me than anyone else in this life? More than your sisters, bless their souls, and more than even your fair mother, may she rest in peace. And certainly more than me ne'er-do-well son Stewert! Be pleased with what I have done! It was no easy task to send you to Rome, of all blessed cities."

Rome. And what of his friends here—Marlon and Lady Regina? *Regina!* Though there was little hope to own the heart of a damsel of royal blood, he could not get her out of his mind. Regina, with her dark hair and eyes . . .

"At the monastery you will do wonderful works of mortification. And you will pray! You will serve the church."

Slowly Justin could feel the bars closing about him.

"When your father speaks, answer! Do you understand?"

"Perfectly."

"Good. I will be proud of you, my son." He drank from the goblet, finishing its contents in one breath. He sighed again, wiping his mouth on the back of his hand.

Justin heard the goblet thud against the table. It reminded him of a dull bell ringing out of tune.

"Christ will be pleased with us both." His father sounded well-satisfied with himself and his religious decision. "Now, surely peace shall come to me wretched soul." He sank wearily into the chair.

Justin distractedly pushed the chart about the desk, and the words *Christ will be pleased* repeated themselves in his mind.

"He shall not be pleased," Justin told him tonelessly.

His father seemed startled. For a moment they only looked at each other. Then Ewan Brice leaned forward. There was a flicker of anger in the stark blue eyes. "What do you mean? Have you been reading heretical literature?"

Justin held out his hands, palms up. "There is blood on them."

"You speak like a fool."

"There is not only blood but other things that I have done."

"Forget it, me son. Your religious duty for the church will make them into the hands of a sweet child. They shall not only purify with service, but they will lift me from earth to heaven."

Distraught, Justin searched his face. No words would come. His father's confident gaze left him speechless. His father truly believed what he said!

Lord, he thought, and for the first time his use of the Name was a genuine call. *Lord God, what am I to do?*

They bowed before the abbot at Saint Catherine's, Justin and his father. The bell chimed, and the Latin chant monotonously droned in Justin's ears.

"As vowed," his father murmured, "I give my younger son to God for the penance of my soul. He will follow the monastic life from this day on. Neither will he remove his neck from the yoke of his service. Neither I, Ewan Brice his father, nor any family member, will tempt him to leave and thereby sin against Christ. Amen."

Justin arrived in Rome feeling more like a conquered slave brought in chains for a triumphant Caesar than a willing servant dedicated to God.

2

A Monastery in Rome

Justin awoke with a start in the deep, airless dark, and above the sound of heavy breathing he heard the bells begin to ring from a convent elsewhere in the city. The first glimmer of dawn had not yet shone on the seven hills of Rome when the call to rise for prayer repeated itself, echoing down the stone passages like a summons of doom.

The other young monks were hastily on their bare feet, blundering about in the icy cold. Someone fumbled for the flint and candle, and the quick commotion of sharp strikes to steel gave way to a tiny spark.

On a winter's morning the blackness of the chamber seemed impenetrable and the weak illumination of the fluttering candle a mockery. Soon others were rushing by to touch their charred candlewicks to the wavering flame. Justin could see the lanky figures of a dozen young men in monks' robes making swiftly for the door. In a moment they were gone, and Justin realized that he was already late.

Marcus, a nephew of the archbishop himself, was next to last to leave. He paused and gestured wryly at Justin's bed—a stone bench with a log for a pillow.

"Did you sleep well?"

The cynical whisper was the very first communication that Justin had heard from any of the other dour inhabitants of the monastery. He was quick to take it up. "Isn't sleep a transgression?"

"Speech in the vulgar tongue of English is."

With numb fingers Justin reached for his robe, still finding it strange after wearing chain mail and a sword, but Marcus halted him and shoved a prickly garment into his hands.

Justin's brow was quizzical.

Marcus smirked. "Where have you come from, pagan? From the Saracen?" The Muslim East. "The hair shirt must be worn night and day under your robe. The superior will look to see if you have disobeyed. Make haste," he prodded. "The hour strikes."

Quickly Justin dressed, finding the hair shirt a nervous distraction.

They flew from the chamber, racing down the passage to the hall where a monastic chant in Latin was already underway. Kneeling bodies would be shivering for warmth that was not there. Justin found himself wondering why the chanting voices did not themselves stammer from the cold.

The door was closed—they were indeed late—and he heard Marcus groan his apprehension. Above the door was a woven garland of tinkling bells. Each morning after the monks filed into the hall for mass, these were securely fastened in place so that the opening door would strike them. No late-comer could possibly enter unnoticed by the superior.

The bowed heads did not turn—they dared not—as Justin and Marcus slipped into the hall, helpless to keep the clattering bells silent.

They knelt at once, and Marcus joined the pious chant, but Justin groped in his memory for the appropriate Latin. He had mastered enough of the language at the little school in London to be considered far more scholarly than his fellow students there, but here in Rome he had proved to be hopelessly dim.

He heard slippered feet and the rustle of a robe. The superior stopped beside him and bent his dignified head, cupping his ear toward Justin. All at once his lazy Latin fumbled into silence.

"You." The stick prodded his shoulder. "Louder."

Justin's Latin slowly struggled forward.

"What?" the superior whispered. "Will the sun not set before you seek mercy for the morning?"

Justin's chant broke forth into English, larded with Scottish brogue. He heard a slight groan and caught himself at once.

The superior sighed deeply, then snapped in Latin, "The common tongue is forbidden. You shall neither pray in it, nor quote Scripture in it, nor speak it at all. Understand?"

Justin nodded, not trusting his Latin response.

"You shall see me in my chamber after you break fast."

When the superior walked on, Marcus ventured to lean toward him. "Now your yoke has begun. The grammar master shows no pity. His love for Latin transcends his love for wine."

In his great vaulted chamber the superior sat behind a large table with both hands clasped peacefully before him. The walls were lined with awesome books, parchments, and stacks of manuscripts, some sealed with an imposing insignia. The robe he wore over his religious garb was patched here and there and was furred for warmth. On his head sat a battered velvet hat from under which straight silver hair hung limp.

Justin halted, and the superior studied him with unsmiling concentration. The scrutiny was so minute that Justin humorously wondered if he might wish to utter something in Latin and turn him into a toad. But at last the lips curved into a smile, and the sharp eyes softened.

"Your name is Justin Brice. Your father . . . er . . ." The superior hesitated to search his memory and locate a letter on his desk. He held it close to his face, squinting through a single spectacle. "Your father is Sir Ewan Brice of London."

"The same, my lord," Justin said in careful Latin.

"He has written a most moving discourse acclaiming your skills with Latin." He fixed his gaze on Justin, his mouth twitching.

Justin remembered the embarrassment of the morning.

"Your father's parental enthusiasm is, shall we say, exaggerated? For the moment" —and the superior offered a grimace— "you may speak English. But softly," he hastened to add. "Oh, so softly."

Relieved that his superior was not as unrelenting as he had at first thought, Justin apologized. "My Latin, I fear, is born of the grammar school in an English village."

"So I gathered. Your father has wondrous plans for you. Are you in agreement with them?"

Now it was coming. "My lord—" his breath came rapidly, and he became aware of the hair shirt "—I am beholden to my father, yet, if the choice were mine, I would be far at sea."

"That too I gathered."

"I meant no offense to this religious community. It is only that I have not the heart of a monk."

The superior surveyed him through heavy lids. "That is what we intend to change."

Justin felt the chill of the vaulted chamber.

The superior then grew businesslike. "Your father's plans concerning you are noble and to be commended. He wishes, as any good father, for you to become a man of holiness, a man of letters, a scholar of the Latin tongue—and he has sent a most wondrous endowment to the church in order for his wish to be exercised with all speed. Therefore"—and he smiled —"you shalt be given every opportunity to learn Latin as Latin ought to be spoken. You shall speak it with the splendor of those masters who use it as sweetly as their mother tongue."

Justin was aware that his future was taking another turn on the swiftly moving shuttle he had no control over. He had been in Rome only one day, and it seemed a lifetime.

"It is your privilege to have classes each day with the learned scholar Mirandola at the University in Rome. Those chosen from our monastery to attend his classes are young men of notable backgrounds. Know, therefore, that this privilege is to be revered. However, your daily classes will in no wise excuse you from your duties. Prayer vigils and godly endeavors are to continue."

The superior stood now and came around to him. "I notice your body is handsome of flesh and muscled with strength. You must gain ascendancy over its passions."

He pulled back the robe and saw Justin was wearing the hair shirt. "So far, well enough. The victory of chastity and holiness is not awarded to the sluggard. You must strive! Your body is to be used as a farmer uses his ox. Strokes and burdens lighten the soul, though the rebellious flesh quivers beneath the load. Far better the groan of the chastened flesh than its licentious freedom to bring the soul headlong into the bottomless pit. Enough." He turned away with a wave of his hand. "Go to your vigil, and Christ give you grace."

Since his every hour was controlled by ritual and unending demands, it was startling one morning to notice, as a blind man receiving sight, that the dreary winter had given way to spring blossoms in the meditation garden. Then—it seemed but days later—Justin noticed as he labored over his grueling schedule of Latin that there was frost on the ground again and his breath was white in the air.

The monastery in Rome had been his prison for three years, but it had not imprisoned his desires or tamed the storm of doubt growing within his soul. He knew that a life of rigorous self-denial had not brought him internally to a higher spiritual state. Ritual had not quieted the fires smoldering deep within nor had it brought him peace with God. He was more troubled now than he had ever been in London.

For three years the ritual had varied little. He rose before dawn to give himself to the monastic chant, to devotion and prayers. In spite of the required fastings and watchings and the hair shirt, he found his body to be most rebellious in response to the unending demands, and no amount of discipline silenced the struggles going on within his heart or his mind. And when he lay down on the stone bench of his cell, with a log under his head, allotting himself only four hours of sleep, he felt more wretched than ever.

"My body is to be used as an ox," he repeated as taught, but the self-rebuke fell dully upon his senses, neither quickening him to joyous victory nor granting inward strength to overcome.

"If heavy strokes secure chastity and acts of self-mortification make me holy," he argued with a monk named John one morning on the way to class, "why has Christ not seen fit to give my soul peace?"

John was younger than the others, a delightful boy with the most tender brown eyes Justin had ever seen. He was gentle, dedicated, and outraged at such debates, yet he had strangely taken up friendship with Justin and the cynical Marcus.

Now he scowled briefly. "Must you argue with me daily and wear me to the bone? Do you wish to make me into a heretic?"

"To question is heresy? Be you truthful with me, as I have been with you. Do you have assurance of acceptance with Christ?"

John quickened his steps over the cobbled way. "More works are needed to please heaven if His smile is to come upon you."

Justin well knew that John was not at peace. Often he heard him sighing. That sigh had become such a habit with him that it reminded Justin of an old yeoman farmer he had once seen in London, tilling his field by hand, for his ox had died of sickness at planting time. As the plow was tied to his shoulders, and he sought to cultivate the unyielding earth, he would stop under the grueling heat of the sun and sigh deeply, his body shuddering under its heavy load.

Justin pressed him. "Then all your striving has brought the benediction of peace between you and your Lord? You are not burdened as I am with the emptiness of ritual?"

John, a slight figure in his worn robe, refused to look at him. "Heaven is not won in a day."

"No? When? When shall I know? Will I know when the day and hour has struck? Will it be morning or evening? Summer or winter? No, perhaps spring?"

"You speak like a fool, Justin Brice!"

Ahead, Marcus and an exceptionally tall young man with red hair followed the superior. The monk now escorted them up the awesome steps of the university and into the cloistered halls of learning.

Having put his mind to it, Justin found that Latin came far easier than he had anticipated. Of the five young men, including John, who were permitted to attend the famous university, Justin had striven to excel, and his progress had provided the Master of Arts a high level of pleasure.

"Surely you will be chosen to be the abbot's secretary on his journey to visit the bishop at Bologna," John had said. "My Latin falls behind yours."

Justin, however, had more intense ambitions than to serve the Abbot of Saint Athenians. He ventured now to share with John the hope he had not breathed to anyone else. "No, I will seek to work in the university library as a translator. I heard Master Mirandola speak yesterday of an opening for an assistant to the superior."

"A lofty goal. But if anyone has Latin down well enough to translate lesser volumes, it is you. Marcus too wishes the position. Most likely he will prevail since he is nephew to the archbishop."

Justin's schedule began at four in the morning and went well into the night. Even after the candle went out and the other monks sought sleep, he went over his Latin by memory until his eyes shut on their own.

It was not love for the language that drove him but the desire to escape the empty rigor of religious ritual. If his fate was to be cast among those in the Church of Rome, there seemed no better opportunity than to use his mind in the great library where he might have access to important works, especially the Scriptures. And if he could show himself somewhat of a scholar, he might obtain a position doing translation.

So far, among the endless religious activities demanded to sanctify his soul, access to the Scriptures was rare, and the few verses that were used were spoken and not put in writing. Justin remembered the Wycliffe translation of the gospel of Matthew and longed again to have the written words before him, to see them, to speak them, to meditate over them like a cow lying under the cool shade of a tree, chewing her cud.

"Well then, Master Brice, what could be on your mind?"

The great hall of the university was nearly empty. Master Mirandola came toward him dressed in his scholar's gown and academic biretta. His dark eyes were friendly and encouraged Justin to speak his mind.

Speaking his mind to anyone besides Marcus and John had seemed a risky venture. However, Justin believed that the Master of Arts felt kindly toward him as one of his most promising students.

"I am under no illusion as to my abilities as a scholar, being but a junior grammarian when it comes to the language you speak so well, but . . ."

"You are far more learned than you give yourself credit for, Master Brice. As I have mentioned to the other masters at the University, you have untapped resources."

"I am honored, learned sir. I . . . you have mentioned the library and the need for an assistant in translation. I could not hope to fill the position, realizing I am but a learner, but

I had hoped to begin in that direction. The work of translation holds great interest for me."

"I had hoped your interest would be routed in that esteemed direction, Justin. It may surprise you to know I had you in mind all along."

Justin was astonished.

"I must first speak to the bishop about this," said Master Mirandola, "but he is a congenial man where my requests are concerned. And there is urgent need for copies to be made of certain works in order to send them to the rector Julius."

The interview had gone so well that Justin could hardly believe it. Few matters in his life had gone well recently, he thought, and why should this? But now the opportunity to handle precious parchments—including Scripture—nearly drove him to lose control of his grave demeanor, a demeanor he had rigidly practiced. He could almost believe that Christ did look upon him with grace.

"I shall know how it will go shortly," Master Mirandola was saying. "The bishop will arrive in a few weeks to meet with *Herr Doktor* Martin Luther's delegation from Wittenberg. I shall speak to him then."

It was with a lighter heart that Justin resumed his arduous schedule.

The message he awaited arrived during supper one winter evening. The superior, who had taken to Justin with affection, brought the news to the table.

"Well, my son, your father shall be proud of you. You have gained position in the university library under the supervision of the renowned Master Mirandola."

When he had gone, Marcus, who saw himself becoming a cardinal one day, took to groaning. His family was rich and powerful in Rome, and he often mocked them, as well as himself, for the personal use of position. But now he complained, "Alas! How my uncle the archbishop has failed me in the hour of need. He has promised me a secure position where future wealth and power wait. Yet the position of assistant translator to Master Mirandola goes to a pagan Scot," he teased.

"Master Mirandola looks for scholarship, not a powerful family to bribe him," said John with a twinkle.

Marcus grimaced a dry smile. "What scandal do you breathe? You who are so blindly dedicated to the church? Are you so wicked as to even suggest that wealth buys position in Christ's church?"

John blushed. The abuses in the system were offensive enough, but it was shameful to have Marcus unveil them with his irony.

Justin, however, took up Marcus's challenge. "In *Christ's* church, no. Among those who would use religious means to secure unholy ambitions without inward merit, yes. Where is your burning conviction to resist compromise?" he concluded, goading Marcus with friendly humor.

Marcus winced but was quick with a retort. "I prefer—as Erasmus—wine to ale, roast meat to a crust of bread, and friends in high places."

"Erasmus has been offered the position of cardinal," John whispered.

"Erasmus?" said Marcus with disbelief. "Ho! What jest is this? My uncle knows him well. I have often been in the same room with him. Erasmus would sooner stand aloof of the church and ridicule its hypocrisy than wade in and work to cure its ills. This much I will say for him—his writings are work enough. They are meant, like John Colet, to light a needed spark of renewal."

"When you speak of sparks, let us hope with Erasmus that you do not mean wood and fire," offered John.

"Forbid," Marcus said hastily, suddenly grave. He leaned over to Justin with another whisper. "Speaking of heresy, the great Erasmus has left Cambridge, where he taught Greek, to come to Italy. It seems Cambridge is seeded with new thinkers who plot for reform in the church. And it is said that a secret few hope that Erasmus will render a translation of Scripture in the English tongue. Cambridge is now laden with floating ideas of heresy, and so Erasmus has wisely come to sunny Italy, leaving what he began to others."

Justin's attention was riveted. He found his heart pounding. "Erasmus will translate the Scriptures into English?"

"No, Erasmus will not meddle. He will instigate it but take no part. He has promised a new translation in Greek only—and a new Latin without the errors of Jerome's version."

"To admit of errors in the Vulgate brands you too as a thinker," said Justin with a wry smile.

"Erasmus distinctly said that the Scriptures should be placed in the tongues of all people. Why do you think he left Cambridge? It is because, while he believes in the task, he will have nothing to do with the translation. That is left to Colet or others. Perhaps someone even now stands in the shadows."

"The stirring of the bones of the devil Wycliffe," John said.

Justin took the words like a slap across the face. His mind went with painful clarity back to the woods near King Henry's stables. The Wycliffites were fleeing—men, women, even children. The stirring words of the gospel of Matthew in English pierced his heart anew, and he relived the gripping agony of Balin York's tearing sections from the parchment and throwing them into the fire. He saw again the ashes and felt the sting of his former guardian's knuckles against his mouth.

He looked from Marcus to John. "Wycliffe saw what the leaders of the church have no spiritual discernment to see. Or if they do see it, they cower before the cost of such a stand. Does that make Wycliffe a devil? Is he not rather a saint? He was a man before his time, but will the time ever come unless men such as he risk all to do what is necessary? Why shouldn't the common man be entitled to hear and read the Word of God in his own tongue?"

He waxed fervent. "Is the God we claim to serve lord only of the religious cloister? Does He dwell only with scholars in the halls of the university? Then what of the masses who shall die in their sins before they ever hear all the truth? And what of truth itself, if committed only to the few in the cloister? If the trusted few have strayed from the flock to feast alone, what shall become of the sheep left to starve? What should they feast on if not the Scriptures? Tradition and ritual, tarnished by self-seeking clerics?"

They stared at him.

John's face flushed, his gaze dropping to the table.

If anyone knew the danger of these words, it was Marcus. He was grave for the first time, and his dark eyes glanced about to see if anyone besides the few in their circle of friendship had heard.

"If you will be burned as a heretic, such words as you have uttered will surely light the torch to the fagots."

Justin knelt during prayers in his chamber, but he could not concentrate for thinking of his outburst at the evening meal. As his own convictions began to take shape, he wondered just where they would lead him. He tried to pray and could not. His heart was not in the chant. The fixed chant did not speak his true feelings.

3

Rome

For Justin, to translate a work was to know it. His memory was disciplined, and he entered his labors at the university library with a sense of destiny.

He glanced about. The various translators were busy at their own duties. Cautiously he pushed aside the lesser works he was to translate for the village rectory and slipped Jerome's Latin Scripture translation from under the stack before him.

He viewed the Old Testament with awe. How would he ever master this book? He turned to the New Testament. To gain a general understanding of what it offered he began to look through the gospels, then the Acts, and the beginning of Paul's epistles. He intended to move on to what followed, but his attention was arrested by the word *Rome*.

He read, "'To all that be in Rome.'"

Was he not in Rome? And, indeed, a servant in the church at Rome? What did Saint Paul have to say to the church in Rome? This was the logical place to begin, he told himself, and with another cautious glance around the silent room, hearing nothing but the scratch of quills, Justin settled down to read.

The morning light turned to afternoon shadows. How long he had been absorbed, he knew not. An hour? Two? Even three? His mind was swollen with the sheer volume of the written words, as he struggled to grasp their profound meaning.

Justification by faith . . . faith alone . . . apart from works of man's religious endeavors . . . faith in the work of Christ justified a sinner before a holy God . . . Christ's righteousness was imparted to the believer and Christ Himself was his righteousness . . . the believer was *in* Christ and therefore was completely accepted.

The tolling bell marking the close of the day at the university interrupted his concentration. A look around proved that the bell was no noisier than usual. The other translators were calmly putting their work aside until the next morning. Justin reluctantly closed the Vulgate, slipped it under the other manuscripts, put his quills aside, and stood. A moment later he had donned his hat and cloak and was out the door.

That night in the dining hall he managed to secure a private corner where John and Marcus could join him. At once he shared what he had discovered.

John was silent and scowling, but Marcus listened with quick interruptions, pressing hard. "How do you know Saint Paul meant it as you interpret?"

"It is so written."

"But you may have interpreted it erroneously."

"No, the words speak for themselves."

Marcus pointed a finger at his chest. "I would see for myself."

Justin's hesitation was only slight. The decision came as easily as though born from blossoming seed pushing through the earth. "You shall see for yourself. Tomorrow I will make a copy of Romans and bring it here. Where can we meet to debate?"

John looked at them as if they had both gone truly mad. The minor debates they had were one thing, but to debate Scripture within the walls of the monastery? And on a subject strictly forbidden? He sucked in his breath. "Here?" He looked from one young face to the other.

Marcus would not flinch. "In the chapel," he told Justin. "Tomorrow night is my vigil. But remember, Justin, if caught, I have the archbishop to turn to. You have no one."

"I have the truth."

At the library the next morning Justin searched immediately to see if his collection of manuscripts had been disturbed. With relief he saw they had not. He slipped the Latin version from under the stack and found his way more easily this time to the epistle of Romans. With a vast inkwell and a stand of quills at hand, he began to write.

Paul, a servant of Jesus Christ, called to be an apostle, separated unto the gospel of God, (Which he had promised before by his prophets in the holy Scriptures,) concerning his Son Jesus Christ our Lord . . .

That night the three youths met in the chapel.

The candle flames flickered, casting swaying shadows. John said they reminded him of spirits, and he cast his eyes upward to where the chiseled faces of saints and angels stared down upon them from the ceiling. Then he drew his robe more closely around him to keep from shivering.

Justin felt nothing but the burning in his heart.

His handwritten copy of the Roman epistle lay on the floor before them.

Justin read in whispers but distinctly, pausing now and then to search his friends' faces to see if they understood the profound meaning.

John soon hung on every word, though his eyelids fluttered nervously. His figure was as small as a child's, lost within its clerical robe. The candle flame made his brown eyes luminous under the dark lashes.

Marcus frowned and raised a hand to cut Justin off. "Slowly, slowly. With rapidity you do sear the page with the flame of your tongue."

He then leaned over the Scriptures, his forefinger sliding over the Latin text. His finger went back and forth under the same line several times as he repeated the words, but he seemed still to miss the emphasis.

Justin made small jabs at the key words in the passage, repeating them for Marcus with emphasis, and then explaining their meaning.

"'Therefore'—because of what Saint Paul has written previously," Justin insisted.

"'Being justified'—do you see it?" he continued. "'By faith.' Not by works," he pointed out. "'We have'—that means right now. 'Peace with God through'—by the merit of another—'our Lord Jesus Christ.'"

Marcus rubbed his chin. He agreed thoughtfully, wagging his head. "Yes, I see it. But let us move on. There is much to read, and the night wears on. Who has a vigil tomorrow?"

"I do," said John.

"Then let us meet again. And let us invite a few others to see what their minds will tell us."

"Is that wise?" breathed John. "If word gets out . . ." His voice trailed.

"Whether it be prudent, I do not know," said Justin, "but it is good that any who have a desire should read for themselves. The more we discuss this doctrine, the more defined it will become. But our arguments must not stray from what the Scripture says. We must let the words speak for themselves."

"They speak more clearly than I thought," Marcus said. "This is the first time I have heard the epistle of Romans word by word."

John whispered, "I confess the words make my skin crawl. How awesome is the pen of Saint Paul."

"No," said Justin quietly, "it is not only the pen of Paul but also that the words are living with the very breath of the Almighty. Agreed?"

"Agreed," they said.

Justin's smile was disarming. "Good. We cannot walk the same path unless we agree."

"But where does this path lead us?" Marcus questioned ruefully.

"We will follow until the path forces a new direction. Only then will we know. But if these words guide us, then we can be sure of going in the right way."

For the next few weeks they met, until the number of student priests who risked attendance swelled to a dangerous level. They changed the meeting place nightly, and when it was impossible to meet the word was passed with hand signals.

Not all those attending the study agreed with Justin's interpretation of justification by faith apart from religious works. At times the discussion grew tense and voices rose, only to have emotions bridled by the necessity of whispering once again. But the meetings around the handwritten epistle continued.

One night Justin slept restlessly on the stone floor. The events of the past weeks swirled through his sleep like actors on a stage. He tossed about and saw an image of the superior twice his usual size, yet gaunt, illuminated by the candle he held above his head, which made his eyes appear empty sockets of yellow.

"*Recant!*"

Justin awoke in a sweat. He had been startled to wakefulness for no apparent cause other than that his muscles were cramping, but between wakefulness and sleep he imagined someone was standing by his feet. Or had someone really been there? Upon reflection, he assumed it had been one of the other one hundred students who slept with him on the floor.

His mind, filled with Romans, formed the words in his memory. And now it seemed the apostle Paul himself stood before him in chains.

"But to him that worketh not, but believeth on him that justifieth the ungodly, his faith is counted for righteousness. . . . Therefore we conclude that a man is justified by faith without the deeds of the law."

Justin cried, "Then I shall *not* recant! Never! In those words I shall rest my soul!"

A hand grabbed his shoulder.

"Silence," John hissed in the darkness. "You will have the superior in here. Who were you talking to?"

Justin lay back down and in spite of the cold realized that his body was wet with perspiration. Yet peace beyond verbalization wrapped itself with glowing warmth about the inner recesses of his soul. He murmured in Latin, "To my Lord."

John squinted at Justin in the darkness, then lay down. But try as he might, John could not go back to sleep. He began his own rote prayers, then stopped.

Timidly he began again, with only his lips moving, and spoke from the heart. "If you hear me, Jesus Christ, and do in truth offer justification from all things vile, and this justification lasts forever in Your holy presence, and this is based alone on Your sufficiency and not on any merit of my own—then give me boldness to believe.

"Grant to me the courage to act in an hour of darkness. For I quake with trembling in my bones, O Lord. I sense the prison walls of separation coming between us three friends, and the end of our diligent pursuit before it has truly begun. Help me to be true, for I fear greatly the darkness of a dungeon."

The one tree struggling to stay alive near the library wall had leaves of red and gold. The wind blew chill, shaking it to its meager roots, threatening to topple it before it posed a threat of dense shade to the few square feet of ivy now inhabiting the earth and reaching for the university wall. But one tentacle of ivy had already latched hold of the slim trunk and was climbing upward, prepared to swallow up the highest branch, which was poised as if in prayer toward the gray sky.

Justin ran up the university steps. Upon entering the echoing musty halls, he slowed to a walk. The day promised rain and strong winds, but his spirits were light. He had peace, and the joy of his relationship with Christ seemed more blessed than it had ever been.

He wanted to whistle as he entered the library but dared not. So he entered sedately, and it waited for him as it had for the past year. As usual, he removed his hat and the drab woolen cloak that had sufficed him for the three years he had been in Rome. It was getting threadbare at the elbows, but he scarcely noticed. And, as usual, the odor of musty parchments, ink, old leather, and wood greeted him inoffensively. He had grown accustomed to the smell and now linked it in some pleasant way with the Latin text and the great teachings of Paul the apostle.

The other translators glanced up sharply. Justin murmured his customary Latin greeting. He was thinking of the promise of Erasmus and did not notice that one head bent low did not meet his eyes.

Erasmus vowed a better version of the Greek New Testament and a new Latin text as well. As yet Justin had heard nothing, and he wondered how long the church would need to wait.

Of course, the honored task would be a mighty one and would take time. Marcus had told him that Master Colet had called Erasmus the finest scholar in Christendom. He had tried to keep Erasmus at Oxford to teach literature and the Old Testament, but Erasmus did not feel ready to handle the language, and he had come to Italy.

Justin sat down before the stack of uncataloged manuscripts that filled his table to overflowing. It was his job to bring them to some kind of order before the Christmas holidays.

He began work at once, and the silence made the scratch of his pen seem loud.

He paused, and his mind turned back to the new Greek version promised by Erasmus. It dawned on him that if he were ever to study such a translation for himself he must become proficient in Greek. Thinking of Scripture, he reached under the stack of manuscripts for the Vulgate.

It was gone!

Cautious, he dared not draw attention by showing alarm. Affecting unhurried calmness he began to move the manuscripts about. He might have placed it elsewhere. The Vulgate was a seldom-used library copy, and therefore safe to keep at his disposal, but it was not there.

The implications caused a rise in his heartbeat. No one would look among his manuscripts unless sent to do so. And who would bother unless he suspected the Latin version to be there?

He looked up. Every head was lowered and busy as always. Then he saw one head turn slightly and glance in his direction. The eyes of the scholar meeting Justin's were averted at once, and his pen scratched quickly.

Had news of the meetings in the monastery reached the abbot? Justin was sure the man across from him knew the answer.

A moment later the scholar slipped from his seat as if to visit the lavatory perhaps. As he walked past, he dropped a piece of parchment at Justin's feet.

When Justin was sure no one was watching, his foot reached out and brought the parchment closer. He dropped a quill, stooped to pick it up, and read a message hastily scratched in Latin: "Your secret is known. Be prepared in mind and spirit for arrest."

Aware that some of his fellow monks were glancing in his direction, Justin resumed his translation work. Should he make a run for it? But if he did, would he not be admitting transgression? And what would those who had followed his example in the monastery believe of his actions?

He looked quickly about the library. The other scholars all knew of his situation. He sensed the sympathy of some and the satisfaction of others who disagreed with his actions.

He looked past the candle to the door. It swung open, and the translator reentered. He held the door wide open for a moment to reveal several guards in the outer hall.

It was too late for any recourse. The others knew it as well, and one by one they went back to their work, resigned to the outcome. Tomorrow morning they would be one less, and there would be an empty desk.

Justin's internal struggle heightened. Was his newfound conviction worth the danger he was now in? He immediately thought of John and Marcus. Had they been found out too? But of course. The superiors would have to know. Whoever reported them would be sure to give the name of every young monk who had attended and how much involved each man was. The leaders were sure to be singled out first.

To his right, lying on the table in a leather envelope, was the handwritten copy of Romans. Cautiously he pushed it to one side, but there was no hope he could keep it. Soon the precious parchment would forever be out of his reach.

It had been his intention to commit the entire letter to memory, but with all his studies and religious duties he had memorized only the first chapter. He now saw that it would have been wiser to memorize key verses.

And he should have hidden the epistle somewhere in the monastery instead of carrying it daily back and forth. He had been overconfident. He might have known that, as the meeting around the Scriptures grew, someone would turn against them.

Hindsight is always the best teacher. The hour for better planning had passed. Perhaps his youthful zeal had carried him away, but for the joy of those months of study with his fellows, it had been worth the risk. Who knew what new seeds of faith the Word had planted in their hearts? He could only guess the harvest. He waited for the footsteps of his superiors.

Recant? His hand rested briefly on the leather envelope. How could he forget those astounding words written by Saint Paul while they resounded within his brain like the beat of a drum? The dream of the night before stirred in his memory. Recant? No.

The click of sandals on stone brought him back to the moment. He prayed for strength to remain true. Two superiors stopped at either side of his table. "The abbot will see you in his chamber."

Justin scanned the epistle of Romans. He sensed he would not see it again.

As Justin and the two superiors walked swiftly and silently back to the monastery along the cobbled streets, a few drops of rain fell. They passed through the gate of the high wall that encircled the monastery compound, through the cloistered garden where he walked each day, and down the passage to the door of the abbot's chambers.

The door swung open. Justin stepped inside and heard it shut solidly behind him. There would be no turning back now. It was one thing to be brought in question by a superior, but the abbot was a powerful man.

The head of the monastery school sat behind his desk with an open ledger before him, quill in hand. Once he had enjoyed his work at the monastery of Saint Athenians and had satisfied his interest in scholarship by involving himself within the university. But the favor conferred upon him by the archbishop, and the prospect of an esteemed position within the Vatican Palace, now owned his ambitions. If he distanced himself from unorthodox opinions, both religious and political, his opportunities would blossom into a distinguished career.

He looked at Justin, then reached for a letter on his desk. "Your name is Justin Brice, and you are from London. You have been here at Saint Athenians for three years. You have excelled in your scholarship at the university. Master of

Arts Mirandola writes highly of your use of Latin and your position in the library." The dark eyes now fixed upon him.

A small fire crackled on the hearth, but in spite of the cold Justin felt too warm. Beads of perspiration formed on his forehead as he struggled over what he would say. Words now eluded him, and his previous confidence fled.

Suppose he could not defend his position? How would he answer this distinguished man? That he might have no answer disturbed him more than the thought of punishment. What would he say? His throat suddenly constricted. He felt as though he had been stricken dumb.

The pressure of the strained silence mounted as the abbot stood. He was tall and lean with a shock of silver hair and keen dark eyes. He reminded Justin of a military man, a handsome Roman with the noble manner of royalty. Instead of a robe, Justin pictured him with a toga tossed over his shoulder and a laurel wreath about his head.

The abbot scanned him and tossed a familiar parchment to the desk. "I was told you see yourself as an authority to judge between the original writings and the teachings of the church."

The dark eyes were satirical, yet not altogether angry. A glimmer of amusement turned his lips into a smile as he took in Justin's youthfulness.

Justin felt the humiliation of his scrutiny.

"Yes or no?" asked the abbot.

Justin cleared his throat and bowed his head. "The abbot is a very wise man. Surely he knows that I see myself as a mere humble student. No less than a worm."

The abbot was amused. "I once heard of a humble worm from Wittenberg who came to Rome and kissed the ground. Martin Luther has since sprouted butterfly wings. He now debates heretical teachings on justification by faith. A growing and popular theme, so it seems, among humble worms."

"The monk you speak of I do not know, my lord abbot."

The abbot scrutinized him.

Was he satisfied? Would he accept this token or would he press for more?

"Brice, you are a hypocrite, truly a worm of compromise." The abbot arched his brow. "A Latin scholar who deigns to teach the epistle of Romans, 'humble'?" he jested and smiled.

"What a rare find! But for such a humble worm, young man, you hold lofty opinions. Strange ideas that breed conflict and disunity within the monastery of Saint Athenians."

"I have not sought nor do I wish conflict with you or the church."

"I am pleased to hear that. Obedience to the will of your superiors will put an end to all conflict."

The silence locked them in. It was an awful stillness to Justin. As their eyes held, Justin lowered his gaze, for the fire that burned within contradicted his words.

The abbot's voice was toneless. "Questions can be healthy. But then again, it is no light matter to undermine the foundational teachings of one's own house. The house can come crashing down upon one's head. Tell me, I would hear from your own lips and not the lips of any who may be jealous of you."

He then fixed Justin with a grave stare. "To willfully undermine any foundation ordained by Christ is heresy. A wise priest will work to maintain that ordained system." He paused. "Do you agree, Justin Brice?"

"The abbot speaks wisely. But, my lord, what if the foundation is discovered to be newly laid by men and not by Christ? What if it is contrary to what has already been set forth in the Scriptures? Then is not change necessary to recover forgotten truth? The questioning of such foundations would then not be heresy but vigilance."

The moment seemed endless. Under the probing stare of the abbot, Justin felt like a dismembered frog.

"This necessity," the abbot inquired. "Do you see it as a need for reform in doctrine?"

Justin chose his words cautiously. "I would see it as a necessity to differentiate between written Scripture and the growing emergence of tradition. Such tradition, if not differentiated from the written words of God, will surely lead the church into a path of further error."

The eyes of the abbot glinted. "I must be sure I hear you right. Did you say 'further' error?"

Justin froze. "Yes."

"Ah, so the church is smothered with the darkness of tradition?" he mocked. "Our lamp has gone out? Is that it? The voice of the church is the voice of men and not of Christ? And so you, a mere 'humble worm,' have felt inclined to teach your erring brothers."

He held up the parchment. "The writing of Saint Paul," he explained, as though Justin had never seen it before. "The epistle of Romans. I understand you consider yourself familiar with it and qualified to teach it."

"I never considered myself to be anything. But I would wish both great and small to labor over its awesome truth. Therein we will find light to lead us from darkness."

"Indeed! But who will lead with book in hand? You? Even as I gaze upon its truths, I often find myself a mere child before a fathomless sea. Are you tempted to think you have plumbed its depths? Perish the thought! Where is your humility, your mortification before the feet of teachers better than you? You have but captured in your cup a drop of water! Do you think yourself wise enough to understand what is written without the guidance of your superiors? Do you believe that you can teach the writings of Saint Paul?"

"I confess to be but a learner. Yet, even as a student, I have stumbled upon vast differences between what the writings say and what I am taught."

"Great minds within the church have wrestled to understand the high and lofty words of the apostle from the beginning of Christianity—yet you can expound his words with confident authority?"

The abbot thrust the epistle into Justin's hands and sat down quickly, arms folded. "Will you teach? Will you confuse the young minds of your brethren under cover of darkness? Be so bold now as to teach me. I wait with bated breath."

The ridicule stung, and Justin felt himself getting hot.

"Or do you want me to wait for the archbishop? Perhaps I am not audience grand enough for scholarship? Perhaps the pope? Shall I hustle you off to the Vatican Palace?"

His mockery provoked Justin to match his satire. And before he could control his tongue he blurted out, "Surely I have sinned, my lord abbot. For in reading the Scriptures

59

and in discussing its contents, I did not know that God gave them in order to hide His truth in a sea of profundity.

"Nor was I aware that He gave Scripture to frustrate the minds of great scholars for centuries with words that cannot be understood. I did not know, my lord abbot, that the words were to be kept under lock with the key given only to the few whose religious position, often bought by temporal wealth, has then authorized them to teach the ignorant multitude— but only in Latin.

"I have grievously erred, my lord abbot, for I believed God gave Scripture to reveal, to quicken, and to teach His church His will on earth. And that of all epistles, the letter written to the church at Rome could be understood by us at Rome. Unworthy though I be, I confess to have learned more truth in one year of studying the Scriptures than all my vigils, fastings, and strivings in prayers have gained me."

The abbot slammed his fist down on the desk. "You insolent and stupid young fool. You are hereby declared a heretic." He stood. "You shall wait in the dungeon until I bring your case before the archbishop."

"I meant not to be insolent, sir, but you mocked my sincerity as the babble of a fool."

"Babble aside! You are here to receive just correction, and do you audaciously seek to correct me with your cynical tongue?"

"I will receive correction if I am shown wherein I have erred."

"Shown? Is it not enough that your spiritual superiors by their very position have called your behavior into question? You sin now by refusing to accept their correction. Your obedience to the church is demanded. I warn you now, Justin Brice, if you do not recant of your errors, your situation will be grave indeed."

"Sir! Since when has reading the Scriptures in Latin become an act of heresy?"

"I would remind you that Savonarola was tried and put to death on charges of disobedience alone."

Justin recalled the Dominican who was assigned to Florence. He had tried to reform both state and church, but his cries against the evil life of church leaders had resulted in his death.

"Answer me. Have you, or have you not, copied Holy Scripture without authorization?"

"Yes."

"All or some?"

"The epistle of Romans only."

"And smuggled it into the holy cloister to teach to your brethren in training?"

"I saw no sin in bringing the Word of God into the cloister nor meeting about it with those who willingly came to hear and see. I have uttered nothing in the ears of my fellow brethren but what was written in this parchment."

"And is it not also true that you preach the need to translate the Latin into—" he spread his hands "—God forbid! English! The language of peasants! Answer me, Justin Brice. Do you see yourself a man called of God to translate the Scriptures into the common tongue?"

Trapped, thought Justin. *If I do not speak, I will despise myself as a man and even more as a Christian.*

"Yes, my lord abbot."

The silence seemed to thunder.

The abbot threw up his hands, stood, and turned away. After a moment he said very quietly, his back still turned. "For that you can be burned."

Justin stood silently, his emotion now leaving him spent.

The abbot turned back. "Don't you see that translating from Latin into the carnal language of peasants and slaves would corrupt the holy words? The original writings must be preserved."

"Preserved, my lord? Preserved to sit silent in musty rooms in a language few can speak or understand? Should they not be translated and fed to both priest and people?"

"Are there not enough problems in trusting student-priests with the Scriptures? Do you expect us to also turn them over to peasants?"

"The Scriptures should be in every man's own tongue."

"Ah."

Justin imagined the clang of the cell door, the key turning. "I have said no more than scholars such as Erasmus. Has he not said the Scriptures should be in the common language?"

The abbot took up the parchment and for a moment stood reading it. "A pity. Your work is quite good. Master of Arts Mirandola was right. He had plans for you. That was the reason he chose you for work in the university library. He was wrong, however. You cannot be trusted with such an awesome task. If your education proceeds beyond Latin to Greek and Hebrew, you will soon be at the bazaar peddling handwritten portions of Scripture along with leeks and fish."

He walked to the hearth and tossed the manuscript into the coals.

Justin watched the writing disintegrate.

"This is a dangerous time for the church. The winds of heresy are stirring in unlikely places across Europe. I must bring your case before the archbishop. Perhaps a year or so in the dungeon will be enough to bring you to your senses."

A year!

"My lord abbot! Since I have not yet earned my ordination, is it not enough to banish me from this diocese and return me to London?"

"So you can sow seeds elsewhere? I could wish, Justin Brice, that it were so light a matter." He rang a bell. "The archbishop will decide your fate. It is out of my hands. I have no more to say." He turned away.

Justin stood in resolute silence. It was evident that further argument would be useless.

A servant came in.

"Put him in confinement until the bishop comes."

4

A Dungeon in Rome

The dungeon was black. His body ached from lying on the cold slab of the damp cell, and the wind blew rain through the small barred window above his head. He had no idea of the time or what day it was. He pulled his soiled cloak about his head and moved across the filthy straw to another corner, hoping to get away from the rain.

He felt the loathsome movement of the rats who were so accustomed to his presence that they brushed against him without fear and only smelled him inquisitively. He had learned to move about in the gross darkness to keep from being bitten.

How many days had passed? How many weeks? It seemed months. He never knew, for his questions of the monks who brought his food were greeted with silence. He had tried to use his fingernail to scratch a mark for each dawn that lightened the window, but the stone was hard, and he could find nothing sharp enough to keep record. Even his cross had been ceremoniously removed from around his neck.

Where was the archbishop? When would his trial begin? Or had they decided to just let him remain in the dungeon? What had been the fate of John, Marcus, and the others? Were they too in dungeons, or had they recanted?

The nights were always the worst with their darkness, the cold seeping through his clothes, and the stench of lumbering rats. Again he rebuked himself for not memorizing the epistle. If he had done so, how much comfort would be his.

Instead he concentrated on prayer and found that the mercy of the Lord knew no bounds or lack of patience. During his endless night vigils, the warm peace he remembered so well upon resting in the written Word again came to brighten his mind, and he found his courage strengthened.

"Christ of goodness, give me the faith to rest my case confidently in Your hand and to believe Your will shall prevail. If it is here You wish me to stay, grant me peace. And if it is death, do not let me recant in fear of the hot fagots. Let me die knowing my conviction is not in vain."

He took consolation in remembering the sufferings of Christ and in knowing that his own, however presently miserable, were light in comparison. The One who had suffered and died now lived to come beside him as Sustainer and Helper, and not even the dungeon could diminish His sweet presence.

He slept, and when his eyes opened upon a new dawn the rats were out of sight. He stirred. Someone was coming.

At the end of the outer passageway a flight of chiseled steps led up to a small door. A rattle of keys was followed by the sound of footsteps. A torch gave light, and a monk came hurriedly down the steps. Even before he came into clear view, Justin recognized the form and face.

Marcus! He was free! Had he recanted? Or had his uncle, the archbishop, moved on his behalf?

Marcus reached inside his tunic and removed a supply of smuggled apples, bread and cheese, and a flagon of cider. Justin took them through the bars, feeling relieved to see his friend well, yet faintly disappointed.

"So you have recanted?"

Marcus arched a mocking brow. "Have you no confidence in my integrity? No, say nothing. It is enough that I have the keys, is it not?"

Victoriously he turned the lock, and the cell opened. "Come."

Freedom? Justin could hardly believe it.

Marcus lit a second torch and passed it to him. With an upward glance at the steps he said, "A friend waits for you in the meditation garden. He masquerades as a priest and calls himself Felix. He has a message and says a Brice ship is docked in Italy."

Felix! Ewan Brice had first bought the Saracen out of slavery in the Muslim East. Changing his name from Tahir to Felix, the servant had been in the Brice family since Justin was a boy.

"All things have come together for your escape. If we make haste, you will soon be aboard ship sailing for London."

"God be praised, but—" Justin felt a twinge of dread "—what of John?"

Marcus stiffened. "He became ill in the dungeon and died. Grieve later. We have no time to linger. There is a passage through the lower dungeons. This way."

Justin fled after Marcus, who darted down the passageway. They walked for several minutes before Marcus paused at a crossway to consult the small drawing that he held to the torchlight. Justin knew better than to ask where he had gotten the drawing. They stopped before another door, a key rattled, and a dark passage loomed before them.

"There is an aqueduct that takes water to the orchard."

"Who told you of this exit?"

"The archbishop." Marcus looked at him squarely. "He is not my uncle. He is my father. My mother is of the Italian nobility."

Justin began to understand why Marcus had been able to get himself out of trouble.

"Escape from Rome is your last hope," Marcus said. "A trial would condemn you to death."

Their torches had burned down, and Marcus pointed ahead with his flickering flame to a narrow passage. Justin heard the sound of water, and then they were lowering themselves into the cold flood. Now their light was gone, and they edged forward blindly through the tight tunnel. The water was waist deep.

The distance seemed endless amid the pitch black, and the rush of water tore at Justin's body. Marcus was much lighter, and he gripped Justin's arm as they moved forward together.

Then they emerged, unexpectedly. Light greeted them, and the water echoed ahead.

Marcus was shivering. His teeth chattered. "Y-you up first. M-my strength . . . is lacking."

Justin grasped the top of the conduit and clambered up and over. Then, placing himself flat to the rock, he reached down for Marcus's hand.

65

They rested against the outer flume of the aqueduct. A gust of cold wind blew the rain in their faces.

Justin listened for voices, but the garden was silent. A glance about proved the area deserted. The grove of fig, apricot, and olive trees stretched before them, and still farther was the large monastery garden. Little of the summer harvest remained except tired squash vines and the yellow and brown leaves of the abbot's prized grapes.

Marcus led the way. In one corner of the grove, a sheltered path took them through an isolated arbor of climbing rosebushes. The sky above was like granite, and the steady drizzle dripped through the overhead tangle of thorny branches.

They walked hurriedly in silence, and after a time came in sight of another path angling toward the outer back wall of the monastery.

"It is here we must say good-bye, my friend," said Marcus. "Your father's servant waits by the fountain."

It seemed unthinkable that having arranged for his escape, Marcus would not join him.

"Together we may accomplish something of lasting value for our generation," Justin urged.

"No, brother, I cannot go with you to London," Marcus said firmly. He avoided Justin's gaze, resisting, it seemed, the inward tug of friendship and—something else. What was it? "I believe as you. Only I will work here in Rome. The power of my father, the archbishop, can open doors that neither of us could open alone. And it offers a safe haven from which I can work toward reform. What good to die in a cell like John, or to be burned? Who remembers martyrs?"

Justin gravely considered. "It matters not if the world pauses to remember. It matters that Christ does."

Marcus stood shivering in his dripping robe.

Justin knew well his friend's ambitions, and he knew what was possible if one had influence and wealth. His own escape and the fact that Marcus could remain in safety was proof of that. The abbot would not touch Marcus because he was thought to be the nephew of the man who held the key to the abbot's advancement into the Vatican Palace.

But what of future controversies? What would befall Marcus when he was older and the archbishop was no longer there to protect him? Would his convictions then lead him to death?

Justin warned quietly, "Think not that position alone will give you room to bring about reform. Good men have tried in the past to be rebuked into silence."

Marcus smiled thinly. "One could learn much from Erasmus when it comes to walking the cliff's edge. I will be leaving Rome and going to Florence where Savonarola served. I will attend the Platonic Academy to pursue my studies and Greek." Marcus grew thoughtful. "Remember the night in the chapel when you spoke of the path branching? It branches now, and I choose another way. Nay, I have not recanted. My father did not ask me to, and I did not offer. The abuses in the church must be stopped. But I will seek reform within the institution. I cannot, and will not, break with it."

"And I respect your decision. Let us leave to the sovereignty of God His method to bring reform. It is enough we agree on the need. The bodies of heretics may die, but their ideas, if born of the Spirit, will live. And if the light of truth burns brighter through the death of men like Savonarola, then it must be."

They paused together at the place where their paths would part and for a moment said nothing. Behind Justin lay the past. Marcus would go to Florence with the promise of a bright future, and he would return to London and—what?

"Then here we part," he said. He smiled into the face that usually bore a cynical expression. "I wish you true peace, my friend and protagonist Marcus."

"And for you, said heretic, true answers."

Then Marcus removed his silver cross and handed it to Justin. "The peace of Christ be with you."

Justin quickly embraced him, and Marcus hurried away, his emotion to be seen only by the silent friends of nature who told no tales.

And the last of the nodding roses, whose withered petals drooped, moved gently in the silent rain, and a lone bird, who sat in a branch of his once secure summer home, took flight as the leaves fell, leaving the limb stark against the on-coming blight of frost.

When Justin reached the end of the path he looked back. He had thought he heard Marcus following, but no.

There was no time for disappointment. And who knew the variance of God's ways when it came to His own? He was sure His hand would be upon Marcus. And John? John's memory was everywhere in the garden, but his soul was with Christ.

The ancient Roman fountain lay in ruins. Moss grew on its stones, and a few flowers, unwilling to say good-bye to the summer sun, bravely turned their faces into the rain.

Justin paused and looked about for Felix.

Then from the shrubs came the familiar voice he had not heard in years.

"Heaven be praised! You are still in one sizable piece, Master!"

Justin turned as Felix crawled out of the bushes, his black eyes gleaming with relief.

Justin laughed and embraced him, then held the lean figure in monk's robe at arms' length. "Felix! Your hair is turning gray."

"Yes, Master. The years pass as swiftly as the flight of a raven. You have not kept count."

"So you think! And where did you get the monk's cowl?"

"Anything can be bought in Rome."

"I knew matters were bad, but things are worse than I thought when even Felix can buy a priest's robe," Justin jested. Then he grew serious. "Did my brother Stewert send you?"

Felix's eyes became troubled. "Nay, 'twas the fairest of women, Lady Regina."

Mention of her name took Justin by surprise.

"There is much to tell you, Master, but it must wait. We should leave at once. After I spoke to your friend Marcus, another monk saw me and knew I was a stranger."

Justin halted him. His head jerked back toward the path. The sound was unmistakable. There was a rush of feet and more than two voices.

Felix motioned ahead. "That way! There is a wall!"

They raced through the tangled shrubs. Felix surged ahead, then tripped over his robe. "A robe is a curse, young Master. How have you borne it?"

"Not well, but better than you. Hoist it up under your belt. Watch those vines."

At the corner of the wall Felix had a rope in place and was instantly up and over. Justin climbed swiftly, seized the top of the wall, pulled up the rope, and dropped to the other side.

"They will never get over," Felix said confidently. "They must turn back to the gate."

"Never underestimate hounds after a fox—two foxes now. Hurry."

Below was a steep slope. They slid and twisted their way to the bottom where a quiet dirt road waited. In the distance several riders on horseback were approaching. From their dress they looked to be mercenary soldiers.

"Master Justin, quick! Cross the road!"

Sprinting as though huntsmen were at their heels, they darted into the welcoming shadows where trees grew close together. At long last they emerged on the other side of the wooded area, apparently safe for the moment. They sank into the grass, gasping.

Finally Justin's heart ceased to race. He stared up at the sky, enjoying the soft drizzle on his face and the lightening clouds that seemed like sailing ships.

Lord, thank You.

5

Rome

Inside the Roman inn, Felix sat cross-legged on the floor. Justin leaned against the wall, tasting his new freedom.

The room was long and had but one entrance. The hostel would soon fill with travelers, though only a few vagabond soldiers were presently at the inn. They sat wearily in a corner talking among themselves and drinking from a shared jug.

Felix used his dagger to carve a chunk of meat from the leg of lamb. His eyes twinkled. "A woman with wit and courage," he said of Lady Regina. "I would trust her with my life—and yours, Master."

Justin remembered his younger days near Windsor Castle. Regina had always been adventurous, much to the dismay of her father, Lord Simon, and her brother. She rarely, however, gave them true cause for concern.

She was, in truth, not only a girl of wit and courage but owned the charms of a lady of nobility. He remembered how she had sent her servant to Saint Catherine's with the price of his indulgence for helping the Wycliffites to escape. He remembered the time shared in the woods when they read the forbidden English version of the gospel of Matthew.

"What news do you bring from her ladyship?"

Felix reached under his robe and handed Justin a letter. "'Tis with sadness I bring you this news, Master, but we thought you should know."

Expecting the worst, Justin opened Regina's letter dated in August from King Henry's palace. Her artistic handwriting leaped up at him.

"Learning from Felix that one of your father's ships was soon to set sail for Rome under the command of your brother, I have given this letter to Felix, your faithful friend and mine, to deliver to you at Saint Athenians. Since my other letters and parcels have gone unanswered . . ."

His jaw tightened, and a feeling of frustration seized him. So she had written to him, and he had not been able to answer. What must she have thought of him? Did she believe he no longer cared? And yet, what hope was there?

When Felix first came to me about your father's condition, I traveled at once to Antwerp to find him in the home of a merchant friend, Thomas Poynitz. I found your father just as poorly as Felix had described. He is a man tormented in soul, and I fear for his eternal state. I have tried in vain to console him with hope in Christ, for I have learned much recently under the lectures of Dean John Colet at Saint Paul's Cathedral. Yet it seems I am not the one to break through your father's spiritual barrier. The dear man is twisted by guilt and regret over your fate in the monastery.

I regret to tell you that your sisters, Catherine and Mary, died of the sweating sickness this winter. Your father is sure that he is to blame. He is woefully convinced that he is doomed to abide with heretics in hell. I shall let Felix explain his thoughts to you.

Justin paused. So his little sisters were gone. Stabilizing his emotions he read on.

I have written, hoping you might receive permission from the bishop in Rome to come to London to visit your father, for I do not know how much longer his mind will hold. Through the kindness of his friends in Antwerp, I have managed to bring him to my father's estate in Devonshire. The countryside, I felt, would do him good.

I wish also to tell you of a wonderful happening here in London. Dean Colet is lecturing on the Pauline epistles to overflow audiences. I have attended whenever possible, though my father is upset with my independence. I have talked Marlon into coming with me on several occasions, and he is quite excited at hearing the Scriptures so plainly taught. I could wish for you to hear also.

At the lectures, Lord Marlon has met a most interesting young Oxford scholar by the name of William Tyndale. You must meet him. I dare say no more on paper except that his scholarship is noteworthy. His zeal for Christ and the Scriptures is like a flame of fire.

As ever, Regina

Justin sat staring at the letter. His emotions were divided in several directions. Being in touch with Regina if only by letter awakened a strange desire within his heart. The thought of John Colet lecturing on the Pauline epistles thrilled him. Of the Oxford scholar William Tyndale he knew nothing and could only wonder why she would mention him along with a Master of Arts such as Colet, who taught the Word of God as no one else was doing in the university.

But his father . . . He tensed, his appetite gone. He must go to him at once. He must share what he had learned from the epistle of Romans before it was eternally too late.

"And Stewert," he said, "where is he? I would see him at once. Where is his ship?"

Felix scowled. "I wish not to speak evil of your brother, Master, but—" he spread his hands "—what shall I say to you?"

"The truth, Felix, as always. Spare nothing."

"The Brice ship is docked at Genoa and will be there for a few weeks. Captain Stewert is about his business, buying cargo to return to Antwerp. Most of the crew is on leave, and he thinks I too revel in the city. Your brother does not know I am here. He warned me not to come to you."

Justin frowned. The years between him and his older brother were many, and the boys had never been close. Adding the years Justin had spent with his studies, he realized they hardly knew each other. Yet was this reason enough for Stewert to forbid Felix to bring him news of the death of his sisters and his father's condition?

"Captain Stewert is a jealous man," said Felix darkly. "He thinks ill of you."

A ghost of a smile touched Justin's lips. "Jealous? Of a brother in a monastery? While he sails the open seas?"

"Stewert fears the love your father has for you. The bond your father feels between you and your mother has always been deep. Stewert's mother, poor woman, was never loved. Wherever Captain Brice has sailed, it was you, Master, that troubled the mind of your father. Stewert fears that your return to London will mean the Brice galleons will be left to you and not to himself."

"My father expects me to remain in the monastery. Why would he unexpectedly change his will?"

"That his own conscience might find a token of rest." He leaned closer, and his voice lowered. "Your father is a tormented soul. After your journey here to Rome, we sailed to Cadiz and on to the Golden Horn of the Turkish Empire. He knew no joy, Master. He would not eat nor even drink his ale. He took to badgering your brother until there arose a great argument between them over you. Stewert accused your father of caring nothing for any of his children except you.

"One night Sir Ewan called me to his cabin, greatly disturbed. 'Felix,' he said, 'I did well in sending my lad to Rome, did I not?'

"'Aye,' I told him. 'Heaven is pleased, Captain Brice.'

"He looked at me squarely and said, 'Then why does the peace of God still elude me?'

"'I know not, Captain,' I told him.

"'Why does the blood on my hands gleam red in the dark?'

"'I know not, Captain,' I told him. 'It is but a wicked dream sent by the spirits of those you slew fairly in battle. They rise from the sea in wrath to goad with pricks. Pay them no heed.'"

Justin groaned deeply within. *My Father, your conscience is aware of sin and has no knowledge of the sufficient work of Christ.*

Felix went on in a whisper. "'I did the lad ill,' your father kept saying. 'I forced him. God is not pleased. Even the ghost of me wife comes to scowl upon me.'

"'Tis but a dream, Captain Brice,' I keep assuring him, but he will not listen.

"It was then your little sisters took ill, and the news reached him of their death, both in one night. He became like a ranting lunatic. I grew fearful for the health of his mind and pleaded with the Honorable Thomas Poynitz to send word to Lady Regina about his state, thinking she might influence the bishop to seek your release from Saint Athenians."

Justin was greatly troubled. "I wrote my father that God had mercifully turned my journey to Rome into a discovery of light. There is no reason for guilt."

"No letters came, Master. Nor does it seem that you received those from her ladyship."

The morning sun broke from behind the clouds to send a glimmer of gold upon the dark blue of the Tiber. Slaves stroked the oars slowly as a guard galley passed the water gate, and their voices chanted in time with the oars.

Justin and Felix walked the flagstone road to catch the small ship that would bring them to Genoa.

"What city is like Rome?" Felix exclaimed with awe.

Justin stopped before a great cathedral and read aloud the inscription. "Christ our God, guard Thy city from all disturbances and wars. Break victoriously the force of the enemy."

"A noble prayer," said Felix piously.

"Yes. It was taken, if I am correct in my history, from one of the gates of old Constantinople. But one must remember Jerusalem, Felix. There the glory of God once dwelt. When the priests departed from His word, He departed from them. Is this great city any less responsible?"

Felix made no comment, for his eyes were beholding the many fine cathedrals. With so many great and awesome buildings dedicated to the honor of God, he thought, *How could this city be said to have departed from Him? My mother was a Moor. But I, Felix, am not a follower of Muhammad. No, indeed. It is Christ who is the light of East and West.*

He felt pleased with this pious thought and glanced at Justin's robe and cross. His satisfaction increased. *Why, I, Felix, walk beside a very priest of God!*

Justin threaded his way through a throng of merchants and buyers, and the jostling, bargaining, and arguing fell upon his ears an irksome babble. He came to a particular stall where a lean, bearded man was in charge. Justin caught sight of the weapons he sold, and he paused.

The keen eyes of the dignified Arab merchant fixed upon him, and he raked the clerical tunic with the controlled insolence of a race who had conquered the East.

The Arab would consider Justin an idolator. A worshiper of women. Belonging to a race that looked upon women as little more than personal property, he would consider Christianity to be worship of the virgin Mary.

Justin pointed. "A Damascus dagger?"

"What else, my friend?"

Justin ignored the hint of pride. He priced the blade.

"I will take it." He nodded toward Felix. "My friend will pay."

The merchant smiled for the first time as the exchange passed hands. "May Allah twice bless you," he said, too piously.

Justin started to walk on, but Felix apparently felt obliged to reveal his zeal. He leaned across the booth and pointed a finger toward the man's well-kept beard. "Beware, you infidel," he whispered.

The merchant drew back, insulted.

But Felix grabbed a basket of oranges from a neighboring booth and tossed the seller a coin. He joined Justin, peeling one with vigor. "Eat, Master," he said.

Justin had never seen so many churches, yet beyond the chanting of voices, the glimmer of candles, and the rising of sweet gray incense, there was no distinction between truth and error. Did anyone know? Did people or priest? Growing traditions mingled with Eastern mysticism, while the culture of Plato and the philosophy of the humanists were incorporated along with the words of the apostles. Clarity was needed.

"And what could unveil historic Christianity more completely than the renewed teaching of all the Scriptures?" Justin asked aloud.

Felix was cautious. Yet he had traveled enough with Captain Brice to understand the thoughts of the common man toward Rome. He mingled with them, and he knew their growing resentment over the apparent wealth of Rome and the drainage of their tax dollars into the papal treasury. Rome's attempt to get more money out of Saxony by the selling of indulgences would anger the Augustinian monk Martin Luther into nailing his ninety-five theses to the church door at Wittenberg.

The rulers of Western Europe had also begun to resent the loss of money and, along with the nobles and middle class, were casting eyes toward lands owned by the church. Moreover, political independence from the decisions of Rome was growing. King Henry would one day battle the pope for the right to marry Anne Boleyn by divorcing Catherine, who bore him no sons to inherit his throne. By doing so he would eventually break his ties with Rome and declare himself head of the church in England.

Beside the drainage of wealth, complicated by inflation and rising prices, the middle class saw corruption in the church and the abuse of clerical power. It angered them that self-seeking clerics could buy and sell offices—sinecures—where they were paid a salary yet did none of the work.

Justice too was bought and sold in clerical courts. For the right amount of money, ruling could be obtained that permitted acts that the Scriptures clearly condemned.

"Your friend Marcus said that you are in trouble with the abbot," whispered Felix. His black eyes rolled.

"It is good you have come, Felix. I must escape Rome. If caught, I will be tried as a heretic."

Felix's mouth dropped open. The dark eyes widened. Words temporarily failed him. "A heretic?" he repeated at last. "I cannot believe it, Master!"

Justin paused on the wharf, and the cool wind off the water blew his cowl. "Can you read Latin?" he asked innocently.

"Master, you mock me."

"It is not I who mock you, Felix. What value would you place upon the words of Christ if you possessed them in your own tongue?"

"You mean . . ." Felix hesitated to voice the suggestion. *"English?"*

"Yes. The tongue of merchants, sailors, yeomen, peasants, and slaves."

Felix hesitated again. He glanced about. He watched the dock workers loading and unloading cargo, and a peasant child running past carrying his breakfast and lunch in one hunk of bread. Then his eyes searched Justin's face.

In response to the question, Felix impulsively emptied his pocket of his remaining gold pieces and sent them rolling into the cobbled streets like flecks of light. "To possess such words in my own tongue would deem gold cheap, Master."

Beggars and waifs converged on the spot and fought for the coins.

Justin raised a brow at the dramatic act, but Felix lifted his dark head with dignity. "A profound question demands a dramatic answer, Master," he explained.

"It is for my desire to put the words of Christ into our tongue that I am branded a heretic," said Justin.

"What will you do, Master? Become another Wycliffe?"

Justin smiled and repeated his words. "Such honor would deem gold cheap."

A beggar tugged at Justin's worn sleeve. "Alms, my father, alms? For the love of the saints?"

Justin held palms forward to signify he had nothing and, grabbing Felix's arm, hurried him through the gathering crowd. Shouting waifs followed them.

"Now you've done it," Justin said.

They darted down the street, ducking here and there among shops and other buildings until they found themselves nearing the harbor. They paused then to walk.

Jason was awed by the morning's magnificent view extending southwest toward the Mediterranean. He looked at his companion and smiled. And then he was hurrying Felix down the steps to the wharf, which groaned with the movement of the water's swells beneath his sandaled feet.

The private boat slipped quietly from the waterway and moved west on the landward side of Italy toward Genoa, where the Brice ship waited to take on cargo.

Moving astern, Justin watched Rome slip from view. A thousand memories played with his emotions. The sea, still tumultuous from the storm of a few days before, was picking up again. The cold spray blowing against his face tasted salty on his lips.

Felix came back and fixed his gaze not toward Genoa but southward toward the open waters of the Mediterranean. Justin thought he understood his concern. "Stewert is late in bringing the ship to harbor in England."

"A mistake if you ask me, Master. We have delayed too long. The year is far gone to be risking the voyage."

"Is he a good man with the sea?"

"Already as good as your father. But proud and arrogant he is. You cannot tell him a thing. Yes, the sea will be no friend to the ship of Captain Stewert Brice. The weather will be sore enough."

"How long will the ship remain in Genoa?"

"Another four to five days."

"That will give me time to get aboard. And Stewert must not know until we are far at sea. I wish no argument with him now."

6

Genoa

Genoa was known for its merchants and ships, which aggressively competed in the world's markets. There the Brice ship had been loaded with the sort of fine, rich materials that had swept the palace of King Henry VIII, especially brightly colored velvets and cloth of gold.

It was night when Justin and Felix neared the vessel, huddling among the numerous masts docked quietly in the harbor. The night was still, the sky clear after the storm, and the moon was a silver crescent in the black canopy.

One of the men on watch recognized Felix. The crewman cast a glance over his shoulder. The others had their faces to the sea, undoubtedly anxious to put out again and return home to Antwerp. They only waited for Stewert and the crew to return.

The watch tossed a ladder over the rail of the tall ship, and Justin latched hold and climbed up. A few strides across the deck brought him to the cargo hold. He took the ladder down and was about to close the hatch over his head when above, in the ship's mast, he saw a young lad with flaxen hair.

The boy swung from a rope like a monkey, watching Justin with wide eyes transfixed on his monk's cowl—and probably on his cross as well, which caught the light and glinted.

Justin felt an uncomfortable twinge.

The lad stared at him in awe, as if he believed a monk possessed special powers. Because of the lack of knowledge of the Scriptures, the Christianity of even the most devout often mingled with superstition. And as their eyes briefly locked, Justin sensed that this could mean trouble.

Felix followed him down into the hold. "You will be safe here."

"That boy. Who is he?"

"Only a lad. 'Tis his first voyage. He will say nothing. He fears Captain Stewert."

In the cargo hold Justin lost himself among the barrels and caskets of goods to be brought home to London. How easy, he thought, to smuggle things into the belly of a ship.

They had been at sea several days when Justin awoke to find the vessel being tossed and battered by the Mediterranean. The hold was in total blackness. His bed of cushions in the bowels of the ship pitched up and down, and for a confused moment he could not remember where he was.

His head buzzed strangely. Felix had given him some exotic tea from an Eastern port. The last thing he remembered was the meal he enjoyed the night before, smuggled to him by Felix. "Eat, Master. Drink. You will need much rest."

Much rest. How long had he slept? He sat up in the darkness. What had been in that tea? He studied the movement of the ship, obviously struggling through high wind and heavy seas. The vessel lurched, its timbers groaned and shuddered as if ready to split apart. A gale. As Felix had warned, the sea was not easy to master this time of year.

Justin struggled to his knees. His head still buzzed, as he tried to keep his balance. Years away from the sea made his stomach churn. His robe—where was it in this blackness? And his dagger was gone! He felt blindly about the floor, bumping into a wooden barrel. At the sound, he heard something—someone—startle, then freeze.

"Felix!" he whispered fiercely. "Come here, you scheming practitioner."

It didn't take him long to realize that it was not Felix. But whoever it was had taken his cloak, his cross, and the dagger. Now, in his hurry to get away, he was bumping into barrels and sending them crashing and rolling.

It had to be that boy! What he wanted with his belongings, Justin did not know. He staggered toward the sound of the boy's stumbling feet.

"Wait," Justin called. "I promise not to hurt you."

His ears told him that the thief had reached the ladder and was now scampering upward. Justin followed, feeling his way. He grabbed an ankle just as the boy started through the hatch.

A sudden blast of wind and spray against his face shocked Justin out of his grogginess. He heard voices shouting above the wind, and the thud of running feet.

The strong booted legs of a crewman now halted above the hold. The man thrust a swaying lamp into the opening. "All hands on deck! Who dares cower down there with the rats?"

Another crewman joined him. "It's the lad," he called above the din of wind and sea. "Trying to escape your duty, are you? You scurvy bloke!"

"No sir, no sir, the gods of the sea are angry, and I was seeking relics to bless us!"

"Now look here, boy. Did not the captain warn you to keep out of the cargo? You have got the fingers of a thief! This is your last voyage on a Brice ship—what you got in your hand?"

The seaman grabbed the robe as the boy cowered against the ladder top. He held up the lantern with one hand and shook out the garment with the other.

"A priest's robe?"

The men looked at each other.

"Where'd you get this?"

The boy shrank back farther.

"Up here, you worthless cur! Eh, and what's that you're clutching to your heart!" He pried open the boy's hand. "A blade! And a cross!"

They grabbed his arms and hauled him through the hatch.

The boy landed hard on deck, shouting for mercy.

"You'll tell us where you stole these or—"

"I did not steal them! I only meant to borrow them. They are blessed."

"Whose are they? Speak, boy!"

"I found them below in an old trunk."

"You're lying. You're a thief and the son of a thief."

The boy yelled and struggled as they strung him out. "A lash is too civil for the likes of you. Tie him to the mast."

"Let him go," Justin said.

The crewmen whirled, hands to their sword hilts.

"I am unarmed. The tunic and cross and blade are mine."

They stared at him, astounded. "A stowaway! Call the captain."

Captain Stewert Brice appeared to be already angry at being called away from the helm in such a storm.

"What goes here?" he demanded.

"A stowaway, Captain. He is a priest."

Every eye fixed upon Justin.

For a moment no one spoke. Away from the lantern the night was inky black. Not a star was visible. The wind lashed against them and sent Stewert Brice's cloak flapping. Like the other men, Justin struggled to remain upright.

"I was going to return them, Captain," the boy whined. "I only wanted them because they are blessed. The wind screams danger. We are doomed!"

"Hold your tongue," Captain Brice demanded.

Justin turned to the boy. "Nothing of mine can ward off the storm. I shall want back my belongings," he told the crewman.

Stewert stepped back as if struck. The voice apparently had ended any doubt as to who the stowaway was. *"You,"* he breathed.

"It has been a long time. Greetings, my brother."

Stewert stepped forward and peered at him. "Hand me the lantern," he told the crewman.

The light shone in Justin's eyes, and he could see nothing, but Stewert seemed satisfied. He sucked in his breath and muttered. His face hardened.

Other crewmen gathered, recognized Justin, and shock turned to relief. They looked at each other and began to laugh. It was Justin! The fair son of their true captain, Ewan.

"Silence," Stewert ordered.

"Captain," one man cried as if Stewert did not understand, "this is your brother!"

"I can see who it is," Stewert growled.

"Are you not going to . . ." The seaman stopped as the icy blue gaze above the lantern confronted him.

The man sobered and stepped back.

The wind gusted. Great swells, black and threatening, sent the ship heaving and plummeting.

The boy appealed to Justin like a frightened animal. "The wrath of God is upon the ship! Bless us, my father, and we will live!"

Stewert squinted at the sky. Nothing but blackness there. The rain splashed against his face. He turned in cold rage to Justin. "Blessing?" he shouted. "His presence brings a curse." He thrust an arm toward Justin. "You run from Christ. You bring your sin with you onto my ship!"

The crewmen stared at the clerical robe and cross as if they were now the omens of a sinking vessel. They glanced at each other warily. One man touched his lips with his tongue and swallowed. "The wrath of God," he whispered.

"No, a storm," corrected Justin. "It is the season for storms on the Mediterranean. Any good English seaman knows that. And you are all good seaman. God is not angry. There is nothing supernatural about our danger."

A murmur of relieved agreement arose. Yes, he was right. Justin looked at his brother. "You should have finished your voyage and docked at London two weeks ago."

"Your mouth, my brother, has always opened the way for your trouble. Hold your tongue, unless it is in prayer." He seized Justin's possessions and turned on the crewmen. "Get back to your posts! Can you not see the storm is upon us?"

The men scattered, leaving Stewert with Justin. Large raindrops heralded worsening winds. In the distance sounded the rumble of thunder.

Stewert hurled Justin's belongings at his chest. The cross fell near the boy's feet, and he gave a fearful gasp, as though expecting terrible judgment to strike them.

"Have you fled your duty to God to meddle in matters best left alone? Leave our father in peace!"

"Peace? Is his soul at rest? Is yours? Far be it from me to trouble either of you, but to bring the true message of Christ."

"You flee from God!"

"If I flee, it is not from God."

"No, you stow away till we be far at sea, then bring curses upon my ship. Your presence is the work of Felix. I warned him to stay away from you."

"Had Felix not shown mercy and brought news of my father, I would still return to London. If not on this ship, then another. I will not return to Rome nor to any monastery. You must accept that, and Father as well."

"So. You *have* run from the monastery like a wicked son. Your broken vow dishonors the name of Ewan Brice."

"If a vow be broken, it is not your concern. It is between my God and me. But come, my brother! Your self-righteous indignation shows you a pious fraud. Is it a broken vow that you are concerned with? Or my return from a grave you hoped I would stay in?"

Stewert's eyes narrowed. "If I wished you dead, I could do it now. The sea could be your grave."

The ship lurched and sent them both sprawling.

The boy, still tied, cried for mercy.

Stewert was first on his feet. Leaving his brother, he staggered back to where the pilot was clinging to the helm. A crewman lay propped against the bulkhead, bleeding from a head wound. Felix was attending him.

"Captain, there is land ahead—perhaps the Balearic Islands," the pilot gasped. "But the wind demands her own way, Captain Brice. I cannot hold her."

"We are cursed," breathed the injured crewman.

The thought of losing the ship was more than Stewert could stand, and it was easy to fix blame on Felix for an ill omen. It was he who had smuggled his brother aboard.

He jerked the Arab to his feet. "You conniving Saracen! Infidel! You went to your master Justin. Do not deny it. Confess!"

Felix did so, bravely, and bowed his head. "As servant to Justin Brice these many years, Captain Stewert, I could not forgive myself if I had not brought him word. It is your father I think of, not only your brother. Captain Ewan would wish to see him before he dies."

"I am captain, and you have disobeyed my orders. And I think I know why. With Justin Brice as your captain, you would seek to rule the ship yourself!"

He hurled Felix to the deck. The man took the maltreatment without flinching, and his bravery provoked Stewert further. He defended himself with angry words. "You have cursed me by bringing him aboard my ship. He has come between me and everything I strove to attain. My father would leave him sole heir for love of his dead mother. And now you jinx my ship, infidel!"

"No, Captain Stewert, no. I am a Christian. Master Justin will give me the words of Christ in my own tongue."

Stewert drew his sword and seized Felix by the throat. He dragged him to the side of the ship and pressed him to the railing. The point of the blade pricked his flesh. The wind raged against them, and the black swells curled upward toward Felix's head like anxious fingers ready to pull him into the deep.

"Your life for his, Saracen," Stewert shouted above the wind.

"Captain Stewert, please! I am no infidel! Lord, save me!"

Water cascaded over the side, sweeping them both to the deck. Stewert held onto the wooden railing, then staggered to the helm and shoved the pilot out of the way.

Justin desperately struggled to loose the boy from the mast before another surge of water crashed over the side. The foam swirled about his feet.

"Get below," he ordered.

But now the boy went to his knees before Justin, his eyes wild, clutching at him. "Bless me, lest I die," he shouted above the wind.

"Get off your knees!" Justin seized him, but the boy fell on his stomach and clung to him all the more. The despair on the still-childish face pierced Justin like a sword.

The ship heaved, and the sea swirled about them. The vessel tilted. The boy still clung to him, and together they slid across the deck.

"Bless me!" he kept shouting until Justin thought the words would drive him mad. The hunger and fear in the voice would forever burn within his soul. "Bless me!"

Seawater dashed over Justin's face, he came up choking. He tried to speak.

The boy clung to his ankle with one hand.

"Have you no hope? Seek Christ! Seek His sacrifice alone! You will find that sufficient."

"Bless me!"

"I cannot bless you! I can only give you His Word."

His Word!

A streak of lightning blinded him. The sea momentarily lit up. And as it did, a shout of alarm from aloft mingled with the gale. "Ship ahead! Ship ahead!"

A second flash split the sky. Thunder echoed. And now the rain drenched them. The Brice ship attempted to turn to avoid collision.

From the second vessel a desperate alarm sounded, followed by shouts of sailors so near at hand that Justin could identify the words spoken.

The Brice ship took the full force of the impact, and Justin was flung against a mast. With a shudder the vessel groaned. He felt the shock that doomed the ship—it throbbed through his very skull.

Then there came an abrupt cracking of timbers. The vessel reeled out of control, and the dark waters rushed in. Justin caught sight of a threatening wave and shouted for the boy to grab hold. Before his eyes the billow lifted the lad over the side and swept him away.

Dazed, Justin clung to the mast. Gone. The boy was gone. One moment he was there, alive, asking for a blessing in the face of death. And now he was gone. Forever gone.

I lost him, he kept thinking. *He was my responsibility. I lost him.*

An alarm was still sounding.

His mind remained fixed on the boy. As if hurled back with the raging wind and sea, the boy's face appeared in his mind, but now it became many faces, many boys. "Bless me . . ." And his voice merged into the cry of a multitude.

Now, mingled with the sound of running feet, came the cry to lower the boats. But the swells were high. Crewmen hung from ropes and ladders and were being slammed against the hull until they fell.

Justin was still clutching the mast when Felix struggled toward him, clinging to the rail. "Quick, Master. A boat. This way."

"Where is my brother?"

"In one of the boats!"

At the side of the ship the rope ladder swung precariously. A lifeboat rode the swells, and the sailors strained to hold it. Felix descended, and they hauled him aboard, but the waves worked against Justin. He swung over the side and slipped badly. Relentlessly, the wind and waves beat him back against the hull as he gripped the moving ladder, scraping his knuckles until they were raw. Felix shouted desperately for the sailors to bring the boat nearer.

The swells beneath Justin were first mountains, then valleys. Again there came a hammerlike impact against the hull, and this time pain weakened his grip. His right hand slipped, and he swayed hopelessly from side to side.

"Lord," he prayed, his eyes looking not above but on the raging black swells beneath, "if I brought them Your Word, would I not bless them? Was it not Your Word that the boy cried for, though he knew it not? Lord! For the many—like the boy—and like Felix. I do not know how, but . . ."

The rope slipped from his numb hand. Down he rushed and struck the water with a splash. He was immediately sucked under. The cold shock, like needles, stunned him.

He sank deeper into the black pit, then surfaced, gasping, choking, only to meet a towering swell that drove him still farther from the bobbing boat. The voices of his comrades shouted in alarm, then ebbed into the distance. The mammoth sea claimed him. Again he went under.

But then it seemed to Justin that stronger hands, unseen, were lifting him upward, claiming him for their own, and the sea had no will to contest. This time, when he bobbed up choking, he found himself close enough to the lifeboat to be tossed a rope.

Felix hauled him over the side.

Justin lay on his stomach, gasping. He was aware of the sailors' murmurs of amazement. It was, they said, an act of God.

"Master, I saw the giant swell bear you away, and I thought I would never see you again." Felix wept now, unashamed. "Christ is good to us, very good. We will live to serve Him."

7

Off the Coast of Spain

Justin awoke, alert to the threat of danger. He was alone.
Ahead of him lay the stormy beach, and behind him, carved
into the windswept cliff above, stood the dread castle of Baron
Soleiman. It would not take long for the baron's corsairs to
gain sight of the disabled Brice ship and begin searching for
them.

Justin listened without moving. Nothing stirred but the
wind in the branches overhead. A steady drip of rain monotonously ran down the back of his neck.

Where was Felix? He had lost sight of him just before
the swells capsized their small boat. Justin had been hurled
along, choking, swallowed up by the flood until he found
himself upon the sand and lapsed into unconsciousness. When
he awoke the rain was beating down, and in the darkness he
could see none of the crew, only pieces of wood making their
way to shore with the heavy pounding of the surf. Had all
drowned? Or had they righted the craft and gone on without
him? He clawed his way up the beach to the shelter of some
trees and lay gasping.

Hours had passed since then. The first light of dawn
was breaking through the clouds, and the great storm was
moving on, but still the wind blew.

A twig cracked, and he tensed. He waited, listening. He
gripped his dagger, expecting attack.

Then a crewman stumbled into sight, clutching his
wounded arm. Justin grabbed hold of him and pulled him
into the thick shrubs.

"Where are the others?" Justin whispered.

The man shook his head. His eyes were bloodshot and
dilated with fear.

He is out of his head, Justin thought.

"Do you know where we are, priest?"

"Yes."

The crewman was not satisfied with Justin's toneless response. He seemed to want the black words to be mouthed with as much dread as he felt surging through his heart. He rasped, "Baron Soleiman masters this islet."

"I know."

"He serves the enemies of your father. We are trapped, priest." He clutched the front of his tunic. "Trapped! Where is your God?"

"Watch your tongue. Speak His name with awe or speak it not at all."

"No man on this isle has ever escaped the baron's slave castle or his evil galleys!"

"Where is Captain Brice?" Justin demanded.

"On the Spanish galleon that struck us."

"It survived?"

"Your brother intended to leave you."

So Stewert was willing to sail without me.

"There is still a chance to catch the galleon. But we must hurry." Justin pulled the man to his feet.

"The baron's men are searching the island. They will catch us before we get there."

"We must try."

The seaman was bleeding heavily. Justin ripped a piece of cloth from his shirt and bound the wound. The man did not look good and was paling.

"Leave me not, I beg of you!"

"Neither a priest nor a warrior abandons a friend."

With the man's arm about his neck, Justin stumbled through the wet overhang, plodding, often tripping over fallen limbs. And then they were out of the trees and facing the beach.

The gray waters still thundered onto the shore, overtaking the sand and scattering debris. Several dead seamen were sprawled at the water's edge, and waves washed over their bodies. Apparently there had been a fight for the remaining boats, and the strongest had prevailed.

Automatically Justin's eyes sought Felix among the dead. With relief he saw that his servant was not there. *Yet he is lost, or Stewert has forced him to go on without searching for me,* he decided. *He would never leave me of his own will.*

The crewman caught his arm, pointing. "And there she is, priest! There is still time!"

Then Justin caught sight of the Spanish treasure ship.

They stumbled down to the seaside, where the oncoming waves threatened to tear the sand from under their feet. It was all Justin could do to stay upright. He waved frantically. Could those on the ship see them? Would they send a boat?

Justin could swim, but the swells were heavy, and he could not keep both of them afloat. He made a quick search of the shore for a piece of wood large enough to lay the crewman on. Anything to keep the man's arm from strangling his neck. The sand was barren.

He must try to swim.

They waded into the water, but it was too late. Out of the trees behind them burst the baron's men, hundreds of corsair warriors brandishing Toledo swords, lances, and crossbows.

Another party carried boats and shoved off to scale the Spanish galleon, bending their oars with a will as they fought the shining dark swells.

An arrow whizzed by, striking the water beside Justin.

Another struck his companion, and, with a cry, he went under the rolling waves.

Justin grabbed for him, but a blow to the back of the head sent him face down into the cold water. A great hand took hold of the collar of his tunic and dragged him back to the beach.

A corsair stood over him, tall and muscular. He had a shock of golden hair and a square jaw. His conical helmet was absent, but he wore a mesh shirt of iron chainwork reaching to his elbows.

"I am unarmed, corsair!"

The man's sharp blue eyes fell on the cross glinting against Justin's dark tunic. He hesitated.

"Or does that matter?" Justin challenged.

The granite blue eyes sparked, and a smirk crossed the pirate's lips. "Well, what have we fished from the sea! A warrior-priest without a sword? You must be a Greek," he mocked.

"I am a Scot!"

"If you insist that so great a blood is yours, where are your knightly weapons, lad?" The eyes continued to mock him. "Is it not an ancient law that a warrior-priest possess helmet, mail shirt, sword, lance, and horse?"

Justin was well acquainted with the militant state of mind among certain sects within the church. The church and its lands were ruled mainly by Spanish bishops and abbots who were often the brothers of those fierce barons who ruled the rest of the land.

He was also aware that this grinning corsair was enjoying the opportunity to sport with him.

"I am willing to do without the great horse," Justin mocked in return. "I would be content with a ship, however. Surely there are a few about that you have pirated. What of the Spanish galleon?"

"Fear not, priest. You will travel by ship again, but not until we have taken its treasure. Content yourself with a sword." Glimpsing a dead seaman still clasping his blade, he seized it and tossed it at Justin's feet. A malicious smile crossed his face. "Now, what is your excuse? Get up and fight, lad. You are among warriors."

"And if my conscience forbids me to take off your arrogant head?"

The corsair grinned again. He unsheathed his sword from the scabbard strapped to his left side. "Then I will lop off yours."

Was he serious? There was something affable about the man, but he reeked with violence. Still, Justin hesitated to take up the sword.

The corsair apparently perceived his internal struggle, and it aroused his interest. Nevertheless he took the toe of his boot and flipped the hilt of the sword closer, now within Justin's reach.

"Get up, lad. Learn to fight, or you will die. If not by my hand, then by Baron Soleiman's. He will wish you to go to sea with him on future ventures."

"No, corsair. I go nowhere but to England."

"We shall see, lad." He swung his sword.

Justin ducked as he felt the breeze of the blade. In response he seized the dead seaman's sword and jumped to his feet.

"That is better." The corsair lunged.

Justin parried his blow, but the man swiftly countered with such force that Justin lost his footing. The pirate unexpectedly laughed, then began to taunt him for his poor use of the blade. He toyed with him, backing him toward the rolling sandhill beyond.

"Come, lad, where's your stuff?"

Painfully Justin began to recall some of what he had once known well, but not until he had retreated halfway up the beach. He found himself growing angry and sensed that the corsair knew that and was enjoying himself.

This only made Justin feel more ashamed. His conscience smote him. *Am I a servant of God or a half-wild barbarian?*

Then Justin's sword crashed against his opponent's. He thrust, and parried again. The blades rang.

"Ah! Better!" But then the corsair charged, and the force again sent Justin sprawling back against the sandhill. A hearty laugh followed.

"Forget your boast! Get it over with," Justin challenged.

"Surrender, do you? Look at him, will you! And his sword still in his hand! Get up and fight!"

Justin's left hand lay across the sand. He threw a handful of grit into the corsair's face, and in defense the pirate covered his eyes. Had Justin been on his feet, his sword could have pierced through his heart.

The corsair rubbed his eyes, blinking. He shook his head. "You have a good wit about you in the heat of a fight. A strong body as well. Who are you, priest?"

"I should ask you that question. But from your murderous attack, I can easily see you are one of Baron Soleiman's thieving corsairs. You have killed my friend."

"You are in no position to hurl insults, lad. I did not kill your friend, but I could have killed you. Your garb stayed my arm. Be thankful. What is your name?"

"Brice! Justin Brice! That should tell you a lot."

It did. The corsair fell silent. His pale blue eyes swept the young man from head to toe. He would know that name well. His own liege, Soleiman, served an enemy of Justin's father.

"A Brice! Soleiman will be pleased I have spared your innards from being washed upon his beach."

"No doubt. Gold from my father is worth more than any head," Justin said dryly. "But my father is in no position to pay ransom."

"The cross about your neck, lad, will be worth more than all the gold your father could pay."

"The cross is worth little to a pirate such as Soleiman."

"Ah, yes, Soleiman has his castle looking like the finest in Cordoba, but the worth of the cross is not in its gold but rather in your office as priest."

At once Justin was uneasy.

The corsair nodded in the direction of the forbidding castle. Justin followed his gaze to the windswept cliff where the castle stared down upon them.

"Soleiman is a religious man." The glint in the corsair's eye told his intended irony. "He wishes to have his own priest. Where did you come from?"

"Rome."

"Ah . . ."

"I joined my brother's ship at Genoa. We were on our way to London when we collided with the galleon. My father is ill, perhaps dying, and I must reach him. I beg you, let me go."

"If Soleiman has his way, you will not be going to London, lad, but serving our entire company as priest."

"I will not serve as hired priest to any man, least of all a clan of pirates. Do you think I can evoke God's blessing on thievery and murder?"

"What, lad? Not partake of gold?" he mocked. "Duty calls!"

"And Greed calls for her, does she not?"

"I shall give you serious words of advice," said the corsair. "If you value your life, you will do nothing to provoke Soleiman. He is not a man given to wisdom, though he prides himself as a scholar. You may find his religious beliefs to be

93

mere superstition, but for the present—like it or not—your one hope for survival rests in your position as a priest."

"For the present I shall consider your advice."

"Now about that sword, lad. One day I may teach you how to use it. They call me Andrew. I am first in command of Soleiman's affairs."

The Spanish ship was being taken over by Soleiman's corsairs. The wind carried the distant sounds of battle—or was it the thunder of the waves? Justin could discern men fighting on the deck and many falling over the side. His concern was for Stewert. He was an egotistical warrior. His pride would not permit him to surrender easily.

Andrew's sun-bronzed face was unreadable.

"Even without the storm we would have taken her. Word was sent to Soleiman weeks ago. She bears wealth untold from the New World. Now let us go. Soleiman comes. He will be delighted to find the son of Ewan Brice as an unexpected prisoner!"

It was raining again, and the wind had picked up.

The prisoners from the galleon stood on the beach, guarded by rugged corsairs. Baron Soleiman was so pleased with his catch that for a time he could not control his sometimes silent, sometimes wheezy laughter. His bulging eyes restlessly swept over them.

"Ah," he said long and deeply, "ah yes, ah yes."

The Spanish captain bore the unconquered elegance of a ruling monarch. He was handsome, dark-haired, and boasted a fine-clipped mustache. His hat, although damaged by the sea, yet bore a cocky plume, and his cape was decorated with gold brocade and gemstones. "You will pay for this act of piracy, Senor Soleiman! You will have His Excellency Ferdinand after your head!"

"The king has his old enemy France to worry about," said Soleiman. "A Spanish ship to decorate Soleiman's island is too little to concern him now."

He turned then to Stewert, who lay sprawled against a tree. His wound, taken in the battle for the galleon, appeared to be severe.

"So, the son of Ewan Brice!" A wolfish smile spread across Soleiman's jowls.

"The one," growled Stewert with a challenge.

"A double blessing from the sea!"

"I will live to double your woe," breathed Stewert. "You will pay for taking my men prisoner. My father has loyal men in many ports, including Cadiz. They will take this islet."

"And they will find you swinging from a tree on the beach. Let that be their welcoming flag!"

The corsair Andrew, possibly hoping to avert some deaths, quickly pointed to Justin.

"Ah! But there are two sons of Ewan Brice. Are they not worth a great ransom, my liege Soleiman? Think what the old retired pirate will pay to receive them whole? And—" he bowed toward Justin "—this goodly lad is Justin Brice." He clasped Justin's shoulders. "A priest!"

Soleiman's eyes riveted upon Justin, and he seemed to forget all else. He took in his attire, then smiled broadly, his temper receding as waves washing out to sea.

"A priest? Is this so, my son?"

"Yes."

"Where?"

"Rome."

"Excellent, excellent," he kept repeating.

Every eye fixed upon Justin, taking in the black woolen tunic, the soiled maroon cloak, the cross. His hair was brown, just tinged with red-gold, his features strong and handsome, his eyes a clear blue-gray.

"He is no priest," came a cold voice from behind Soleiman.

Justin turned toward the voice. For the first time he saw a tall, lean man wearing some sort of religious garb. A deep scar ran across his left eyelid and down his cheek. He carried a whip. Justin judged him to be Soleiman's personal soothsayer. Had the man taken an immediate dislike to him?

"I suggest that he is no more than a common mercenary in disguise," continued the man. "Give him and his brother to me. I shall put them in the dungeon."

The corsair Andrew stepped back into the circle and

bowed to Soleiman. He was obviously trying to make matters go as well for Justin as he could.

"O Soleiman, man of wisdom. Surely he is a priest and also a lad of wit. Look at him." His hand smacked hard against Justin's stomach. "Fine looking lad! He has good Scottish blood and the arrogance of a Frenchman! Strong too. Look at those shoulders! Look at that height! What baron will own a more awesome warrior-priest? When I have finished his training, he will be fit for battle on any ship we take to sea, as well as for prayer. Who could ask for more? Ah, Soleiman, my liege, you have yourself a prize."

Soleiman smiled broadly. He grunted, then laughed, slapping his muscled thigh. "Rome, you say? Are you also a scholar? Can you read Latin?"

When Justin paused, a warning glint in Andrew's gaze prompted him to relent. "Indeed, O Great One."

"Ah, and write letters?"

"With a prolific hand."

"He will know what secrets are written in the parchment taken from the North Africa churchman," suggested Andrew. "Unlike your soothsayer—" he bowed mockingly to the man with the scarred eyelid "—Justin Brice can read Latin."

"A parchment from a churchman?" Justin asked, his interest instantly aroused.

"It was accidentally taken during the capture of an enemy ship," explained Andrew, tongue in cheek. "I thought the leather envelope contained jewels. Alas."

"I would be anxious to translate it."

Soleiman beamed at Justin and rubbed his big hands together.

"He lies," said the man with the scar. "No one can read the magic writing of the gods."

"If the soothsayer cannot read the writing of the gods," Andrew taunted lightly, "then may I suggest, my liege Soleiman, that the priest be permitted to try?"

The soothsayer glared at his antagonist Andrew, for the two men vied relentlessly for the highest position in Baron Soleiman's council—Andrew, in order to obtain his own ship and escape his slavery; the soothsayer, to gain prestige and the subservience of the superstitious corsairs.

The fortune-teller's good eye burned hot with jealousy as it fixed on Justin. "I say it is secret writing, profane priest!"

"If it is written in Latin, it will be no secret to me," Justin replied. He turned toward Soleiman. "I should very much like to see this parchment, Baron."

"Indeed," Soleiman told him. "I have waited more than a year for someone who could translate it for me." He glowered at the soothsayer. "You told me no one could read the writing. My patience is coming to an end. Are the spirits of the gods in you or no? Ah, this has been a great day, Andrew! You shall be thrice rewarded for saving the holy man. What will you have?"

Andrew said smoothly, "I shall think long and hard, my liege Soleiman. Perhaps to captain my own ship and to foray with the ships of Portugal and Spain to the New World. To bring you back treasure and slaves, of course."

"We shall see, we shall see." Soleiman again appraised Justin with delight. "Priest, you will serve me in the castle, then travel at my side upon the sea. The capture of fine ships laden with treasure will need your blessing. Do you not know how generous Soleiman is to the church? Yes! How often have I given great treasures from my booty to the bishops of Spain."

"No doubt, Baron Soleiman, the bishops are in your humble gratitude," quipped Justin.

Soleiman took the remark at face value. "I will treat you well. You will perform your religious duties and entertain me with tales of wisdom. But I shall be the judge of whether you tell the truth! Even a priest can lose his head. Remember that, Justin Brice."

Here was a man whose vanity urged him to become wise, but Justin felt certain that he had no true heart for wisdom. Nevertheless, the baron must be humored. Realizing that he would be given training with the sword and have some freedom in the castle—and therefore gain opportunity to escape—Justin bowed with feigned humility.

"As it is written by the wisest man who has ever lived: 'Receive my instruction, and not silver; and knowledge rather than choice gold. For wisdom is better than rubies; and all the things that may be desired are not to be compared to it.'"

Soleiman beamed. "The wisest man who ever lived? Who? Who wrote that?"

"Solomon."

"Ah! Soleiman!"

"No, Solomon, king of Israel. He reigned in Jerusalem."

Soleiman appeared disappointed and a little irked. "Then if he is so wise, why did he not rid the Holy Sepulcher of the Saracen infidels? Why are the pilgrimages to Jerusalem halted by Muslims?"

Justin could see that he was in for a difficult time. He said nothing.

"Fools," muttered Stewert Brice from his place against the tree. "You stand there in the rain speaking of wisdom, and I am bleeding to death."

Soleiman turned to Andrew. "Look to the Scot, then put him in the dungeon! Let the famed Captain Stewert Brice contemplate with the rats the folly of contesting my corsairs on the sea! Wisdom cries that his old fox of a father will pay very much gold to free him from my galleys. Send what remains of his crew to the fields to tend my pigs," Soleiman jeered. "I was told that pigs are wiser than sheep. Perhaps Captain Brice's crewmen shall learn a thing or two. You also," he added, gesturing with disdain at the indignant Spanish captain. "And give me his plumed hat."

Soleiman placed the dashing hat upon his own head and smiled broadly.

8

The knifelike figure robed elegantly in brocaded blue and gold stopped before the door to Soleiman's private chamber.

"He sleeps," warned the guard. But squarely fixed by the soothsayer's gaze, he pressed the seer no further. *The soothsayer can bring curses or blessings,* he thought. The guard was a large man and courageous with a sword, but, like many of the other corsairs, he feared this strange man.

To the corsair, the one good eye of the soothsayer was a curious novelty because it never appeared to blink. It was the blind eye, however, that was chilling, for its cloudy color reminded him of darkness and thunder. In fear of bringing down on himself the soothsayer's curses, he mumbled something unintelligible and stepped aside.

The soothsayer crooked a jeweled finger and rapped three times on the door.

The door swung open, and a great Nubian servant barred his entrance, an ivory dagger at his waist. He stepped aside when he saw who it was, however, and the soothsayer passed into the room as silently as a shadow.

The chamber boasted rugs from Baghdad and wall hangings of scarlet and deep blue. Soleiman sat among cushions. Around him lay a rich assortment of pillaged loot newly taken from the Spanish ship.

The baron chuckled as he admired vessels of gold, honey-colored agate, and containers of little brown beans that the Spanish captain assured him should be ground and boiled, then drunk hot. *Coffee,* he called it. Soleiman handed the treasures he wished to display to the Nubian and consigned the others to a chest to be stored in the castle treasury.

Soleiman was a heavy man but solid and an expert wrestler. He enjoyed nothing better than to hold matches with his tallest corsairs, whom he delighted to pin helplessly to the floor.

Fool! the soothsayer thought, watching him. *I should sit in your seat!* Outwardly, however, he stood with a frozen smile and waited for Soleiman to beckon him forward. When it came to the soothsayer's desire for power and gold, it was fortunate that his liege reverenced fortune-tellers as well as priests.

The soothsayer had served the baron for three years, having beguiled Soleiman with his mysterious peepstone, a device that he claimed had been passed down to him from Moses on Mount Nebo in the Holy Land.

Soleiman looked up from his treasures and grinned for he was in a celebrative mood. He hadn't been this happy since the day he proclaimed himself a baron.

"Ah, soothsayer, come, come! You are just the one I wish to see."

"My liege, I must speak to you alone. It concerns the danger that Brice brings to your castle."

Soleiman cut him off. "Captain Brice is below with the rats. He poses no danger to anyone but himself."

"It was not Stewert Brice I had in mind, my liege, but the younger one. Yes. The heretic who masquerades in a monk's robe!"

"Heretic?"

"I have not been idle, my liege. From a crew member aboard the Brice ship I have learned that Justin Brice fled the monastery in Rome to avoid being burned at the stake for heresy."

"A heretic! Surely these are the lies of jealous men. He boasts a robe and a cross, and he reads and writes Latin. What else is needed? It is enough."

The soothsayer stiffened. "He must be destroyed at once, my liege."

"Destroyed! What is this you say?" Soleiman's voice rose. "Destroy him?" He stood. "My priest? My very own personal priest? Are you mad, soothsayer?"

At the baron's display of indignation, the Nubian servant stepped forward, and the soothsayer shrank away.

"The priest sails my ships!" Soleiman stated. "Is that clear? And if we embark to the New World, he shall bless our voyage with fair weather and good health. I will hear no more lies to upset my plans."

The soothsayer hastened to bow low. "I meant no offense. Only—" he hesitated "—he must be watched." He looked up, his good eye cautious. "For your sake," he whispered.

Soleiman's eyes narrowed. "What do you mean?"

"My liege must keep in mind that although the man claims to be a priest, he is still a Brice. Are you not a known enemy to his father? Have you not fought Captain Ewan Brice with sword and ship?"

Soleiman scowled at the reminder. "Andrew believes the priest can be trusted."

The soothsayer leaned toward him. "Andrew schemes, my liege."

Soleiman pondered the words. He had heard similar words before from the soothsayer. A few times Soleiman himself suspected that Andrew might be thinking of stealing a ship and going to sea as captain of his own corsairs. The Nubian servant, however, assured him it was not so.

The Nubian's deep voice was silky. He bowed from the waist. "Baron Soleiman, you know Andrew is a brilliant captain, and one who is passionately devoted to your service, as am I. If we sail to the New World as the ships of Portugal and Spain do, we will need him. He once sailed on a Spanish ship and knows the way."

The soothsayer stared coldly at the bodyguard. "Andrew claims to have sailed on a Spanish ship only to Brazil. He comes from Antwerp. He was the son of an English merchant until taken a slave by Baron Soleiman."

"Hold your tongue, soothsayer. Is it not envy which drives you to these charges?" Soleiman suggested.

"I wish only your honor, my liege. I am your truthful servant. I have gazed into the peepstone, and the gods warn of deceit in the imposter."

Soleiman frowned.

Seeing his troubled scowl, the soothsayer pressed ahead. "Shall I seek his true nature with the whip, my liege?"

"If one ugly mark tarnishes his handsome flesh, I will have you thrown in with the rats."

The soothsayer went down on one knee, head bowed. "The peepstone does not lie."

Soleiman hesitated, obviously irritated that his delight in owning a priest was being marred by the soothsayer's suspicion. "I am beginning to wonder. Walk softly, old crow. If Priest Justin proves himself false, it is I who will be his executioner."

The soothsayer bowed again in stiff silence.

Soleiman was appeased and sighed deeply. He motioned across the chamber toward his private sanctuary. "Look not as if you were weaned on sour fruit, soothsayer. I have not forgotten how you served me these three years. I have an honor for you. Come!"

At the word *honor*, the fortune-teller lifted his head and followed his liege into the sanctuary.

Smiling, Soleiman swept his arm toward the prayer bench, where lay a prized scarlet robe embroidered with stars and crescents.

"My liege! Surely you do not mean . . ." Overwhelmed, the soothsayer lapsed into silence and stared.

How he had coveted this robe, how he had plotted ways to convince Soleiman to honor him with it. Who among the other wise men in the baron's castle dare claim it? The soothsayer stood riveted, as the fever of excitement raced through him.

The robe!

Taken from a pirated vessel, it had become a religious status symbol. Soleiman was so taken with its texture, color, and design that he declared it would be worn only by the counselor among his religious wise men whom he most delighted to honor. Almost at once, the robe became a mark of supremacy among all of Soleiman's counselors. None dare ask for it, but all desired it, and none more than the soothsayer.

To this day Soleiman had not been impressed enough with any of his advisers to bestow it. So it remained in the sanctuary. Here it greeted the soothsayer each time he entered. And the longer the robe lay unclaimed, the more he desired it.

"Me? Me, my liege? I am not worthy," he murmured.

Soleiman seemed not to hear him. "The coronation will take place tonight in the sanctuary. O Soleiman, how the gods have looked down upon you. How you have been rewarded for your piety. And they said I was but a corsair! That God was displeased with my sin. Hah! How could He be displeased? Has He not brought me a priest to wear the holy robe? To teach me wisdom? To interpret the secret words?

"See to it, soothsayer. I want everyone of importance here tonight." The broad face widened in an indulgent smile. "And you, soothsayer, will have the honor of escorting the priest into the sanctuary."

With a flourish Soleiman handed him the robe. "Have Justin Brice brought to the bath and prepared. He will look splendid in the robe! Are you well, soothsayer? You have turned a strange color. And posthaste bring me the religious parchment. I will present it to him tonight. He will translate the secret words. Who knows what majestic mysteries lie within my reach?"

Soleiman turned and knelt, murmuring a prayer. He arose, then glowered.

"Do you still stand there? Go! And send Andrew to me. He has an important function in the ritual as well."

The Nubian giant wore a faint smile, and his eyes gleamed with amusement. He watched the soothsayer depart wearing the expression of a man about to be hanged.

The soothsayer disappeared into the castle library. Here, he took a bunch of keys and unlocked a small drawer. Slowly he removed the churchman's parchment.

"The secret words of the gods," he muttered. Could Justin Brice interpret them? If he did, the seer's own position before Soleiman would be undermined. Soleiman was a fool. The soothsayer had worked for three years to trick him into believing in his magical powers to know the future. Justin Brice and the parchment could easily destroy all this with one stroke.

He lay the robe on the desk and picked up the candle. His hand shook as he brought the parchment close to the flame. Could he not claim that the rats gnawed it to rubbish? His heart pounded, echoing in his ears.

Yet what of Andrew? He would remember that the parchment was safely locked in the drawer. Andrew did not reverence his position as soothsayer. Andrew was not superstitious. Andrew mocked him.

But he must destroy Justin Brice before they sailed for the New World.

The soothsayer whirled at the tread of boots.

Andrew stood behind him.

"Do you spy on me?"

Andrew smirked. Then his eye caught sight of the parchment and the candle, and the way the soothsayer's hand shook. His smirk vanished, and his eyes hardened.

"Beware, croaking toad. That parchment will be given to the priest tonight. Be sure of it."

"Do not I always honor Soleiman's wishes?"

"To his face, you are always his humble servant."

"And you, O great military lord?" the soothsayer challenged. "Is your loyalty only with your tongue? Do you think I don't know that you intend to break away from your master?"

Andrew knocked the candle from his hand and stamped out the flame. The chamber dimmed.

"Babblers have died for saying less. How much more a servant of darkness?"

The soothsayer paled. For a moment they stood eye to eye. Then the soothsayer whispered hoarsely, "Only a frog babbles. My lips are silent, O great lord."

"Good. The 'great lord' does not like frogs who croak in the night. I dislike soothsayers even more. Now then, see to the prisoner I have brought you. His name is Felix. Put him with the cook. When you do, tell the baker you have a message from Andrew. If one more varmint ends up in my bed, I shall pay him a visit."

At the end of the passage, the Nubian waited for Andrew. "The time is near. Tonight the boat will be unguarded."

Their strategy to escape the islet in a small boat for Valencia, a port on the coast of Spain, had long been in preparation. Andrew felt confident the plan would work. Soleiman would expect escaping slaves to confiscate one of the galleons.

"We must bide our time and wait. The sea is too rough for a small boat."

"The longer we wait the more risk we take," said the Nubian. "The soothsayer is suspicious. Who knows who else?"

"It is a chance we are forced to take. If we take to the sea now, we will never make Valencia."

"What of the priest?"

Andrew shrugged. "We shall take him—and Felix."

"What of Captain Brice?"

"Can he travel?"

"He has the strength of a bull."

"Can you get him from the dungeon?"

The Nubian held up the keys.

"Then let us also take the Spanish captain. For our generosity in helping him to escape, he can repay us with supplies to reach Bayonne. Breathe nothing yet to the others. A secret is best kept by two."

Unexpectedly someone unbolted the door to Justin's chamber, and the Nubian entered. His strong body rippled with muscle, and his skin looked as though it had been polished. He wore ebony trousers edged in gold.

Justin thought he saw a ghost of a smile on the man's lips, but his voice was toneless. "Tonight a special honor is to be yours from Baron Soleiman." The dark eyes scanned Justin's shabby tunic.

"An honor?" Justin asked cautiously. "Will I be given the parchment to interpret?"

"Among other notable things. But come."

The chamber to which he was led was larger than his own quarters and lavishly decorated with pirated goods. There was a marble bath and bench, fine rugs, and carved vessels for filling the tub. He watched the Nubian pour scented oil from a gold urn.

When Justin emerged from the bath and put on a clean robe, his reflection appeared that of a stranger. Nothing remained of his clothes but the cross lying on the bench.

Now he followed the Nubian. The door to another room was thrown open, and three guards stood there. Justin gazed upon an assortment of rich clothing.

"Baron Soleiman bids you accept these gifts from his hand," the Nubian said, spreading his arm wide.

There were black woolen trousers, silk shirts, brocaded vests, mantles trimmed with marten fur, and boots.

The soothsayer stood somewhat hidden in the shadows. "So, imposter! You managed to beguile Baron Soleiman."

The fortune-teller moved into the light. Over his arm was an elaborate scarlet robe, embroidered with gold stars and crescent moons.

"Do you wish the honor of putting the robe on him, soothsayer?" asked the Nubian innocently.

The fortune-teller scanned the Nubian as if he were an insect. Face taut, he placed the robe on the table and, sweeping his cloak about him, walked out.

With the robe across his arm, the Nubian came to Justin. He bowed deeply, murmuring, "Tonight Soleiman will proclaim you chief of his wise men—a position most coveted. This robe too is coveted."

"Coveted? The soothsayer may have it. It fits him well." Justin walked over to the pile of garments. It was satisfying to put on the black trousers and white shirt. Over it he wore a long-sleeved doublet, full of sleeve but gathered at the wrist. The masculine boots of fine cordovan leather were the best. Three years had passed since he had worn boots!

He finished dressing, ignoring the guards until suddenly aware of the silence. Looking up, he saw the Nubian still standing patiently with the robe. Justin sensed his determination.

"There is no choice, Priest Justin. You must wear the robe."

Justin's determination was a match, but he smiled. "I think not, friend."

The guards smiled slightly. The Nubian sighed and gestured to them. "Then force him."

Before Justin knew what was happening, the weight of several bodies impacted his own. Jarred, his breath knocked from him, he was slammed to the floor.

"Do not mar his flesh," the Nubian calmly commanded. He circled the struggling bodies.

"Careful of his face! Hold him!"

Justin could not move. With determination the Nubian knelt, robe in hand. The garment was soft and smelled of some sweet perfume that Justin found repulsive. The face of the Nubian was blank. He avoided looking at Justin as if afraid he would smile. The three guards were now scowling, perhaps angry because it took all of them to hold him down.

"I will not entertain your liege like some troubadour," Justin warned. "Rats are preferable to this."

An amused voice sounded from the doorway. "Rats make for unpleasant company. Especially when the night holds pleasant surprises. There will be feasting and singing—and tomorrow night? Who knows?"

Justin recognized the voice of Andrew. The corsair approached and stood looking down upon him. Unlike the others, he did not hold back a smile as he took in the robe.

Andrew was dressed in the substantial clothing of a warrior, but the clothing was of quality, and his manner had taken on some surprising elegance.

Still pinned to the floor, Justin gazed up at him. "Well, corsair," he said dryly, "so you actually can look civilized."

"Ah, lad, my one hand bears the golden manners of English nobility." He bowed. "Do you not know I am a respectable merchant-adventurer from Antwerp? Ah, but on my other hand—" he held it up "—is the fist of a warrior! Be glad of your privilege of serving such a future captain."

At the term "future captain," Justin eyed him.

A promise glinted in the corsair's amused eyes. "I will yet teach you how to use a sword," suggested Andrew lightly. "Let him up."

The warriors released Justin and stepped back.

Justin was on his feet at once. His eyes locked with Andrew's, and he removed the robe with emphasis.

"If he does not wear it," said the Nubian, "Soleiman will be in a rage."

"There is only one way to handle this. The lad will not submit to force," said Andrew. He took the robe and flecked off an imaginary speck of dust. Deliberately he made no attempt to put it back on Justin's shoulders.

The others watched, apparently wondering what he had in mind. Andrew sat down on the table and folded his arms. His blue eyes glistened.

"Do you remember the parchment taken from the North African ship?"

Justin remembered.

Andrew paused, clearly waiting for the words to sink in, baiting Justin before going on. "It is a portion of the Writings."

Justin was alert. "How do you know?"

"The good churchman told me. He was quite upset. And alas, he died, good man though he was. I made him a vow at his last breath. If ever the Lord sent the right man, I would see to it that it was put to proper use."

"And you haven't told your liege what it is? The soothsayer beguiles him into thinking it is secret writing."

Andrew shrugged. "Even if I had, he would need a man to read Latin. None of us can do so. How much is it worth to have the Scripture portion in your hand, Justin? To read it, to translate it, to know its words as one knows a familiar path?"

Justin wondered that the corsair had the sensitivity to understand his feelings. He wanted the Writing as much as he wanted freedom. Andrew knew it. And that told Justin more about the character of the man than any of his actions.

Andrew smiled. Calmly he handed Justin the robe. "If you behave wisely before Soleiman, the parchment will be given to you tonight."

Justin hesitated, then grudgingly took the vestment. "Where did you get this monstrosity? Did you pirate it from a ship as well?"

"What! You insult the baron's taste in fashion?"

"I will wear it. I make no other promises. I will decide from minute to minute if I can proceed with what he has in mind."

"Opportunities may be yours," Andrew hinted, "if you cooperate."

Justin scanned him. What was the man implying?

They turned at the sound of footsteps.

Andrew turned from the table and bowed pretentiously. "See who arrives to lead the pompous ceremony! Soothsayer, do I notice a livid complexion? Does your peepstone forecast some gloomy image to disturb your peace this night?"

The soothsayer clutched two lamps burning with fragrant oil. He was dressed in his own religious garb—representing what, Justin had no idea.

"The only image I foresee is your head rolling from the block, Andrew. And it affords me no gloom." Then, seeing Justin attired in the robe, his one eye hardened.

"Come, imposter. Entertain the baron with your masquerade. But when you gaze upon the Writing you shall be blinded by the gods. Soleiman waits in the sanctuary."

Justin found him as annoying as a buzzing fly.

"Remember my advice, Justin," Andrew told him quietly as Justin walked past him. "Soleiman is a man to be humored. If you anger him, you will be cast below with your brother."

9

The Baron's Island

With sullen face, the soothsayer led the procession down the passage. Candles flickered.

Justin's eyes were busy as he entered the sanctuary. Soleiman was seated on a dais with a number of men standing behind him, and Justin guessed them to be his counselors. The Nubian, his chief bodyguard, stood to his right. Torches blazed along the walls, and beneath them stood a line of corsair warriors, each wearing his weapons and a fine mantle trimmed with fur thrown about his shoulders.

The soothsayer bowed stiffly before the baron and placed a lamp at each side of the dais. Spiraling gray incense, too fragrant to be pleasant, drifted upward.

"Come forward, Justin," Soleiman cried jubilantly. "You look splendid!" He gestured to Andrew. "What do you think? Is he worthy of the robe?"

"Soleiman, my liege," Andrew said exuberantly, "alas. What can I say at this awesome moment?" He turned toward Justin and deliberately hesitated.

Wondering what the corsair could say, Justin met his gaze squarely, affecting sobriety.

"Magnificent! Auspicious! Sanctimonious!" Andrew declared. "Surely such a robe makes a man of God!"

Soleiman seemed unsure of the intent of his words.

Justin suspected that with Andrew he was never quite sure.

"Are you asking me or telling me? Never mind, let us proceed." He stood up from the dais. "All bow in reverence to God. Any remaining on his feet will be deemed an infidel. Posthaste he shall be hanged from Soleiman's gallows."

There was a shuffling of feet and a clinking of metal as the warriors went down on their knees.

Soleiman, however, remained standing. He smiled, appearing pleased at the sight. "Very well."

He began to pace back and forth, carrying his halberd. "Let it be known from this day and forward that I, Soleiman the Great, a devotee of Christianity—" he paused and cleared his throat with a wary glance toward the soothsayer "—and all other gods of the deep do hereby choose Priest Justin Brice to be the chief of all my religious counselors. All in agreement with my wise decision, give praise."

The assembled men were now on their feet, giving a great cry and stretching out their arms. Above the din of voices, steel clanged as the corsairs jerked swords from their sheaths in a salute first to Soleiman, then to Justin.

Soleiman smiled, then beckoned for Andrew to proceed.

Followed by two warriors bearing the gift of weaponry, Andrew stopped before Justin. A slight smile was on his face.

Soleiman's oratorical voice rang out. "Soon we embark upon the greatest of expeditions, joining our forces with those of Portugal in a journey to the New World. Notorious though we be, piety hovers over us like the wings of an angel!" He paused, then spread his arm in Justin's direction. "A warrior-priest will sail with us. He shall lead us forward with sword and cross! Bestow knighthood upon him, Andrew!"

"On one knee," the corsair commanded.

Justin hesitated. Instantly he felt the heavy hands of the guards pressing him down. Andrew gave an extra push against the back of his head, forcing his face to the floor. Justin unwillingly stared at the silver buckles of Andrew's polished black boots.

The flat of Andrew's sword struck the base of Justin's neck, and his clear voice rang out. "In the name of God, I make you also a knight. Now arise, Justin Brice, a warrior-priest fit for battle and for the duties of God."

The corsair lifted him to his feet. "Be proud," he said. He took a weapons' belt from a guard and thrust another sword into its sheath. He smiled as he handed it to Justin. "Use it well."

There followed other pieces of armor—a mesh shirt of iron chainwork, a hood of similar mesh, sleeves, gloves, hose of mail, and a conical helmet.

Justin's mind went back to his youth. He had been in training to be a belted knight when his father sent him to the monastery. Then, he would have given anything to become a knight; now, he found himself sobered by the truth.

"The warrior-priest!" exclaimed Soleiman. "Together we shall claim territory for England—and Soleiman. What say you, O great seamen?"

"For the splendor of God!" came the great male chorus, echoing the cry of William the Conqueror.

The splendor of God, thought Justin. *What do any of them know about the splendor of God?*

Only the soothsayer, standing near by, held tight lips, his one eye burning. Amid the noise, Andrew spoke in a low tone. "Soleiman will call you before him. Do as he demands. Humor him. You will be commanded to dedicate the men and ships for sailing."

"Is it a light thing to engage in pretense in matters concerning God?" Justin whispered.

Andrew ignored his determination. "Your honor impresses me, but it will not impress Soleiman. If you want to live to return to England, you must do something. Listen—and I may be able to get you to London."

Not until Soleiman raised his arm did silence come over the room.

Justin stood before the baron as the elaborate ceremony continued. Andrew was at his right and the Nubian to his left. The brocaded cloak was about his shoulders.

A servant drew near bearing a silken pillow on which a parchment lay.

Justin's eyes were riveted to it. Andrew had said the parchment was a portion of the Scriptures. Was he right? It must be. Why would the cleric on the pirated vessel lie?

"You will now speak good words of courage to us and dedicate us for our upcoming journey."

Justin grasped the scroll, aware that he was about to risk Soleiman's anger. Could he turn events to the Word? He lifted it in the fashion of those lifting their swords.

"Baron Soleiman, though I offer a hundred prayers to evoke His blessing, I cannot evoke His favor. Therefore, you are wise when you say 'Speak good words of courage.' I hold some of those words in my hand. True words. His words. I would give them to you now, from Christ Himself. Surely a man of your religious zeal will not waste this noted gathering on ceremony alone or on my prayers. Now is the opportunity to hear a true word from the One you claim to serve."

Confusion made Soleiman's bushy eyebrows rush together. What was this? He presumably had wanted the ritual to move as simply and ceremoniously as the incense pouring up around him. Yet he had just been pronounced wise.

"Then the secret words are from God?"

Andrew had better be right. "Locked within this parchment is the word of truth, knowledge, and wisdom."

Soleiman's eyes gleamed. "Ah?"

"It is so, Baron Soleiman."

"I would possess this wisdom. Read the secret words of truth, Priest Justin."

Justin released a silent breath of relief and began to open the parchment, but Soleiman halted him like a child whose attention was fixed on a brightly wrapped gift.

"But first bless my sword and our upcoming voyage," he said with petulance.

The soothsayer interrupted. "He speaks of written words few can read," he mocked. "How then may we judge? And yet he claims the ability to tell us the meaning of the secret words of the gods. We have no proof he tells the truth. Pardon my presumption, Baron Soleiman, but have you not been hasty in making this man your chief counselor? But I! I have seen with my eye visions in this stone, visions that transcend mere words."

The soothsayer held forth his famed peepstone, a clear stone that sparkled in the torchlight.

"I have seen such stones," said Justin. "My father brought several back to England on his ship. I believe they are mined from the earth and called quartz. One thing I do know, Baron Soleiman—God does not speak to this soothsayer through that stone."

"Not so! On my pilgrimage to Jerusalem I came upon Mount Nebo where the great priest and king Moses ascended to paradise on the wings of a great horse."

Justin interrupted. "Baron Soleiman, far better that you make the soothsayer your minstrel than your counselor. Beside his exaggerated humor, his biblical facts are in gross error. Why will you hear folly when you may hear the words of God? Do not let him deceive you. He seeks not your welfare but his own greedy ambitions. I challenge the tales he has told you these past years. How many have come to pass?"

Soleiman's shaggy brows lowered as he fixed his eyes on the soothsayer.

Silence.

"Not even one?" said Justin in mock surprise.

The fortune-teller hastened to extol his wisdom, growing exuberant in his eagerness to convince Soleiman of his powers. His arms flailed, his voice rose to heights of passion, yet as he proceeded, faint laughter began to be released by the rugged corsairs until even Soleiman began to chuckle.

The soothsayer tried harder. "A little spirit took my hand as I bowed in prayer and led me to a hole in a rock. Behold! The peepstone of King Moses gleamed as fire. 'Take it,' said the spirit. 'You, Olin, son of the great Norman Viking Odo, have been chosen to bear this awesome revelation. A revelation handed down by King Moses himself. It is the very stone he used to speak with God. This stone gave the twelve commandments.'"

Justin interrupted firmly, his eyes riveted on the soothsayer who now refused to look at him. "The soothsayer would convince Baron Soleiman that truth is progressive. God has already spoken once through His Son and the apostles. Their words alone are final authority."

"I have beheld great mysteries!"

"Neither man nor angel dare add to that revelation, or else he will be found a liar," Justin said.

Soleiman leaned toward the soothsayer. His eyes narrowed. "I think you have been beguiling me with your stone," he said through clenched teeth. "I am a wise man, but you seek to make me into a fool."

"My liege, you are too wise to be deceived these three years."

Soleiman had but to lift his sword from his scabbard.

"Toad, I grow weary of your croaking. Away! Let the man of God read the writing."

The soothsayer shot Justin a daggerlike look, then slunk away into the darkest corner of the chamber.

The servants drew near with torches.

Justin cautiously unrolled the parchment, and his heart hammered. Andrew was right. It was indeed Scripture. He felt a surge of excitement. The scroll was a portion of the book of Acts, handwritten in Latin.

The light was poor, and he strained to read the sometimes faded lettering, searching for a clue as to what section from Acts he held. He was unfamiliar with it, but the moment he grasped the content, a strange joy came over him. Had he doubted the providence of God to this moment, he could doubt no longer. The Scripture portion in his hand seemed the perfect document to read to the manner of men assembled. Silently he thanked God for His guidance. The assurance of the nearness of the Lord persisted. God was not only aware of him, He "knew" him. And He knew all those assembled.

With a confident look toward Soleiman, Andrew, and the Nubian, he nodded, then glanced about the chamber to the corsairs to show they were included. He began to read clearly, first in Latin, then in English:

Then Paul stood up, and beckoning with his hand said, Men of Israel, and ye that fear God, give audience. . . . God according to his promise raised unto Israel a Savior, Jesus. . . .

For they that dwell at Jerusalem, and their rulers, because they knew him not, nor yet the voices of the prophets which are read every sabbath day, they have fulfilled them in condemning him.

And though they found no cause of death in him, yet desired they Pilate that he should be slain.

And when they had fulfilled all that was written of him, they took him down from the tree, and laid him in a sepulchre.

But God raised him from the dead: and he was seen many days of them who came up with him from Galilee to Jerusalem, who are his witnesses unto the people.

And we declare unto you glad tidings, how the promise which was made unto the fathers, God hath fulfilled the same unto us their children, in that he hath raised up Jesus again; as it is also written in the second psalm, Thou art my Son, this day have I begotten thee . . . .

David, after he had served his own generation by the will of God, fell on sleep, and was laid unto his fathers, and saw corruption. But he, whom God raised again, saw no corruption.

Be it known unto you therefore, men and brethren, that through this man is preached unto you the forgiveness of sins: and by him all that believe are justified from all things, from which ye could not be justified by the law of Moses.

Justin stopped, and a great silence permeated the hall. He sensed the reading of the Word had gone forth in God's power, and for that he knew joy and satisfaction. It was the Word of God that was needed in the English tongue! This Word was the sword needed to cut through man's spiritual density and religious error. The Sword of God must be recovered from the darkened cloister and used to set his generation free.

The torchlight flickering on the faces of those assembled revealed men moved by the presence of the Lord.

Justin rolled up the parchment and faced Soleiman. "The apostle has written of justification by faith through the finished work of Christ. Baron Soleiman, and all those among us who have listened with sincere heart, this righteous position before a holy God is given freely by grace. It is by no means attained by any merit of our own, no, nor by any religious work, however sincere or costly. Forgiveness of sin and acceptance by God rests alone in the merit of the death, burial, and bodily resurrection of His Son Jesus Christ. A resurrection that has declared Jesus to be, as Paul has written in the epistle of Romans, 'the Son of God, with power.'

"If salvation began with Christ, and is made complete by His work, and if it is kept operative by His resurrection life, our faith must rest in that God-oriented work and not in our own. I now declare that work unto you, Baron Soleiman, and to all the men here gathered. Believe, and as He has said, 'perish not.'"

The silence continued, but Justin knew the words had penetrated their souls. Then Soleiman leaned forward, and the moment was broken. His great hand, outstretched toward Justin, trembled.

"You have given us good and fair words, my son. Words that will not be forgotten—no, nor go unheeded. May this great God be blessed for sending you to us to interpret the secret words. And now we know the truth, and now you have given us true wisdom."

The silence was further interrupted only by the awkward clink of metal and the scuffle of boots as the men in the hall stirred.

Soleiman stood. "You will read them to us again, Priest Justin. Tomorrow."

"I would do more than that, Baron Soleiman. Give me paper and a quill, and I will translate them this night into your spoken tongue. Then you may read and meditate upon them yourself wherever you go. And they will be yours to read to others also, for who knows where you may traverse?"

Soleiman gestured to the Nubian. "See that he has all he needs." He then turned hard eyes upon the soothsayer, who remained in the shadows. "I will have the words of Christ for myself. No longer will I trust others to speak for God to me. His words and only His words will I hear from henceforth." The baron gave a gesture of dismissal, and the chamber began to empty.

Justin stared at the parchment. God's truth is revolutionary. Who would have expected a man such as Soleiman to receive His Word? Yet he had. An unlikely man had responded with humility to the grace of God in Christ. What it would mean to Soleiman's way of life in the future, and to his corsairs, Justin could not guess. Instead he found himself pondering the results of such a proclamation.

What would happen in the church if this truth were taught from one end of Europe to the other? What would be the outcome? Peace or wrath? Liberation or imprisonment?

More than ever Justin was convinced that the Scriptures must be translated into English. Were there others who believed as he did? He must find men who would join with him in that endeavor, whatever the cost. If a man such as Soleiman would listen and wanted the words before him, what about the common man in England and Scotland? They must not be denied access to the Scriptures.

Throughout the night Justin translated. When he had written until the darkness turned to dawn and his last candle burned low, he went to the window where the cold wind awakened him anew.

Far over the sea came the golden streaks of dawn and strong winds off the water. Below, in the courtyard, soldiers moved about and would soon come for him. He was to meet Andrew for sword practice.

Under guard, he waited for the corsair on the beach. The smell of the sea after a storm and the chill of the sharp wind was stimulating after the long night in his chamber. He had not realized how much he missed the out-of-doors, and he anticipated the training session with Andrew.

To his surprise the corsair came accompanied by Felix and the Nubian. After dismissing the guards, Andrew motioned for the two to join him and Justin.

The Nubian knelt, and with his finger drew on the white sand. "We leave tonight by small boat for the Spanish port of Valencia. From there our journey will continue by land to the port of Bayonne."

Andrew gave Justin a measured look. "There is risk involved. Will you come or not?"

"I shall be ready! But what of Stewert?"

Andrew questioned the Nubian with a raised brow.

The Nubian's gaze was confident. "He and the Spanish captain will join us."

Night had fallen upon the Mediterranean. Justin waited in his dark chamber. The time was near.

He had delivered the English translation to Soleiman that day, and tonight he placed the Latin version in his bag with his other possessions and waited for the Nubian to appear at his door.

A cautious step sounded in the hall and then the rattle of keys. The ebony giant appeared, clad in armor and cloak.

Grabbing up his leather bag, Justin followed him.

On the beach, he found the others waiting. Stewert's arm was in a sling, his cloak was flung carelessly over a shoulder, and his sword was in its sheath. He was silent but watched Justin skeptically, as though trying to judge the reason for his generosity in seeing to his release. When Stewert had sought to escape on the Spanish galleon after the shipwreck, he had left Justin behind. Yet he said nothing and took a position at one of the oars to use his good arm.

The Spanish captain was horrified when he saw the size of the small boat. He stroked his dashing mustache and raised his brows. "*Senor* Andrew! To Valencia in this?" But he threw a backward glance toward the silhouetted castle on the cliff above, and he boarded, to man his place at an oar.

The Nubian strode aft. He drew from his tunic a chart and handed it to Andrew.

Felix whispered to Justin with an anxious glance toward the incoming clouds. "May the God of creation be with us, Master."

The boat slipped away, the oars surged in powerful strokes, and the hull made headway through the dark, glassy waters. An offshore wind picked up, and the small vessel took to the open sea. The wood creaked, and the roll of the sea became deeper as the shoreline disappeared. Then dawn gave way as the rising sun shown on the full sails, and an exuberant shout arose from the men on board.

Andrew, an experienced navigator, headed west toward Valencia. A few drops of rain fell, but otherwise the weather held stable. For days they edged along the coastline of Spain until the port came into view.

Once ashore, the Spanish captain made grateful provision of horses and provisions for their journey on to Bayonne. They traveled the trade route north toward the border between Spain and France, and reaching Bayonne in good weather, they caught a ship sailing around the coast of Brittany and through the English Channel, bringing them to port in London and the Thames River.

On the morning of their long journey's end, Andrew stood on the galleon's deck with Justin as the ship nosed her way slowly into the fog-bound estuary. All were on deck for the cautious berthing of the fine ship.

A cry from the man at the masthead echoed through the misty salt breeze as sailors in the shrouds barked orders. The gray water slapped the hull, and crying gulls wheeled and swooped overhead. The vessel was made secure, and planks were laid to join the cobbled quay.

Justin picked up his leather bag and faced Andrew. "Where now, corsair? Are not the laws of London too civilized for you?" he jested.

Andrew's answer took him by surprise. "To Antwerp to visit a merchant friend at the English House. And you? Once your father is on his feet, will you not join him and your brother and take to privateering? You are good with the sword and at the pilot's helm. Be careful, or Stewert Brice will be jealous of his younger brother."

Andrew didn't realize his jest was true. Justin knew Stewert resented the competition his younger sibling offered. He cast a lingering gaze to the sea. It was still in his blood, and there was no doubt of that.

"My future is yet unknown. If I am to translate the Scriptures into English, I must master Greek. I am thinking of attending Cambridge."

Andrew's brow crested into a frown. "Remember, you are no longer among corsairs or merchants. Your speech must be bridled. This is the England of King Henry and Cardinal Wolsey. Heretics are burned here."

"I know that only too well. I have recently escaped Rome from where I also could have been burned at the stake."

Andrew's surprise at hearing this faded into an impassive expression. "Then you know what you are about and are determined to see it through."

"Yes, though I do not know the means."

"Should you come to Antwerp, you may find us at the English House on the harbor."

"I owe you both a great deal. I will seek a journey to Antwerp to repay you if my fortunes prosper."

"You owe us nothing. But come to Antwerp. We would hear again of your endeavors at Cambridge. Speaking no

Latin myself, I am in sympathy. Even I would muse deeply over such a book if I had it in the tongue I know."

To hear the rugged corsair admit this pleased Justin more than he was willing to show. "Then I will come. And I shall see to it you have the Book."

"Caution, lad, caution. This is one battle where Toledo blades are rendered useless. And since it is the only sword I know, I could be of no aid to you in danger."

Justin remembered the fleeing Wycliffites. In spite of danger, they had risked meeting in the woods to hear the Word of God. "Some things are worth risking one's head over. But let's not think of it now. The sun breaks through the mist, and it looks to be a fair winter's day. I shall see you in Antwerp."

Stewert had gone on alone, and Felix waited for Justin on the wharf. They walked the crowded cobbled streets among rotting two-storied wooden houses crammed together, and around them sailors carried loads on their backs. The street vendors were busy, and the pieman and fish peddlar had their carts loaded for the day's work.

They paused to buy meat pies, still holding some of the heat of the old man's morning oven, then hurried on.

A hubbub of voices filled the mist-shrouded streets. Sea birds bickered over discarded fish bones and decaying debris, and cats stalked. From the upstairs of a wooden structure, a woman leaned out and emptied a bucket of water onto the street below.

By the time they reached the landing stage by the Tower of London, the morning sun had burned through the fog. Here they caught a small hired boat filled with vendors on their way to the better part of the city to sell their wares. London Bridge came into view, and Justin recognized the leaning frame buildings that had seemed so curious to him as a child. As the foundations rotted, the structures tilted more and more precariously toward the water.

But beyond the Bridge the scene changed, and he and Felix entered another world. Here were the magnificent palaces of the Strand, where gardens ran down to the water's edge, alleyways offered climbing roses with sweet fragrance and a maze of varied greens from the intricately clipped bushes and low trees. A large fountain shot a glistening spray of blue into the air, and white-winged doves flew through the mist. Small private boats belonging to lords, bishops, and abbots docked between the landing stages and carried their masters and mistresses over the water under gaudy awnings of scarlet and gold.

It was here that he would meet Lady Regina Redford after nearly four long years.

10

London, 1518

Lady Regina dressed quickly in a ribbon-trimmed gown of green velvet. It had a long skirt and belled elbow-length sleeves. Her dark hair was swept gracefully up from her shoulders and secured with combs of jade. She turned quickly as the door of her chamber opened and Lisbeth stood there, flushed with excitement.

"Sir Justin Brice is here, m'lady, and waiting in the garden. And," she breathed in wonder, "he wears no monk's robe."

Regina tried to calm the thumping of her heart. "Have Trigg bring the coach to the gate." She snatched up her fur-lined cloak and started toward the door.

"Trigg's already waiting, m'lady."

Regina was in such a rush she almost forgot the prized gift she intended to give Justin. She couldn't wait to see his expression or to show him how knowledgeable she was.

Whereas her fluency with Greek and Latin offended Lord Robert, the earl's son, surely it would please Justin. And the extensive notes she had taken on the lectures of Dean John Colet on the Pauline epistles were scholarly enough to have belonged to a Master of Arts.

She smiled. Justin was the one man who would appreciate her labors. Carefully she slid the portfolio into her leather bag.

Lisbeth watched with puckered lips. "One day, m'lady, I fear you'll fall into dire trouble over your interest in such forbidden things," she whispered. "King Henry holds no sympathy for—"

Regina cut her off with a good humored pat to her cheek. "Tsk, tsk, Lisbeth. You fret like a stewing hen. Mind your tongue, and let us go. Is everything packed?"

"Yes, m'lady."

In a manner her father would frown upon, Regina picked up her skirts and ran out into the hall. Then she sedately followed Lisbeth down several ornate corridors to the southwestern section of the palace and to a flight of stairs.

Wide-eyed, Lisbeth watched over the banister as her lady descended in a swirl of shimmering green.

Regina paused. From where she stood on the stairs, the view onto the private terrace showed an absence of guards. Past the gallery, a stairway stretched down to the scenic garden sitting silently in the noon sun. Beyond the sloping garden, the water was gray blue and dotted with small boats traversing to and fro.

Pulse pounding, she forced herself to breathe regularly, trying to gain a measure of control before she faced him. One . . . two . . . three . . . her heart slammed in spite of the effort.

Lisbeth, dressed in hat and cloak for the ride to Redford House, now ushered the servants bearing Regina's trunk to the waiting coach.

"Shall I send for Sir Brice, m'lady?"

"No, wait for us in the coach."

Regina walked down the grassy slope toward the Thames, where Justin waited by the landing stage near the barge.

He turned as she approached.

She stopped when her eyes fell on him. Still expecting a cleric, she stared. His costume was equal in brilliance to his appearance. The suit was black velvet, the shirt made of fine white linen, and a riding cloak was draped about his broad shoulders. His boots were polished, sporting silver buckles, and on his head was a dashing hat of the French fashion.

He came toward her, sweeping off the hat with a deep bow. "Your servant, m'lady."

Regina rallied her floundering courage and became at once Lady Redford. She clutched the leather folder behind her back, wondering. This could not be the young man who had spent years in Rome at Saint Athenians? She had expected a monk's cowl, a subdued if not altogether "religious" demeanor. Instead he looked a lord, at least a cavalier, and she was both wary and pleased all at once.

His propriety and formal tone were quickly matched.

She lifted her chin with studied nobility. "Sir Brice, how pleasant to see you again."

Regina had no idea how Justin had dreaded this formal moment. Felix had accumulated the fashionable clothes, declaring he could not possibly visit Lady Regina Redford in anything less dashing. The plumed hat Justin had considered twice. Yet Felix had won. "And when you meet her, Master, be sure you bow very deep and sweep it wide. Offer your servanthood with profound dedication."

"I remember the customs, Felix," he had said dryly. He could have added that he had also once raced with her on horseback through the woods around Windsor Castle. But the years had considerably changed matters. They had grown up.

He looked at her now, and his poised manner showed nothing of his inward dilemma. He dare not contemplate the feelings raging in his heart.

"Your kindness to my father is graciously accepted, my lady. How can I ever repay you?"

"Perhaps I shall think of some way," she murmured and dragged her eyes away from his. "Shall we go? The coach waits."

Two fine coaches were parked in the cobbled driveway, and the attendants waited in bright uniforms of red and black. One coach was for her and Justin, the other for her servants. Felix waited beside Lisbeth and, seeing Lady Regina approach, made an elegant bow.

Regina went to him at once and planted a kiss on his cheek. "I shall reward you for your faithful service, Felix. I shall not forget your voyage to Rome on my behalf."

Felix grinned and hastened to bow over her extended hand. "'Twas an honor, my lady. And no easy task. Wait until Master Justin tells you of our shipwreck."

"*Shipwreck!*" She looked over at Justin.

He bowed.

"And being made slaves by pirates, my lady!" Felix added.

"*Pirates!*"

"A harrowing tale, my lady," said Justin, too gravely. He opened the coach door and handed her in.

"I will hear everything, Jus—Sir Brice. I must hear every detail."

Justin cast Felix a slight smile. Felix grinned back.

Ah! thought Justin. *By the time I explain my life in the monastery, the wondrous discovery in Rome, and the adventure bringing us back to London, the formality between us will once again melt into a comfortable relationship, I hope. If she is still the Regina I remember, she will relish every moment.*

The coach bearing them to Redford House left the crowded streets of London and took Whitechapel Road past the many small villages that, despite their proximity to London, differed little from countless other villages throughout England. The church of Saint Anne stood beneath a cluster of trees, and the half-timbered cottages with overhanging upper stories were thatched. Each hamlet had a village green, used on festive celebrations such as May Day. There was the blacksmith's cottage, an apothecary, a small tavern-inn whose aged sign hung on a wrought-iron arm over the street.

When Justin at last finished recounting his discovery of the truth found in the book of Romans and concluded with his escape from Saint Athenians, they were well on the road taking them into the English countryside where Redford House was located.

"You must be cautious here, Justin. Returning to London will in no wise give you the liberty to criticize the teachings of the church. Emotions run high since that Augustinian monk Martin Luther found public support for his teachings in Wittenberg. The word *heresy* is bandied about on the wagging tongues of everyone from Cardinal Wolsey to King Henry. If they find out that you were to be tried in Rome, I wonder if you will be able to enter Cambridge. I myself have recently been rebuked in a letter from Cardinal Wolsey for having 'erring feet.'"

Justin had remained calm and unflinching until she mentioned the danger to herself. He searched her face at once. "The Cardinal took time to question you? Why? What have you been doing?"

Her lips curved into a demure smile. But if his concern pleased her, she swiftly masked her pleasure and grew serious. Her brown eyes became remote. "You could risk all to stand for truth before the Roman abbot. But I must stay to the safety of my chamber and to my embroidery."

He lifted a brow. "I know you too well to believe anything so comforting. Tell me—" he winced "—you did not publicly criticize the cardinal?"

She smiled wryly. "Even I know better than that. It was not criticism of Cardinal Wolsey but support for Colet. It seems I have been too vocal in my praise of Colet's teaching. But once you have seen what he has written, you will understand my enthusiasm, if few others do."

She then produced the leather folder that he had been eyeing with curiosity since leaving London. She handed it to him, and her eyes shone. "I have something for you. I was going to wait until we reached the manor, but I cannot hide my excitement. Here!"

Justin raised a questioning brow and opened it. He stared with shock at the contents—the Greek New Testament of Erasmus!

She smiled, her dark eyes gleaming. "My tutor of many years, Master of Arts Whitfield, knows Erasmus. This is one of the first printed copies of his Greek scholarship."

Justin opened the precious leather-bound book and turned the pages slowly. The thought of holding in his hand the Word of Truth from Matthew to Revelation was as awesome as it was disheartening. He tried his meager knowledge of Greek and found himself woefully lacking. He must learn the original language from the Masters at Cambridge. Erasmus was no longer there, but his work was and those whom he had taught.

"I might begin to teach you some Greek," Regina said cautiously. "If you would not find it offensive to have a feminine teacher." She proceeded as though according to carefully laid plans. "I was hoping you would stay at Redford House through the winter and spring. It may take that long before your father is well enough to return to Antwerp. I thought we might study the New Testament together."

He met her eyes squarely. "When do we begin?"

His readiness seemed to take her off guard. She hesitated. "Anytime you wish. Tomorrow?"

"Tomorrow I shall be waiting for you, Master of Arts Redford."

She smiled, embarrassed, and then quickly diverted his attention to what else was in the folder.

"Erasmus's New Testament is not all. This is my own portfolio on Colet's lectures. I wrote it in Latin. Since you could not hear him at Saint Paul's, at least my notes could be of benefit to you. They are quite extensive," she apologized, glancing sideways as though to judge his reaction. Was he pleased with her education, or did he feel threatened?

Justin quickly leafed through the pages. The lectures of Dean John Colet on the Pauline epistles! He could hardly contain his joy.

"There was so much to write down," she apologized again.

But she couldn't contain her zeal. "Oh, that you could have heard him. Instead of quoting the teaching of the church on the Writings, he taught the Writings himself. He straightforwardly quoted what the Scriptures themselves say. He expounded the very words from their original meaning in the Greek. And this he did with all of the Pauline epistles." She nodded toward the ponderous notes in his hands. "Romans, and the letters of Corinthians, Ephesians . . ." She halted, coloring under his gaze.

He was focusing upon her now, unable to conceal his pleasure. Perhaps she had found no one to share her enthusiasm for the Scriptures. The unity between their spirits around Christ and His Word gave him a sense of warm delight.

She averted her eyes to the papers he held. "I . . . I . . . wrote in Latin . . ." Her voice trailed. There was a moment of silence in which the clip of the horse's hooves was loud.

"Your work is excellent," Justin stated. "This means more to me than you can know. How I envied your opportunity to hear him. And to think you have actually captured so much exposition on paper for me."

"I must confess that Marlon also took notes for you."

"Marlon! Now I *am* overwhelmed. He who hated the sight of pen and ink."

"He has changed, Justin. He met Colet and talked with him for hours. He has a great hunger for the Scriptures."

"Marlon?" He was delighted.

"Yes, and he also met a young man by the name of William Tyndale who—"

"Your gift is priceless, Regina." He began to leaf through the work again.

"I wanted to send it to you at Saint Athenians but thought better of doing so. It would surely have been greeted as a heretical work."

"You were wise not to do that. What is the reaction of Colet's own colleagues?"

"As expected, his work has created a stir among other scholars at Oxford. Even the New Thinkers are cautious."

"As well they might be. To see expounded the literal meaning of the Pauline epistles, when most theologians are more interested in allegory, must be a shock. So this is what you have been endorsing in King Henry's palace! No wonder Cardinal Wolsey took time to write you an admonition."

Justin grew sober. "My lady, you must do nothing that will call you before the king. The Tower is no place for one of your beauty or learning. I would have to give up all plans of going to Cambridge in order to attempt your rescue."

Her expression now looked like anything but that of a young scholar. She dimpled. "I find your chivalry quite flattering. Would you indeed, Justin Brice, risk your head to save me?"

His gaze was unwavering. "I would, my lady."

Even among the conservative scholars at Oxford and Cambridge the essence of biblical teaching was unknown. The lecture halls of the two universities, being the foundation of Christian learning in sixteenth-century England, were governed by inflexible laws laid down centuries earlier. The ideas of nominalism and realism were always at odds. The Masters of scholasticism lectured not on the biblical text but cited what the authorities said about the text.

The theology of Thomas Aquinas permeated the doctrine of the church, and, as Erasmus had said to Colet, to speak against Aquinas now was to speak against the church itself. It was to John Colet's credit that he told his students to keep to the Scriptures and the Apostle's Creed.

"His lectures were so crowded one could hardly find room to sit or stand," Regina said. "They stood for hours. Not students only, but monks, and the other Masters of Arts."

"All men should teach as he does," said Justin. "The words should be given in literal context and explained clearly, not only to those who understand Latin, but in English. For too long the church has taught dogma and neglected the foundation of Christianity, which is the Person of Christ and His Word."

"So I agree, and Marlon too. We tried to get our father to attend the lectures and to speak of them to the king, but he would not," she said quietly. "Yet recently Marlon has spent time with him in hearty discussion. His interest is awakening. And now that King Henry will send him on business to Cambrai, we hope Father will take time to visit Wittenberg to also meet with Dr. Luther."

Justin thought of the stalwart Lord Simon Redford. He was highly respected by the king. But today's favor could be tomorrow's trip to the Tower.

Lord Simon walked softly—a necessity for anyone in service to King Henry, as Cardinal Wolsey was to find out. Unable to get the pope to grant Henry VIII a divorce from Catherine to marry Anne Boleyn, the cardinal would be sentenced by the king to die for "treason."

"What does your father think of Colet?"

"He is thoughtful but will say little. He warns us to be cautious about offending Cardinal Wolsey. But I did get him to read Erasmus's *In Praise of Folly*. He thought this satirical work identifying the abuses within the church very clever. But then, Erasmus is such a gifted satirist.

"Marlon and I mistakenly thought we might get our father to aid William Tyndale, but he will not."

"You mentioned this William Tyndale before."

"He is a godly man, a true scholar with a destiny. I am sure of it. He has acquired a masterful knowledge of the biblical languages and abhors obscurantism. I want you to meet him. You have much in common."

She fell silent.

He hesitated. Perhaps now he could ask what had been on his mind for so long. "Felix told me you had not married. I could hardly believe it. How is it that you have escaped Robert's wish to marry you?"

"Like you, I too have been in a cloister."

She touched her volume of handwritten work. "When a young woman buries herself in her chamber and is content to stain her fingers with ink rather than jewels, a frivolous man such as Lord Robert quickly grows bored. It is as I planned it, for I do not love him. And so he is content to busy himself elsewhere."

Justin was relieved, but he rebuked himself. Her disinterest in Lord Robert did not mean that she loved *him*.

"I was offended when you refused to answer my letters," she said.

"I never saw your letters, my lady. The abbot destroyed them."

"I soon understood that."

He hesitated, wondering if he dare express his feelings. And if he did say he loved her, then what? Lord Simon would never consent to their marriage. Was it not wrong then to test their love further? And what of his personal commitment to the Lord? How could he risk involving her more fully in what he knew would be a future racked with danger and uncertainty?

"At least marriage to Lord Robert would mean your safety," he stated.

She turned on him at once. "Do you think I am frivolous? That I care for nothing but ease and baubles? That I have no commitment to things of value? That I fear the harshness of reality?"

"You are a rare woman of valiant spirit. I would be a fool to question either your courage or your devotion to matters of serious import."

Her eyes shone. "Remember Wycliffe's translation of Matthew?"

"How could I forget?" he whispered emphatically.

Her emotion matched his. "Neither can I forget. When we shared the Word together in English for the first time, I knew I had found something important, something worth risking not only the comforts of my position for, but my life."

"I would not see you risking your life!"

"Yet you will risk yours. If I find myself involved in heretical views, they began before your return to London. I told you about William Tyndale, but I have not explained his ambitions. He intends to translate the Bible into English. And I vowed to do all I could to make it possible."

He stared at her, struggling with torn emotions. Hearing of another who shared his greatest desire caused the blood to pound in his temples. But the risk was great. And it was one thing to risk himself—but Regina?

"Regina, you are sure of this? This William Tyndale spoke to you of his desire?"

"Especially to Marlon. You will think highly of him, Justin, as we do. He is dedicated."

"He has impressed me already. I must meet him."

"You shall meet him. Marlon and I have mentioned William and his ambition to our father, hoping he might speak to Cardinal Wolsey or to Bishop Tunstall about receiving authorization from the church to work under their supervision. But Father turned red with rage."

"More likely he would have taken on the ghastly color of fear," said Justin quietly. "Wolsey is the last man in England to ask. William Tyndale's name or whereabouts was not mentioned to the cardinal, I hope?"

"No! And now it seems Master Tyndale must one day go to Bishop Cuthbert Tunstall himself for permission to translate. But he will need a letter of introduction."

The Bishop of London seemed the best choice in seeking patronage for Tyndale's work. Tunstall was a scholar in languages, and he embraced some of Erasmus's ideas of church reform.

Justin, however, was skeptical. "Even if William Tyndale seeks the patronage of Bishop Tunstall, it is not likely he will get it."

Lady Regina scowled. "Why not? I still hope to talk my father into writing him a letter of introduction to the bishop."

"For the same reasons the abbot in Rome failed to risk his position to religious and political criticism when I mentioned the possibility of Scripture in the common tongue—ambition and fear."

"You are too cynical. Not every bishop in the church is so concerned with his position."

"There are good and dedicated men in the church. I meant not to claim otherwise. But there are few in authority who will risk being called a heretic. Like Erasmus, they may satirize or denounce the evil, and by doing so they sow the seeds of reform. That is needed surely, and every man has his own gift. The teacher exhorts his student to put his knowledge into action. And Erasmus has been a great teacher, as others have been.

"But more is now needed. Now the time of harvest must come. Something positive must be done. Some action must be taken. If William Tyndale is a scholar of the original languages and is zealous to put the Scriptures into English—if he is willing to risk his life to do it—then I will do anything I can to help him. And I will consider it the greatest privilege the Lord has given me."

"And you do not think the work can be done with the church's approval?"

"No. Therefore, your father was right to turn red when his son and daughter came to him and asked him to speak to Cardinal Wolsey. I only wonder what Master Tyndale will do when he is refused permission from the church?"

"Tyndale made no comment on what he might do. But I believe he will go ahead with the work anyway."

"Undoubtedly he knows the consequences. I too am willing to do what is necessary. But you—"

She interrupted tonelessly. "But am I to remain safely cloistered in the palace and watch the smoke rise from Smithfield?" Smithfield—the place where heretics were burned.

"Neither I nor presumably this Master Tyndale has plans of visiting Smithfield," he hastened soberly.

"If risking your future to help a man like Tyndale is deemed a worthy sacrifice to serve our Lord, am I to be denied my loyalty?" Regina sounded determined. "Did I ask to be born at this hour in history? And if I possess the authority and goods to help so noble a cause, am I not held responsible to use these things in good stewardship? Or, because I am a woman, does that mean I should shackle my wits to my bed-post?"

A smile crossed his face, for he could not resist. "Your wits, my lady, should be shackled only to a man who appreciates them."

She stared at him. Her energy seemed spent.

But Justin looked away. He could not involve himself. He must go to Cambridge and study.

And she did not ask, "Are you that man?"

11

Redford House

The sixteenth century was a time of sweeping change in Western Europe, shaking the foundations of both church and monarchy. More than eight years had passed since, in 1508, a teenager named William Tyndale entered Magdalen College at Oxford.

Tyndale enrolled at the university as the closing Dark Ages overlapped the beginnings of the Renaissance, the discovery of the New World, the Spanish Inquisition, and the Protestant Reformation. But Tyndale, involved deeply in his studies at both Oxford and Cambridge, and later as a fugitive from the church and the king, was unaware of his crucial role in the movement of God.

In 1515 Tyndale received his M.A. from Oxford. In 1516 Erasmus edited the first printed and published Greek New Testament and also wrote his negative work *In Praise of Folly*, satirizing the abuses of the church. On October 31, 1517, in a town in Saxony called Wittenberg, Martin Luther nailed his ninety-five theses to the door of the Castle Church. And in 1519 Tyndale moved to Cambridge to master Greek.

During his stay at Redford House, Justin was lost in his own studies and unaware of what was taking place in Wittenberg. With Regina's help, his command of Greek improved, but he was ever aware of his need to attend university and earn his degree.

As for his father, Ewan Brice's dark mood worsened. Justin visited him one day in the small cottage at the end of the garden.

Captain Brice lay brooding, his mood as dark as pitch, his brows hunched low over his stormy eyes. No matter how Justin tried to reason with him, his father would not hear.

Felix shook his head. "What will you do, Master? You have spent months with your father, and yet he remains iron in his resolve to do himself harm."

"I do not know, Felix," he said wearily. "Lady Regina returns to London for the Christmas holidays. We dare not impose on the Redfords much longer."

Yet Justin was reluctant to leave his father in his despondent condition. Time was fast slipping away. Even one such as Felix had come to faith in Christ, but his father remained imprisoned in the darkness of his own doom, in spite of Justin's greatest efforts to free him.

And Stewert? Somehow Justin felt he would never be given the opportunity to tell his brother of the peace he himself had gained. As long as Stewert was jealous and bitter, Justin's words would fall on stony ground.

But his father . . .

In the darkening sky lightning flashed above the trees, followed by the sullen rumble of thunder.

"My Catherine and little Mary are dead," Captain Brice said. "Dead like their mother, lying cold in the ground. And, as for your mother, I am to blame for the little ones' sleeping cold. Soon now the rain will come again and drench their beds."

Justin had heard this tale of gloom a multitude of times. And when it rained, his father's mood worsened. That was why Justin had joined him today in the cottage.

"Catherine and Mary died of the plague, like Balin York, and a thousand others, Father. God has not taken their souls to punish you. Know that your sin—and mine—is covered by the blood of Christ. Rest with quiet confidence in that scriptural fact."

Captain Brice lay on his bed staring darkly before him, his mind tormented. At the sound of Justin's voice, his remote gaze turned to fix upon him.

He blinked, then scowled. And again, for the hundredth time, he murmured, "You are not in your robe, nor does the cross grace your neck."

"I have told you, I am no longer a monk. My service to the Lord will be invested in what I believe is a far greater endeavor."

"Do you not hear the thunder of God against heretics? Be quick to seek forgiveness. 'Twas no light matter to flee the very city of Rome."

"The righteousness of Christ is my armor—and can be yours. Be at peace."

"No, lad, you have wrongly returned from Rome to ease my torture. I will return to Antwerp and to my ship. I have a destiny to keep with a storm at sea. The Almighty awaits to send me to a just death."

"Father! Have you not heard a word I have said to you these past months?"

"Neither your presence nor your fair words will convince me otherwise. I have committed an unpardonable sin. The death of my innocent damsels was a judgment against Ewan Brice." He groaned. "I gave my son to Rome—what else more was there to do? Yet there is no peace. My hands are still stained. I have lost you, for I sent you against your wish. And now both of my daughters are dead. Only Stewert lives, and he to curse me."

"I bear no grudge concerning your decision to send me to the monastery. In Rome I found truth, for I found the Scriptures. I have returned to London the better for going. And Stewert is loyal to you, though he bears a root of bitterness against us both. He can be won back by letting him know your feelings toward him."

"No. In my dreams a thousand screaming demons come to gnash upon my soul."

A lightning flash and a rumble of thunder brought him upright. "Yes, the God of wrath thunders against me. Behold, my way is dark, my soul cast from before Him like rotting leaves before the devil wind."

Justin stared at him, distraught by his father's inability to perceive the truth.

For the first time he saw the man as tired and old. There was nothing left of the virility he remembered so well. The strong personality was shattered by fits of depression that deepened as the days passed.

"Obviously he is too guilt ridden to listen to your logic," Regina said. "He needs something else to free his mind."

The Christmas holidays were over, and they were in the library studying the Greek New Testament with Colet's notes. Her comment, though simply put, arrested his attention. Slowly the profound truth in her suggestion gripped him. Was this the answer to his tireless prayers for his father's release from the bondage of guilt? Had he been depending upon his own arguments to dispel the darkness instead of using the Sword of Truth to cut through the unbelief?

Each morning thereafter Justin met with his father and simply read the Scriptures. He refused to debate the reason behind the deaths of little Catherine and Mary, and when his father interrupted to tread again the worn paths of guilt and judgment, Justin did not argue. He waited in silence until his father's tongue grew weary and said no more.

Then Justin would again read the Scriptures that heralded the liberty bought by the blood of Christ. He would conclude with prayer, thanking God for His guidance in his life while at Rome, then quietly reassure his father that he loved him, and leave.

Ewan Brice seemed not to hear, but as the days turned into weeks, Justin noticed that his father was no longer interrupting as much as he had previously. Eventually there were no interruptions at all, and Justin then began to labor over the sense of the words, explaining the merit in Christ's atoning death, what the resurrection proved, and how Christ ever lived to make intercession for His own.

"God is satisfied with the price of the bruising of His own Son. He put Christ to grief and made His soul an offering for our sin. His travail did satisfy the holy demands of judgment, and by Him many are justified, for He poured out His soul unto death. And though a man's sins be as scarlet, they shall be as white as snow."

The weeks slipped by, and then one day Felix opened the cottage door and thrust his head in. "Lord Marlon Redford is here, Master Justin."

Justin left the New Testament on the table and walked toward the manor. Lord Marlon emerged ahead on the path, a handsome figure in doublet and hat. Justin hardly recognized the man before him, and from Marlon's expression, he too wondered at the masculine figure who had once been the stable boy.

"So you escaped the monastery to capture the heart of my sister, did you?"

Justin wondered.

But Marlon grinned and greeted him with a hearty grasp of his shoulders. "It is good to see you again, Justin. I could not be more pleased. My father is here now with some masters from Cambridge. They have come to hear our guest, a scholar from Wittenberg. He knows Martin Luther."

"A friend of Martin Luther here in your home?"

"My father has interest in the work of Luther," he said quietly.

"I am very glad. But it will mean grave trouble if King Henry hears of it."

"Caution is the reason for meeting here instead of in London." Marlon looked grave.

"Of Luther I know little. It is William Tyndale I wish to meet."

"Ah, then, so Regina told you of William? Good! You shall meet him also."

Justin pressed. "When?"

"When will you return to London?"

Justin thought of his father. "I have stayed here too long. I must leave by spring if I am to enroll at Cambridge."

"Then I will arrange a meeting soon. But as for Luther—" his voice lowered "—it seems lightning has struck over Wittenberg. Think what this means, Justin! He has openly criticized the church in Rome for the abuses of the indulgence system. Not only that, but he has challenged a debate on the subject."

The parlor of the Redford house boasted a fireplace built across one wall, and as the wind flung rain against the windowpanes, logs blazed on a bed of red coals.

Several doctors were present from Cambridge, wearing their scholarly birettas and violet robes, and the Masters of Arts wore miniver-lined hoods with wide sleeves. Whitfield, a friend of Erasmus and tutor to Lady Regina was also there.

Regina stood beside her father, Lord Simon. As Justin met her gaze, her lips curved slightly into a smile, but she now wore the face of Lady Redford, and she made no move to cross the room to him.

The discussion was already going on. At once his attention was drawn to the visiting scholar from Wittenberg who addressed those assembled in Latin.

The scholar was a graduate of the University of Wittenberg, where Martin Luther held the position of lecturer in biblical theology and taught in the vernacular on Psalms, Romans, Galatians, and Hebrews.

"*Herr Doktor* was gravely upset when Archbishop Albert received a papal bull to raise money by selling indulgences."

"Such exploitation of the people is not altogether new," said a Cambridge doctor cautiously.

"Yet the archbishop was given authority to sell indulgences throughout Saxony for the next eight years," said the Wittenberg scholar indignantly. "Doktor Luther has rightly asked, although dryly, whether the poor churches of Germany must go roofless so that Rome may have a roof of gold. But that is not the half of it. The Dominican monk Johann Tetzel is the archbishop's peddler. He goes about stirring up the people to buy. He even claims repentance is not necessary."

"Not necessary!"

"He has promised remission of the gravest sins if the sinner will only buy an indulgence. At his table he has a cash box, like so—" he sketched an airy gesture with his fingers, his lips pursed "—and beside it—hear this!—a written price list of standard fees for indulgences. *Herr Doktor* has in these last years come to assured faith through the Scripture alone. Do you wonder why then he has been outraged in the name of true righteousness?"

The German scholar now jumped to his feet, his cheeks flushed. "*Herr Doktor* walked like this—" with shoulders back he strode across the room to the mantel "—and boldly nailed" —he hammered—"to the door of the church his protestation!"

A rumble of thunder followed, and the German scholar lifted his eyes toward the ceiling.

"What will come of this challenge to Rome?"

"Does Pope Leo know of the action?"

"If not, he will. Then what?"

"Luther will be burned."

"Let us hear these famed ninety-five theses," interrupted Lord Simon Redford. "Our friend from Wittenberg has a copy with him. Proceed, learned sir."

"I indeed have a copy," said he, retaking his seat. "It is so, my brothers, that the original in Latin has been translated into German and is spreading rapidly among the people."

"The trumpet has sounded," said an old doctor. "The call will echo throughout Europe."

The scholar from Wittenberg removed a parchment from his sleeve and began to read.

"'A disputation of Master Martin Luther, Theologian, for the elucidation of the virtue of indulgences. From a zealous desire to bring to light the truth, the following theses will be maintained at Wittenberg. . . . He therefore asks that all who are unable to be present and dispute with him verbally will do so in writing. In the name of our Lord Jesus Christ. Amen.'"

As he proceeded to enumerate each of the ninety-five theses, Justin felt a surge of passion. Oh, that he could have been there!

Rain pelted the window with such sudden fury that the German scholar had to raise his voice. His staccato Latin seemed to dent the walls of the chamber.

Lady Regina slipped from her father's side and came up beside Justin, but no one appeared to notice, so engrossed were they.

Justin was spellbound, for Luther's theses were not a long, wandering apologetic but rapid-fire declarations on the unscriptural use of indulgences.

Among other things, Luther declared that "those who assert that a soul straightway flies out [of purgatory] as a coin tinkles in the collection box, are preaching an invention of man. . . . Those who think themselves sure of salvation through their letters of pardon will be damned forever with their teachers. . . . We must especially beware of those who say that those pardons of Rome are that inestimable gift of God by which man is reconciled to God. . . . Confidence in salvation through letters of indulgence is vain. . . . A wrong is done to the Word of God when in the same sermon an equal or longer time is devoted to indulgences than to God's Word."

When the reading ended, silence fell. Then glances were exchanged among the doctors and masters, and debate broke out.

"He has said no more than what men like Erasmus and Colet have said for years. I commend the learned *doktor*," said one.

Another said gravely, "It is but the beginning. What next? And where will it lead? Have these theses been sent to the archbishop of Mainz?"

The German scholar wiped his perspiring brow. "Indeed. And the archbishop has sent them to the pope."

There was a groan.

"Ah, so there we have it," said a grave doctor. "Know now that Martin Luther will surely be called on charges of heresy."

"The Dominicans," said the German, "even now boast that *Herr Doktor* will burn. But he has appealed to Prince Frederick of Saxony. Since a German must be tried only in Saxony, he will not be sent by Frederick to Rome. He will be required to appear before the Diet of Augsburg."

"Will it be an open debate?" asked Justin.

"Yes. He shall be permitted to speak."

"Then the man will have the words to contend for the faith," Justin replied.

The German's eyes looked kindly upon him, and he smiled. "You are right, scholar. Martin Luther will never recant. It is *sola fide*, justification only by faith, and *sola scriptura*, only the Scriptures are the authority."

Regina took Justin's arm and drew him into the hall. Her eyes shone, and her cheeks were flushed. The voices dimmed behind them. "When we left London, you said the seed for church reform was sown by men like Erasmus, but now bold action was needed. Has Luther drawn the sword of action?"

"Only God knows what the end will be. But I think Martin Luther has sounded the trumpet, and men all over Europe who have needed a leader will rally to his summons."

Her eyes clouded. "And you? Will you also go to Wittenberg?"

"I shall remain in England and seek your friend Master Tyndale."

12

Redford House

Justin entered the cottage, bringing a gust of wind and rain with him. Felix was bent over the cook pot steaming on the hearth, stirring his concoction with vigor.

He looked up surprised. "Master Justin, are you back so soon? I had thought you would dine with the great doctors and masters at Redford House this night."

Justin hung his wet cloak on the post to dry. One look at his face, and Felix stopped stirring. "Are you sick?"

"No. I am leaving with Marlon in the morning for Cambridge. You must take my father to Antwerp."

"Indeed, Master," Felix said in surprise. "I thought we would stay at Redford House until spring."

"I thought so myself, until I heard the scholar from Wittenberg. I can no longer delay my future, Felix. If ever I am to master Greek, I would do it now."

He explained about Martin Luther. "It is time I was about my own affairs in London. The news from Wittenberg has stirred me to pursue what I know to be true."

A sound from the bedroom doorway caused them both to turn. Captain Ewan Brice stood there erect and alert and with a curious arch of his brow.

"How now, Justin! So you will go to Cambridge, will you?"

Justin stared at him. His father looked as robust as the day he had taken to ship in good spirits.

Felix too stared.

Then Justin caught sight of the New Testament in his father's rough hand.

Captain Brice saw his eyes fix on the Book, and he held it up with a scowl. "Are you sure the fine words you read me came from this gibberish?"

Justin's relief brought a smile. "It is written in Greek, Father."

"Greek, Latin—'tis all gibberish to the likes of me. Have you none of the good words in me own maternal tongue?"

"My father, you have touched upon the essence of why I go to Cambridge—so that one day you may read the fair words for yourself."

"'Tis a good thing," the captain said with exaggerated irritation. "I cannot always have me son sitting near the bed reading for me now, can I!" His eyes gleamed, and a slight smile showed under his beard. "Especially since your father will take to sea with Stewert, and you shall go to your Master of Arts."

Justin searched the captain's rugged face, and he saw what he was looking for.

"You have found His peace, my father?" he asked quietly.

Ewan Brice walked slowly toward him and paused, his face suddenly aglow. Then he flung wide his strong arms with unashamed affection. "I have His peace, my son."

Justin embraced him, and for a moment they wept together.

Then Captain Brice gripped Justin's arms Roman style. "What is this I have heard you say—that you have no worldly goods to keep a woman like her ladyship in silks and furs?"

"When did I say that?"

"You have always said so, has he not, Felix?"

"Indeed, Master Ewan, since he was a boy," Felix agreed with a broad smile.

"Do you not own half of everything I possess?" asked the captain, throwing an arm about him. "And what of the Brice castle and lands in Scotland? You are young and strong, lad. Venture forth and take it."

"I have a vow to keep, my father. A vow that will bring God's Word to the people in their own tongue. I made it when I left Rome the night our ship was lost in the storm. It is a vow that will mean great risk. I would not involve Lady Regina any more than I have to."

"If you have made a vow, keep it," said his father firmly. He handed the New Testament to Justin, and the corners of his mouth turned. "I will expect your vow to accomplish much."

"There is something I ask you to do in Antwerp, Father. I have a friend there named Andrew. You will meet him when you arrive at the English House. Reward him. It was he who made our escape possible from Baron Soleiman."

"I shall do as you ask. And now," he said with a gesture toward Felix, "let us eat and be merry for this one night at least. You, my son, give thanks to our gracious Savior. He has removed the burden of guilt from my wicked old heart."

13

Cambridge University, 1519

The lesser parlor of the Inn of the White Horse at Cambridge became suddenly quiet. The lively discussion among the learned men and students who often frequented the Inn, bringing books and notes with them to share about the fire, ended abruptly. In the silence that permeated the room, both masters and students exchanged somber looks, then one by one arose slowly and walked out into the night.

Justin too gathered up his books and papers. A melancholy sense of loss had descended upon his spirits, and it seemed the light of a precious torch had been snuffed out. He hurried along the street and then up the staircase that led to the chamber he shared with William Tyndale.

William was busy at his desk by the window. His candle was burning, his worn scholar's cloak was pulled tightly about his lean body to block the chill. His pen ceased its scratching, and he looked up over the candle flame, squinting to see what drove Justin to bang the door.

One look at his face and Tyndale stood to his feet, ready for important news. He gripped the quill tightly, but his face was outwardly composed. "Have they burned the good and brave man then?"

"No," Justin hastened to say. "Not Luther. It is Dean John Colet. He is dead."

The news of Colet's death brought a quiet moment of reflection on what the loss of such an able scholar would mean.

"The Lord has seen fit to take a valuable man," said William soberly, and he sat down again. "Yet He makes no mistakes." Chin in hand he stared at the paper before him.

Justin lay his books on his own desk. "He will be hard to replace. With the storm of controversy over Martin Luther, we need his voice more than ever. Master Colet had hoped for an English version from Erasmus."

William nodded. "Yes, I know. But Erasmus is Erasmus. He has no wish to ignite a quarrel with the pope. He even dedicated his new Latin version to him, thus stilling his own personal controversy."

Erasmus's action had brought criticism from certain men at Oxford and Cambridge, and they had retaliated by banning his works and books.

Justin, long an admirer of Erasmus, rushed to his defense. "Yet Erasmus opposes those who are unwilling that the sacred Scriptures be translated into the common tongue. Has he not said they should be rendered into the languages of all?"

William's eyes gleamed with passion as he swept up the Greek New Testament and read aloud the foreword, where Erasmus declared, "Let the husbandman sing portions of them as he follows the plow, the weaver hum them to the tune of the shuttle, and the traveler beguile the tedium of his journey with Gospel tales . . ."

Tyndale spoke slowly but firmly. "Then if Colet be gone, and Erasmus will not, you and I—if God permits—will translate the Word of God into the English vernacular."

"When?"

William sighed deeply and ruffled the stacks of papers on his desk. "I have not yet the degree from Cambridge. To study Greek is why I came here. It must not be rushed. And there is Hebrew to learn. And I would first seek permission from Bishop Tunstall."

"You are already a scholar of languages. It is I who woefully lack." Justin went back to his desk and his books. "I shall never keep up with you. If you wait for me, the translation will never get done. And I have doubts about the bishop. Will he risk his approval in a time of controversy over Luther?"

"Yet it is best we try the approved route. When we aim our bow at the target, and when God says, 'Let fly,' we will hit the bull's-eye. Now! To your books," Tyndale jested. "You are right. If I wait for you, the years will turn my hair white."

Justin brought his candle to William's and lit the charred wick. A small flame shot up, and he carried it back to his desk. He sat down, turned to his Greek, and studied until his eyes watered and his mind ached.

Long hours later when Tyndale had fallen asleep at his desk and his own candle was low, Justin's thoughts for refreshing diversion turned as always to Lady Regina.

With determination he resumed his studies. He must master Greek! The original language must burn in his heart. His love for it must set fire to his bones, consume his mind until it flows as a musical river! Only then would he dare set to interpret the Holy Scriptures into his own tongue.

Justin turned and looked across the chamber at William. A feeling of despair came over him. It was a fact—Tyndale was the scholar. Justin was and would undoubtedly remain, for many years at least, the underling. Could the translation wait so long? What was the will of God? Had he been called to work side by side with William as he so desired, or did God have some other purpose for him?

Justin shut his books and wearily blew out the candle, too tired even to tumble into bed. The next moment, it seemed, the dawn peeped through the window, and the watchman's call sounded clearly. A new day of study was already upon them.

The rigorous schedule began with a rush as all over Cambridge the scholars jumped from their beds and shivered in the icy morning as they hurried to the hall for breakfast.

The new ideas sweeping Europe in 1520 shook the very foundations of the old beliefs. It was being said, "Luther has hatched the egg that Erasmus laid." Much in Luther's theses went straight to the root of the religious tree of tradition at which biblical reformers had been aiming their hatchet for years. Traditional views based on a growing church theology of centuries of reasoning were giving way to new interest in what the Scriptures alone had to say on matters of salvation, sacraments, priestly positions, and the abuses of the hierarchy.

Martin Luther refused to recant at the Diet of Augsburg, insisting that the Scriptures were the foundation of Christian truth. In a debate he questioned papal infallibility. Had it not been for the intervention of God through Frederick, the elector of Saxony, Luther would have met his death from the Dominicans. Yet he found support among his own Augustinian order.

Luther's treatise *The Babylonian Captivity of the Church* was circulated and read in private at Cambridge, where it was received with caution. For "Lutheranism," as the movement in Saxony was now called, was frowned upon by King Henry, Cardinal Wolsey, and Sir Thomas More.

But it was Luther's biblical challenge in the pamphlet that went to the heart of the Roman system—salvation and grace dispensed through the sacraments—that moved Henry VIII to write his own thesis attacking Luther and defending the sacramental system.

"King Henry has won from the pope a new title," said Tyndale to Justin, and his expression was wry. "'Defender of the Faith.'"

"One wonders how long he would defend Rome if his own political advantage were at risk," said Justin dryly. "I have spoken to Lady Regina. Queen Catherine fears the king is looking askance at her since no male heir has been born. The king grows restless. The queen believes he may wish a divorce."

"It is unlikely Cardinal Wolsey will be able to get the pope to issue such a proclamation."

"And so we shall see how his religious ardor may soon turn sour," said Justin. "The Defender of the Faith may become the defender of his own political posterity. To those in his court who know Henry," explained Justin, thinking of the Redfords, "they believe the man is capable of breaking with papal authority and proclaiming himself head over the church in England. He will do what is to his advantage to secure his throne."

"God may yet use even King Henry," said Tyndale. "Does not the Lord have His way in the whirlwind and the storm? The wrath of man He can make to praise Him."

As the trying months of 1520 and 1521 lengthened across Europe, the brushfire begun in Wittenberg was sucked up by the winds of religious and political discontent and burned as hotly elsewhere. In Scotland John Knox, leader of the Scottish Reformation, would soon be heard from. In Zurich the Swiss Reformer Zwingli was taking a stand. Later, in

Geneva, John Calvin would stress the sovereignty of God in a development of a formal system of theology. And in England, yet unheard of except among his peers, young William Tyndale was convinced the church was in serious decline and stressed the need for the New Testament in the vernacular.

By summer the Inn of the White Horse, a meeting ground for much debate among distinguished scholars, received a number of masters from other universities, including Wittenberg. William Tyndale stood by himself and listened while the others questioned, applauded, or rejected what they heard.

"Did you expect the outcome to be otherwise? Luther's three papers from Wittenberg have struck in force. One, at the errors in the hierarchy; two, at the sacraments; and three, at the theology of the Roman church. The pope had no choice but to issue the bull of excommunication and arrest."

"Luther meant not to attack the foundation—"

"Of course he did. Are you naive?"

"An appeal for reform is not an attack on the foundation of the church, but it is like lighting fire to hay, wood, and stubble," ventured old Dr. Royce. He then blew his nose, as if to emphasize what he said.

"Be not so bold, Dr. Royce. You too will find yourself defending your speech before the cardinal," warned another.

Dr. Royce tugged at his silver hair. "I can hardly burn for defending the Scriptures and the Apostles Creed." He looked about at his colleagues with sharp gray eyes. "Unless babblers who mistake truth for heresy are anxious to run to Cardinal Wolsey."

There was a silent moment, as the assembled colleagues glanced at each other. Cambridge was now viewed as the seedbed for the Lutheran heresy. It had been threatened that Parliament was to debate the spread of Lutheran ideas at the university.

The scholars from Wittenberg shifted uneasily in their seats.

It was William Tyndale who broke the silence. "Pray go on, sir. Have you said the excommunication bull was sent to Wittenberg?"

Patently grateful for the interest shown by the serious young man, the German scholar turned his attention to William. "It has. It was sent under the seal of the Fisherman's Ring to the elector Frederick."

"Did not Frederick found the University at Wittenberg? Surely he would not proceed with Martin Luther's arrest?"

"He did not. Now *Herr Doktor* has instead been summoned by the new emperor Charles V of Spain to appear before an imperial diet at Worms. He will go with the promise of Frederick's protection."

"Has he made mention of what he intends to say?" Tyndale pressed.

"He has utterly refused to recant, and he burned the papal bull. He goes with one plea—to be shown his error by the testimony of Scripture alone. If so, he will recant. If not, he has vowed to take his stand and to appeal to God for help."

Tyndale considered for only a moment. "The man not only has courage, but he is fundamentally correct. He should be judged for error by the use of the Word of God alone."

One doctor looked at him coolly, eyeing his scholar's robe in clear rebuke. "Are you a newcomer to Cambridge?"

"I have been here since 1519. I received my Master of Arts at Oxford, Doctor."

"If Luther were less inclined to thunder in wrath," suggested the doctor, "he might spare the church the agony of being torn asunder as a lion tears helpless prey. Think so?"

Tyndale smiled. "Which do you liken to a lion—Luther or the Scriptures? Or perhaps both. I prefer to accept what the Scripture says of itself in the book of Hebrews. That it is 'sharper than any two-edged sword, piercing even to the dividing asunder of soul and spirit, and of the joints and marrow, and is a discerner of the thoughts and intents of the heart.'

"Therefore if the church system is being torn asunder as you suggest, honorable Doctor, it is the result of the Word and not of Luther."

The doctor made no further comment. "What did you say your name was?"

"William Tyndale."

The room tensed. Several distinguished men rose to their feet at the same time.

"I fear the hour grows late," said one.

The silver-haired Dr. Royce added, "If one is to get a wink of sleep before the tiresome watchman rings his miserable bell, you had best do as I. Turn in early and stuff your ears with bits of paper."

"I shall try it," said another wearily, groaning as he stood. "Lately there has been much to keep me awake. I grow too old for all of this. Blessed be dear Colet, who is removed from our midst!"

William Tyndale stepped out into the refreshing night breeze and paused below the inn's swaying sign. He was in trouble, and he knew it. He turned to walk back to his chamber and was joined by Dr. Royce.

"If I were you, Master Tyndale, I would remove my presence from Cambridge for a spell. Do you have a family anywhere about?"

"Yes, in Gloucester."

"A pleasant place in the summer, I would expect. I have not been there myself. I come from Canterbury."

"At times I forget how pleasant it was."

"Your family and friends would undoubtedly be quite glad to see you," Dr. Royce pressed easily. "And perhaps you might find a teaching position somewhere until the fires over England cool somewhat."

William Tyndale sighed.

"Your study of the languages could be done in your leisure."

"Your wisdom is respected, Dr. Royce. I shall pay serious heed to your suggestion."

Justin stirred in his bed as William fumbled to light his candle. Preferring sleep to discussion at the White Horse, Justin had remained in the room and now raised himself on his elbow as William began to pack his books.

"What are you doing?" He threw off his blanket, grabbed for his clothes, and began putting them on. "What is it, William?"

"I must leave Cambridge for Gloucester. Tonight. I have portrayed myself a supporter of Lutheran heresy."

"Openly at the White Horse?" Justin groaned. *What will Tyndale's departure from Cambridge mean to our plans?* "And why did you need to speak so loudly?"

"You're a fine one to scowl. You who said more to the authorities in Rome than I have among learned thinkers." William smiled ruefully. "You know I cannot but often speak my mind, especially when men who should know better are ignorant of the Scriptures."

"Yes, and rightly so. But we pledged to be cautious until commencement. You only had a year to go."

Tyndale sighed, then threw up his hands. "I said nothing more tonight than what many there also believe. It was only that a man whom I know not, in obvious league with the king's wishes, was there to call me on it. He wrote down my name, I am sure of it."

"Then we best leave at once."

"'We'? No. You were not involved. They will have nothing against you. Press on toward excellence, my friend. If we are to give a fair translation of a matchless work, we must needs be found disciplined in learning and worthy in our mastery of the original languages. Else we will both go down in history as English clods! They may attack me, but my scholarship is something else. I too shall press on, no matter what else I may be forced to do for the present.

"I may be reached through my brother Edward," William concluded. "He was recently appointed general receiver of lands, including Gloucestershire."

"Nevertheless I will ride with you for protection," said Justin, scanning William's slight figure.

Tyndale bore a ghost of a smile. "Will you also be Master of the Sword?"

After Tyndale's departure, Justin resumed his schedule with monotonous rigor. Only one purpose drove him on—to learn. Months passed, and summer gave way to fall chill. He stayed clear of the White Horse and was careful in choosing his friends.

It was with reluctance that he took on Tyndale's private Bible study. He wished to do nothing that might shut the door to his degree. He was planning for the long future rather than for the need of the hour. But a young scholar rebuked him.

"Your Greek is better than ours, since we are but newly arrived. If you fear to assume William's place, we might as well agree to meet no more."

Thus Justin thereafter ventured to risk the meeting. It seemed to be one risk that the Lord intended him to take.

14

Regina's decision came with cool resolve. This was no time for her to be mastered by fear.

She indeed had much to fear in King Henry's court. Intrigue flowed in the blood of the king's men. It was as much a part of their intellect as the hunts and tournaments. If she were caught trying to warn her father that his sympathies with the work of Luther had been discovered, Cardinal Wolsey would not hesitate to send her to the Tower.

Yet she must try. Otherwise Lord Simon would be arrested when he came out of Parliament this afternoon.

The Redfords' enemies at court bought and sold information that put an end to power. Dare she risk going to Lord Robert? Who in King Henry's court could she trust beside Lisbeth, her maid? With Marlon in France on business for the king, she and her father were alone.

Robert would not fail her, she decided. Hope in his declared love prompted her to risk somehow getting past the royal guards and reaching his private chamber. Little time remained to waste debating her actions.

Suddenly the door opened unexpectedly, and Bishop Constantine entered, dressed in his robes and a handsome cloak of black and scarlet, trimmed with silver fur. His magnificent black eyes, alive with passion and in contrast to his religiosity, ran over her with abrupt appreciation.

Regina met his gaze with icy rebuke. "Do you come peaceably?"

Constantine arched a brow. "With blessings, my dear, if you do as I say."

"Your blessings?" she suggested coolly. "Or Wolsey's?"

"The cardinal did not send me. I have come on my own."

"Do you dare enter my chamber without knocking?"

"You would do well to show more respect."

"Yes, there is the Tower, is there not?"

"You are too much like your mother, my lady. We would have enjoyed an exciting relationship, if only she had controlled her tongue. Alas!"

"To wear the dress of a mercenary soldier would suit you better."

"What! And lose my seat at the king's sumptuous table?"

"No doubt Wolsey agrees."

"Wolsey has his problems, I have mine. I have come as a friend. Do hear what I have to say."

Her laughter mocked the term "friend."

He chose to ignore the taunt and walked over to the gallery facing the Thames. "For your sake," he warned softly over his shoulder, "cooperate with us."

"Neither you nor the cardinal will dictate my beliefs."

"Go ahead and persist in your stubbornness, yet expect no aid from Lord Robert. He is too wise to involve himself in church conflicts. He has unexpectedly decided to take an extended journey to Versailles, there to counsel your brother Marlon on the errors of returning to London. Set no hope in the earl's ability to help you now."

Uneasiness began to erode her confidence. Robert had always backed away from conflict. But with Marlon gone from London, she had been relying heavily upon Robert's influence with the king.

Constantine now fixed her with a level gaze. "Your father has already been arrested and sent to the Tower. The accusation is twofold—heresy and treason against the king. I see no hope of pardon by either court."

Regina felt her muscles turn to water. She was too late.

"Be thankful I have sent Lord Robert to advise Marlon not to return, else your brother, as well, would be arrested."

"On what charges!"

"Support of Lutheran heresy. The king views Lutheranism as a political threat to his own security. There are peasant uprisings in Saxony due to Luther's condemnation of the church hierarchy. King Henry fears the same teachings would bring uprisings in London, and rightly so. Your father is known to have entertained and supported a number of Wittenberg scholars in his house. Men are burned for less."

"My father has done no ill to the king! He is loyal to Henry and has served him faithfully since he took the throne. How can the king accuse him of treason! The scholars merely discussed ideas."

"'Mere ideas,' as you call them, breed revolt. Lord Simon was foolish to risk so much for so little. There is scant hope for him now. And if you would save yourself, my lady, do cooperate with me now before Wolsey moves against you. At the moment he is content with having arrested Lord Simon. He wishes no grotesque display of burnings. But I cannot say as much for some other bishops in England."

Regina turned away, sickened. A thousand thoughts swirled through her mind. *How can I save my father? If I cannot, what of Marlon? Can Lord Robert reach him in time to warn him? Will Marlon be wise enough to stay away from London, or will love and honor force his return in order to appeal for the life of our father?*

"There is still hope for you," Constantine suggested tonelessly.

Regina refused to turn. Her palms were cold. *What does he have in mind?*

"I have knowledge of the heretical works here in your chamber. Your maid became terrified when I questioned her, and she told all."

Regina refused to speak.

"I could call guards now and, before witnesses, produce the works of Luther. And—if that is not enough—the works of Colet and Erasmus, which you have foolishly been translating into English. Such works will call for your trial before the church court. Must I say more of your fate?"

Still she said not a word nor turned her face to him.

Constantine crossed to the hearth, where a log burned on a deep bed of red coals. "Think well, my lady. We are alone. Hand them over to me, and I will burn them."

Regina's heart slammed in her breast, and a trickle of perspiration ran down her ribs. *Dear Lord—*

"If you will not, I shall bring them to Cardinal Wolsey. How much better to burn books than heretics."

"And my father?" she asked quietly.

"I am afraid there is little I can do to thwart his destiny. It is in his own power to recant. If he is wise, he will. Both Wolsey and Henry would prefer to spare his life. But like you, he is stubborn."

"What you mistake for stubbornness is conviction."

"I, for one, prefer not to offer my head to Henry on a charger."

Regina shuddered inwardly. Her thoughts darted to Justin and took a measure of comfort in thinking of his stand before the abbot in Rome. And what of Martin Luther, who at the Diet of Worms refused to recant.?

Luther's books had been burned in great bonfires at Rome, Louvain, Liege, and Cologne. Some hostile demonstrations followed the burnings, and in Wittenberg students had torn the papal bulls from the church doors and splashed them with mud.

Luther had met his enthusiastic, supporting students and faculty at the gates of Wittenberg University, where the young scholars kindled their own bonfire. Luther, who was patient in his own defense before the diets, was angry at the destruction of his life's work. He flung the papal bull into the flames and tossed in a volume of canon law with it. Then the students paraded the street with the edict of Pope Leo on a pole. One student carried a sword with an indulgence spiked to its tip.

Regina knew all that.

"Cooperate, Regina. Become my mistress, and you will be escorted safely to my villa. Your secret will die with the ashes in the hearth."

"Never."

His eyes grew remote. "Think again of your fate, my lady. Are your heretical convictions worth the awful price you will certainly pay?" He walked across her chamber then, staring curiously at the floor.

Regina's heart quickened. Beneath a plank lay the small vault where she had hidden her writings and the three pamphlets by Luther. The first, *An Address to the Christian Nobility of the German Nation,* stated that princes should reform the church when necessary, that the pope should not interfere in civil affairs, and that all believers were spiritual priests of God and able to interpret Scripture. The second paper, *The Liberty of a Christian Man*, asserted that the priesthood of all believers was a result of their personal faith in Christ. The third was *The Babylonian Captivity of the Church.*

Constantine tapped the floor with his toe. "Shall I call for witnesses, my lady? Know that such evidence will be your end."

Regina stood rigid, her eyes fixed downward.

"Call for your witnesses, Constantine. I shall not, in order to spare my life, compromise both spirit and body to your demands."

For a moment he said nothing, and she turned her back on him, hoping her fear was not obvious.

"You are a fool," he stated vehemently. He flung open the door. "Guards, search this heretic's chamber." He pointed a finger at the offending plank. "There—you shall find a rat's nest."

Regina watched as the two Dominicans produced the forbidden writings and her own English translation of the works of Colet and Erasmus. Her stomach turned queasy, but she would not fall before them in abject fear. Her mind was suddenly emblazoned with words from Scripture memorized from Erasmus's Greek New Testament.

Who shall separate us from the love of Christ? Shall tribulation, or distress, or persecution, or famine, or nakedness, or sword? . . . Nay, in all these things we are more than conquerors through him that loved us. . . . I am persuaded that neither death nor life, nor angels, nor principalities, nor powers, nor things present, nor things to come, nor height, nor depth, nor any other creature shall be able to separate us from the love of God, which is in Christ Jesus, our Lord.*

"Bring the books to Cardinal Wolsey," Constantine ordered the Dominicans. "Tell him I shall meet with him this afternoon."

Darkness enveloped Regina like a thick blanket but gave no warmth. She huddled on the stone floor, unable to control her shivering.

*Romans 8:35–39.

Abruptly the door to the dungeon opened, and Constantine stood in the yellow torchlight, guards behind him.

She shielded her eyes from the pain of the light. How many days had elapsed? She struggled to stand, for her legs were weak. "My father?" she whispered.

Constantine sighed. "I regret to say he would not recant."

The expected blow did little to ward off her grief. She slipped back to the floor and wept.

"I am not altogether heartless, my lady. I visited your father before the execution. He was not burned but went to the block. His last words were of hope and in praise of the coming 'awakening' across England. Out of mercy I granted him a last request. It was that you would be taken from the dungeon. I have arranged your incarceration elsewhere."

She lifted her head. "What of my brother?"

"He is safe in France with Lord Robert. Bring her to my house on the Strand," he said coldly to the guards.

He turned and left, and the sound of his steps on the stone pavement echoed the empty thump of her heart.

She continued to sit there, numb and cold, until a guard took her arm.

"Do not struggle, my lady," he said as she tried to jerk away. "We do not wish to hurt you."

"Help me get a message to one named Justin Brice at Cambridge."

"To help you would mean involving ourselves in heresy. It could bring about our own execution."

As Regina was escorted across the courtyard, her eyes fell upon Lisbeth.

The maid was watching from a distance, and her hand came up against her mouth.

Regina's hope was small. What could Lisbeth do? Yet she took her chances and cried, "Cambridge! Cambridge!"

Cambridge? Lisbeth seemed to struggle to grasp the message. Then she looked up quickly to show her mistress she understood. Cambridge!

The guards led Regina to a coach. She had just enough time to glance back at Lisbeth over her shoulder.

Lisbeth was waving her white handkerchief as the coach bore her mistress out of sight.

The horses clipped smartly over the cobbled way and down the street past Westminster toward the Tower, standing against the gray and misty morning.

Simon Redford had gone the way of others before him. And who knew how many more would follow? Regina's heart swelled with pain, and she wanted to cry out.

But as she twisted to see the Tower disappear behind her, a surge of peace and comfort that passed understanding bolstered her soul. She was not alone, however black the night, however hard and painful the future. She was not abandoned to the horrors of suffering and persecution.

One stood beside her, one whose Spirit was within, breathing the promise of strength and peace. The realization brought a rush of joy that was unnatural to her predicament. She had no doubt it was His joy and His peace. She took courage.

Lisbeth huddled with the young groom behind the stables at Windsor. Her cheeks were flushed, and her voice shook, but her hand clutched his arm firmly. "Would you see my poor lady burn?"

"But must I see him in this here Cambridge! I've not traveled outside London!"

"You owe her ladyship this much. Who bailed your mother out of debt last year? Tell me, Hicks!"

Hicks, hardly seventeen, wiped his brow with the back of his soiled sleeve. "And a good lady she is, I'll say that. 'Twas a crime, I say, for old Wolsey to take Lord Simon's head."

Lisbeth shuddered, ashamed at her own cowardice before Constantine and her betrayal of Lady Redford. Her nails dug into the lad's arm until he winced. "*Will* you go, Hicks? Will you bring the message to Justin Brice?"

"Yes, Lisbeth," he murmured quietly and, with more determination, "I will see it through. Have you got the letter all written?"

She pressed it into his hand. "M'lady taught me well. 'Tis all written. Here, take this bag of coins. But do not tarry along the way. Her ladyship's future depends on our faithfulness."

"I will not fail you, Lisbeth, nor her ladyship, but if I'm missed here at the stable—"

"I will see to that. Be on your way, Hicks."

He hesitated, and his eyes dropped as a little smile tugged at his mouth.

She tiptoed, gave him a brief kiss, then a push. "Off with you, Hicks."

He turned and disappeared between the horse stalls, and Lisbeth mustered courage to face the new master of the stables. The man who had taken Balin York's position was hard to please. What would she tell him about Hicks's absence?

15

The frost of mid-December struck Cambridge, and as Justin walked to the dining hall his breath was white on the air.

At the high tables the masters ate alone, while the scholars sat below envying their superiors' fatter meals and warmer robes. A fire burned in the huge hearth, but from where Justin sat it could not be felt.

He was surprised when a fellow scholar came up behind him and whispered, "There's a lad here to see you. He says it's urgent."

A youth stood awkwardly in the hall, seemingly unsure of where to put his feet.

Justin had never seen the boy before, and he scanned the lad's rough clothing. "You have a message?"

"My name is Hicks, Master Brice. I work in King Henry's stables at Windsor."

Justin smiled. "I know the stable well. The message?"

Hicks fumbled in his tunic as his eyes roved around, taking in the halls of learning. At length he produced a letter, and Justin found himself reading Lisbeth's shaky writing:

> Lord Simon Redford has been sent to the Tower and died in the service to our God and Savior Jesus Christ on Monday day five. Her ladyship Regina is being held by Bishop Constantine until she is charged with heresy by Cardinal Wolsey's court. His lordship Marlon is in France and has been warned to stay out of London by Lord Robert, son of the earl of Roxbury. I am sending this message at her ladyship's request by your servant Hicks.
>
> Your servant Lisbeth,
maid in waiting to Lady Regina Redford

Outside the cold wind penetrated Justin's robe.

Hicks was fast on his heels. "Will you return to London then?"

"At once. Wait for me in the street. I must get my things from my room."

The hall was silent, and Justin's steps echoed as he ran up the staircase, past the other cloisters, to the chamber he had shared with William Tyndale. The frigid room greeted him with silent memories, but there was no time to dwell on them.

He grabbed his leather satchel and threw in his books, his writings, his last small bag of coins. He started to run out the door, but it was as if the hand of Tyndale himself reached out to stop him. If he left, would he ever return? How could he? And what of his study of the languages?

Justin glanced about the chamber. Tyndale's worn wooden desk, used by many before him, sat empty. The charred candle was completely burned. He imagined William sitting there now, his face intense as he struggled over some hard passage, and his quill scratching. He saw the other scholars gathered about for their private study of the Greek testament. He heard again Tyndale's exhortation to master the languages. In a moment he saw all that he had worked for slipping through his fingers.

Then Regina's image came before him, burning as pure and bright as any flame.

He must go.

Hicks left Justin in London and returned unobtrusively to the stables, where the master eyed him above his thin nose but said nothing.

Lisbeth had taken the liberty of giving the stable master a pearl necklace belonging to Regina, and he was content to ask no further questions. But why a lad should be gone for so long and then return looking none the richer or wiser for it, he couldn't guess. He shrugged his heavy shoulders and turned his keen interest back to the royal horses.

Alone on the streets of London, Justin spent several of his coins on adequate clothing, in order to be rid of his scholar's gown and dress as a common mercenary. Swords and daggers were for sale as well, fine weapons made of the best steel, and he found himself hesitating before the booth. He chose a blade from among those displayed, and Tyndale's wry words came back. *Are you also a Master of the Sword?*

At once the merchant behind the counter began his discourse on the qualities of the Toledo blade. "Look at it, m'lord! See how it balances in your hand? There's hardly a man who will stand before it, I tell you! It's worth its weight in the king's gold."

He pressed on. Justin was hardly listening. Everything he had ever learned in the art of warfare was embedded deep within his memory. "How much?"

The merchant named his price.

Justin nearly emptied his purse of its last coin, strapped on the scabbard, and left. He felt like a stranger walking in his own boots. His conscience tugged him in two directions.

The waters of the Thames were quiet tonight and misted over with the thickening wet air. The small boat Lisbeth had prearranged rocked gently as it moved silently through the dark waters. London Bridge lay ahead. Tiny lights gleamed among the ramshackle buildings.

The rhythm of his oars was smooth as the waters gleamed past. Between the arches Justin glimpsed the splendid houses and palaces of the Strand. Here King Henry would provide a house for Anne Boleyn as he plotted with Wolsey to divorce Catherine, and here a bishop or an abbot, a lord or lady, lived in comfort and finery.

Justin tied the boat and left it rocking in the wash of the private barge belonging to the bishop. He walked quietly through the hedges and the winter gardens.

Ahead, the gray stone wall of Constantine's villa stood above him, barely visible in the darkness. The night silence was interrupted by the faint stir of the wind rustling dry leaves, followed by the rush of running feet. Justin moved behind a bush.

Then Lisbeth appeared, breathing heavily from her run, followed by Hicks.

Justin stepped out onto the path.

"No one followed us, m'lord," she whispered. "We paused at intervals along the way to make sure."

"Wait for us at the boat, but stay hidden."

Hicks was perspiring, his face intense. "Once over the wall you can reach her chamber through the garden, but you must hurry. A change of guards comes soon."

"The present guard?"

Hicks grinned. "I clobbered the bloke. He won't stir till daylight."

"How many more?"

"None in the garden nor in m'lady's chamber. They stand in the passage."

Justin neared the high wall surrounding the garden of the bishop's villa. He listened. The garden was silent. He leaped, grabbed onto the outer wall, pulled himself up.

For a moment he lay flat on top. He peered below into the darkened trees and shrubs, seeing and hearing nothing. Above, in one of the chambers, a light shone golden. He dropped quietly into the garden and approached the side of the house.

Here an inner wall covered with a rambling vine ran the entire length of the villa. Justin hefted himself to the top. He was about to drop to the inner court when he froze.

Directly below him a guard looked up, startled. Apparently seeing the glimmer of steel in Justin's hand, he made no move. He found his voice though. "Who are you, and what are you doing here?"

Justin considered his crouched position on the wall. He whispered, "I am a guest of Bishop Constantine."

The guard's attention was momentarily arrested by the inconceivable suggestion. Then he said indignantly, "If so, why do you come like a thief over the wall?"

"I thought Bishop Constantine might be used to visitors taking the back door."

The guard muttered and reached for his sword. Justin leaped and took him down. At once he was on his feet, and as the stunned guard staggered to rise, Justin struck hard to the back of his neck, and the man slumped to the stones. He dragged him into the trees, then turned back to the dilemma at hand.

Only the urgency of his position prompted Justin to consider undertaking the precarious climb up the side of the villa. Was it possible? He carefully noted the stone outcroppings he could use for footholds. If he maneuvered himself properly, he could just enter the gallery. But if he did reach her chamber, how could he descend with her?

Regina heard the soft rustling of the vine below the gallery and heard the scraping on stone. Someone climbing? Whoever risked such a climb was no friend to Constantine, she reasoned.

Now someone was on the gallery and moving cautiously toward the entrance. In another moment Justin crouched in the shadows, sword in hand, scanning the chamber.

Regina was about to cry out with relief but caught herself. For a moment she stared at him, then rushed into his arms. They clung together as if they stood alone on a crumbling foundation.

"I was wrong to send for you," she whispered. "I was selfish to involve you like this."

"I would have grieved had you not. You should know by now how much I care, Regina."

"My own feelings have been obvious, have they not? I have never loved Robert. I have done everything to delay marriage. There stands nothing between us now. My position is gone, my father, even Marlon—"

"Think not of that now. It is enough that I have found you safe. We must move quickly."

He crossed the room and extinguished the light. He was at the gallery peering below into the garden by the time she slipped into her cloak and came up beside him.

"Do you see anyone?"

"It is quiet. The guard is indisposed for a time." He turned to her. "What have you that could be used as a rope?"

She crossed the room and pulled the braided cord from the scarlet drapes. "I was going to try it many times, but there was always a guard."

"The climb down will be difficult—and long."

She shuddered. "There is no choice. A number of guards are in the house and two in the passage."

Justin supported Regina with one arm and grasped the drapery cord with the other, and they started slowly down. A gust of wind caught them as they clung to the face of the wall. Then Justin's toe found the crevice, and after descending a few feet, they reached an inches-wide ledge and paused to rest.

"Ready?" he whispered.

She made no sound but let her feet go over the small ledge, and they continued the descent.

His feet groped for the vine-covered wall and found it. Then he was swinging her down, and hand in hand they fled to the outer wall. He pulled himself to the top, then reached for her wrists, and she struggled up.

Regina's dress was torn, she had lost a shoe, there were cuts and bruises, but they were over the wall!

The boat was where he had left it, and Regina embraced Lisbeth. "I knew I could count on you, Lisbeth! Will you come with us to Antwerp?" she whispered.

"Nay, m'lady. I . . . I shall stay in London and marry Hicks," she stammered with a little smile.

Regina squeezed her. "I am happy for you, Lisbeth. Godspeed!"

"Thank you, m'lady, and good-bye. May God's peace keep you both from harm." Lisbeth kissed her cheek, wiping away her own tears, and they smiled at each other.

Justin and Regina left Lisbeth and Hicks watching as the boat carried them into the low-hanging fog over the Thames.

They were free!

16

To William Tyndale, the worn trail he rode on horseback was familiar. He was home, where he had been raised, in the Vale of Berkeley in Gloucestershire. In his saddlebags were his precious books and his meager personal possessions.

He was on his way to Little Sodbury and the manor of Sir John and Lady Anne Walsh to take up his new position as chaplain to the family and tutor of their small children. The position was not exactly what he had in mind, but it seemed to be the leading of God, and William found himself content for the time being.

It was early summer, and the trees were in bloom, filling the morning air with the sweetness of apple blossoms. The Cotswold hills smiled down on the green grass as Tyndale dismounted and stood before the honey-colored stone manor.

Sir John and Lady Anne were there to meet him and usher him with grace into the great hall of Little Sodbury Manor. Before a large fireplace, now empty, Sir John extended a chair. The summer light filtered down through the high windows onto the long, wooden table.

"And these boys, Master Tyndale, will be your two pupils," said Sir John.

Lady Walsh smiled as she produced two youngsters from behind her skirt. Their eyes, big and round and somewhat frightened by this tall and angular Master Tyndale, stared up at him.

Tyndale smiled at them. "I am sure the three of us will become very good friends. We will begin our learning this afternoon with a pleasant walk through the apple orchard. There is much to see that God has made," he told the two boys. "And new ways to pronounce their names. We shall afterward play a game and see if we can match the English word with the Latin. And if we do well—" he hesitated with a look toward the smiling Lady Walsh, who raised her brows "—I am sure your mother will have something pleasant to eat."

She exchanged smiles with her husband and said, as the boys showed sudden enthusiasm for the hike, "I am sure the cook shall have something worth your hearty appetites. But Maurice," she said to the oldest, "you must be sure to do everything Master Tyndale tells you."

Tyndale was well received at Little Sodbury and soon found himself settling down to a quiet and comfortable life. His sermons at the little Chapel of Saint Adeline on the manor grounds were given in English, however, and a few voices were raised in mild protest and brows arched. But Lady Anne approved of his teaching and silenced the objections.

"Why did you leave Cambridge?" she inquired one day after a well-delivered sermon. They were walking back alone since Sir John was speaking with the locals on the green.

"Several reasons, Lady Walsh. In the universities they have ordained that no man shall look on the Scripture until he is saturated with eight or nine years of heathen learning."

"A sorry situation, indeed, Master Tyndale."

"So, armed with false principles, the scholar is shut out of the understanding of the Scripture."

"Yet you must be cautious with your criticism, Master Tyndale. The clergy here in the vale are not as learned or liberal in their conclusions as you. They oft come to dinner on Sundays, and you must be careful for your own protection."

"I shall take your warning to heart, Lady Walsh."

When guests were present at the Walsh table, William had expected to dine alone with the children or even in his room. But neither Sir John nor Lady Walsh would hear of it.

The Walsh home was known for its hospitality to traveling merchants and to the clergy of other parishes. William would sit silently at the table, listening to the comfortable but boring conversations. Country squires and merchants from Bristol discussed taxes, the cheap prices of their goods on the English market, and complaints against the economy. Tyndale's mind stirred restlessly.

After theological debates with doctors and masters and assimilation of the news of Luther's fiery stand in Wittenberg, the price of barley, wheat, and oats strayed unattached through his brain. As the meals ended and the guests lingered over beakers of wine, Tyndale watched the seasons come and go through the window. The leaves greened, then became burnt gold and brown, and the bare limbs of winter moved in the cold wind.

The delight of the Walsh children pleased him. They were especially captivated with the little box he had created, having a peephole in one end and a wheel that, when turned, showed the letters of the alphabet.

On long walks through Little Sodbury, Tyndale watched the common farmers plowing in contented peace, working hard from sunup to sunset, then returning to their humble cottages to gather about the hearths. He watched an older boy plowing his father's field, and as he did the words of Erasmus sang in his mind: *I would to God that the plowman would sing a text of the Scripture at his plow and that the weaver would hum them to the tune of his shuttle.*

"That, dear and wise Erasmus, shall not be . . . no, for these common folk shall die and their children and grandchildren with them before ever a word of Latin or Greek is learned of them so thoroughly."

Life at the Walsh manor, however pleasant and however much he enjoyed the children, began to disturb him. He found he had ample time for leisure, so to satisfy his spiritual desire he began to preach in the surrounding villages and traveled to Bristol to speak to the crowds assembling on College Green.

But the minds of the Gloucestershire clergy were not inclined toward the thinking of Colet and Erasmus, and soon he found himself in arduous theological discussions. The clergymen were startled by his opinions and offended that Sir John Walsh sought to protect him from their criticism. In the absence of the bishop, they hotly accused him to the chancellor of the Holy See.

So it was that William found himself standing before the angry Chancellor Malvern.

"I have preached nothing but the Scriptures," Tyndale defended himself. "Do my accusers find this heretical in belief?"

"Silence! You are accused of daring to portray yourself superior in learning and divinity over the learned divines in Gloucester. You ridicule them before the common man and seek to show yourself the master."

Shocked, Tyndale stared at him. "But my lord Chancellor—"

"Silence! If you wish to remain in this diocese, William Tyndale, you must govern your tongue and your haughty spirit with humility before your fellow clergyman. If not," he warned, "and I hear complaint again of your actions, you shall swiftly and without remedy be dismissed from Gloucester as an arrogant young rebel not to be tolerated here."

Chancellor Malvern stood to show the proceeding was over and that he wanted no further words from the accused.

William had turned to leave, angry over the injustice, when the chancellor added somewhat kindly, "Yet I am satisfied with your orthodoxy. You may depart neither branded as a heretic nor trammeled by any oath of abjuration."

William walked back to Little Sodbury in a disheartened mood. The sun was setting, and it would be dark before he reached the manor. If his teaching of the Scriptures brought such intolerance from the Gloucester clergy and false charges of ridiculing his fellows, what must the state of the church be!

He was strengthened in his conviction that the translation of the Word into the vernacular was the only hope for the common man. How else would they ever learn the truth of God? Certainly not from priests who rushed through the mass, mumbled their prayers, and hastened to a warm fire to eat their meal and drink their vintage wine!

The church was too comfortable. The ecclesiastics did not wish to be disturbed from their slumber or to risk taking a stand for the truth. It was far easier to remain in their traditions and reject the call of sacrifice.

One afternoon he found the old dream smoldering in his heart until the heat burst into a new flame. He returned from a walk in the country to find Sir John Walsh entertaining a group of clerics in the dining hall.

He recognized some as the men who had privately accused him to Chancellor Malvern. At the dinner table one churchman in particular seemed determined to trap him into a confession that would mean his end in Gloucester.

"Surely, Master Tyndale, as a teacher of the Walsh babes, you would not teach theology where simple learning will suffice. The uneducated masses need milk, not meat, else they would choke like newborn infants."

Tyndale guessed where he was headed but refused to back down.

Like wolves waiting for a goat to weaken with illness, they watched his every word, clearly hoping to accuse him again before the chancellor. But Tyndale's anger over their hardness of heart solidified his position. What good was the truth if he could not speak it for fear of rebuke or incrimination? Was the Word of Christ to be so guarded from utterance by human tongue that one did not breathe it for fear of angering clerics?

"Was it not Saint Peter himself who wrote, 'Desire the sincere milk of the Word that ye may grow thereby'? If that be so, the Word itself should be given to the babes to grow into strong and healthy men."

The cleric grew tense as he saw his bait being taken.

Tyndale saw it too, but his mind was made up. He would not turn back. He pretended not to notice the warning glances from Sir John Walsh or to hear Lady Anne interrupting to ask the servant to bring in the dessert.

The churchman also pretended not to hear, and he pressed, leaning forward in his chair. "The unlettered multitude need protection from wolves in sheep's clothing, think you not? The body of truth long since gathered as the theology of the church under Rome is best fitted for those who need discipline and guidance by the superiors. Do you not think so?"

Tyndale stood calmly. "I think the wolves devour the sheep and prefer the Scriptures to remain in Latin that their own ignorance of the Word of God remain undetected by the flock. For if the flock could compare the truth of the New Testament church with the tradition built in Rome over these long centuries, they would too easily discover that we flounder in error and would demand change."

The churchman leaned back in his chair satisfied, and a thin smile crossed his lips as he exchanged glances with the man beside him.

That man gasped. "Do you say we should not follow the laws of church theology?"

"I say we should follow the laws of God contained in the Scriptures and judge all else accordingly."

"Even the words which issued forth from Rome?"

"Whatever decree keeps the flock of Christ in ignorance of His words must be defied by the authority of God Himself!"

"You have heard him with your own ears," the cleric stated to all at the table. "The witnesses are many!"

The Walshes sat stunned. Sir John's head lowered to his plate in dismay.

"Then hear this, sir," said Tyndale, his steady gaze compelling those at the table to fix upon him with breath bated. "If God spare my life, ere many years pass, I will cause a boy that drives the plow to know more of Scripture than you."

William looked from one shocked face to the other, pausing at the churchman who had deliberately set out to entrap him. "Know, sir, that my confession is uttered not in emotional haste, but wittingly. Good day." He rose and turned with a light bow to Sir John, who sat gravely looking on, and to Lady Anne, who bit her lower lip. "I beg forgiveness if I have embarrassed or caused you moments of distress."

He turned and walked from the great hall. There was no turning back now. He would have to leave Little Sodbury Manor. His mind was made up. He would return to London and seek ecclesiastical approval for his projected translation. There was only one man he could even think of going to who might agree to work with him.

Tyndale felt great relief as he packed his meager belongings into one simple bag. The decision was made, and it seemed a great load had been removed from his soul. Whatever the cost, he would go through with it. The call, the desire, the assurance that he was in the will of his Lord burned like fire in his bones. If he kept silent, the fire would consume him.

He would seek audience with the bishop of London, Cuthbert Tunstall. Tunstall was a fine scholar, he told himself, and a friend of Erasmus. Surely the bishop would grant permission to translate the New Testament into the vernacular.

But how would he get into Westminster to the bishop's office to see him? He glanced down wryly at his worn rustic robe. He would look a beggar among princes.

It appeared his prayer was answered and the door opened wide by the hand of God when Sir John Walsh, learning of his planned journey to London, offered a letter of introduction to Tunstall.

"Sir Henry Guildford, comptroller of King Henry's household, is a friend of mine." he said. "I shall ask him to send word to the bishop of your desire to visit him at Westminster. I am sure he will do so."

"Then surely the matter with the bishop will go smoothly," said William.

But Lady Anne looked troubled. "Be not so sure, William. It may be that Bishop Tunstall is more anxious to stop the spread of Lutheranism than he is to risk his position by beginning an English version of the Scriptures. Perhaps," she said quietly, "this is not the time for such an endeavor."

"When, my lady, will the time ever strike with ease? He who observeth the wind shall not sow; and he that regardeth the clouds shall not reap, as it is written in Ecclesiastes."

She sighed. "I hate to lose you, William. The children love you so."

"For other children I will sow against the wind, my lady. And who knows? One day Maurice may have his own Bible to read and obey."

"Do be cautious," warned Sir John. "London is a powder keg. The king will come down hard upon any conceived heretic who is deemed to peddle the wares of Luther."

"Permit me also to sooth my own motherly concern," said Lady Walsh. "I have a relative in London, a merchant by the name of Thomas Poynitz. His business often brings him to Antwerp. Perhaps he may prove of some assistance to you."

"And do go by sea to London," urged Sir John in a fatherly tone. "It will be safer than traveling by land where you may run into robbers. You can catch a ship from Bristol."

Tyndale smiled. "With your advice I am sure to fare well."

A short week later he found himself aboard a vessel making its way around the coast of England from the Channel of Bristol to the Thames River estuary in London.

It was a September morning when William Tyndale climbed the steps of Westminster. The narrow street was crowded with barking vendors. He passed them by, lost in the rehearsed speech that he hoped to give to the bishop.

He found the prelate's palace as it had been described by Sir John and took the side entrance. There he was admitted by the guards into an antechamber, where others also waited for a precious and hard-earned audience with the bishop.

It was afternoon before Tyndale was ushered into Tunstall's chamber. The man who sat with grave dignity behind a massive desk was a courtly gentleman who eyed William with immediate caution. At present the bishop wanted to avoid the slightest hint of reform.

Tunstall shook his head. "Master Tyndale, you ask me for the impossible. The project must be put aside with due haste."

Tyndale felt his stomach lurch.

"Such a worthy endeavor under your jurisdiction, My Lord Bishop, would surely find acceptance."

Tunstall stood. Was this young unknown foolish enough to think he would even consider offering him his patronage at such a time as this?

"In the name of reform, havoc spreads in Europe. There are violent riots among the peasants, the overthrow of local authorities, and attacks on clergymen. And is it not Luther's common-language New Testament in German that is behind the movement of the common man? I am cautious of anything that hints of Lutheranism. Do you think I am foolish enough to risk the incriminating charges that would be hurled against me to King Henry and the cardinal? An English version in the vernacular would light the fagots, Master Tyndale. I have far greater plans than to die a martyr's death at Smithfield."

Tunstall sat down again more calmly. He ruffled through a sheaf of papers. "I have no more to say. Except to warn you to forget this vision of yours. You will find no support in England. Not now. Good day, Master Tyndale." He then pretended to lose himself in some important papers.

Tyndale stood in rebuked silence. It was hopeless to debate. Tunstall, regardless of his own appreciation for scholarship and his support of many of Erasmus's reform-oriented beliefs, bowed to the pressure of politics and state religion. He was unwilling to stand with those in support of an English New Testament.

Tyndale was aware that politics had won. Without another word, he turned and walked to the door.

Bishop Tunstall glanced up over his paper, his eyes scanning the stranger in the worn scholar's robe with patched elbows. The door shut behind William Tyndale, leaving Tunstall alone in his lofty chamber. The great red ruby on his finger caught the candlelight and glimmered red. Tunstall stared at the ring.

Rebuffed, the door to fulfilling his goal firmly shut, Tyndale returned to his lodging. There was little else to do for the present but survive. The way before him seemed dark and the path blocked by insurmountable obstacles. Were these obstacles meant to be taken as from God? Or had the voice of church authority been like the authority of the religious establishment in Jerusalem when they forbade the apostles from preaching anymore about Jesus?

One thing was certain. There was no place in all England where he might translate the Scriptures and have them printed. With his purse nearly empty he did what was most practical—he sought temporary employment rather than return to his family in Gloucester.

That Sunday Tyndale preached at Saint Dunstan's-in-the-West on the parable of the prodigal son. The congregation listened attentively, for he had first read the message, then translated into English. When the service was over and he removed himself into the side chapel to dress in his old tunic, a man was still waiting for him when all others had gone home to dinner.

He was a big man, and rugged, yet had an air of nobility in his manner. "The name is Humphrey Monmouth," he told William. "I listened attentively to your discourse this morning. I confess that your manner of preaching, though different from what I have been accustomed to, is of interest to me. Are you new here at Saint Dunstan's?"

Tyndale did not want to appear rude but felt he must move cautiously. "Are you too a clergyman, Master Monmouth?"

The man laughed. "No, I am a London cloth merchant. My business takes me hither and yon. Will you be preaching here from now on?"

"I shall seek to preach wherever I can throughout London until I have decided on the way God will lead me."

Tyndale briefly explained his meeting with Bishop Tunstall and why he had come to London. Seeing William's situation and that he was obviously hungry and without friends, Humphrey Monmouth insisted he return with him to his home.

"No, do not argue. I insist. My home is in the parish of All Hallows in Barking. Until you know how God shall lead you, my home is yours. No, do not protest. I shall expect some remuneration from you. Let us say I have hired you to pray for the souls of my father and mother and all Christian souls?"

Tyndale opened his mouth again to thank him, but Monmouth waved him to silence. "You will fare better among us merchants. One thing is for certain, you shall eat better. Come, let no more be said."

17

Andrew and the giant Nubian faced Justin on board the Brice ship. "Will you not change your mind and captain your own ship?" Andrew pressed.

Justin had turned his galleon over to Andrew to make the voyage to Cadiz. He was to take on cargo that would be sold in the London markets.

Justin smiled. "No. I must remain here in Antwerp."

His mind was on William Tyndale. He had learned that William was no longer at Little Sodbury serving Sir John and Lady Walsh, but he did not know Tyndale had gone on to London. *Has he fallen into difficulty with the authorities?* Justin wondered. The weeks passed, and his concern increased. He must locate him.

"I have other work to do. I must find William Tyndale and see how it goes with him. The English version of the Scriptures must not be abandoned, even if I will not be his partner in translation."

"Careful, lad. Aiding Master Tyndale will place you in more danger than being a slave to Baron Soleiman."

Justin was grave as he thought of Regina. As her husband, he had a serious obligation to see to her safety. And even more so now.

"Right well I know that, and Regina does too."

He walked the short distance from the harbor to the English House, which was the headquarters for the English merchant-adventurers in Antwerp. The solid building stood within easy access of the harbor and warehouses on the corner between the Rue de la Vieille Bourse and the Rue Zrek.

As Justin approached, he saw his brother-in-law waiting on the cobbled street. Having arrived from France for Justin's marriage to Regina the year before, Marlon had since taken up residence in Antwerp to help in their effort to aid

William Tyndale. They had been looking unsuccessfully for William for months.

Marlon seemingly had important news to report. "I received word today that William is in London."

"But why has he left Sir John Walsh?"

"It seems he came to a disagreement with the church in Gloucestershire."

"So I feared. He is not under arrest?"

"No, but he did dispute seriously with certain clerics over the translation of the Scriptures into English and had to leave."

Justin was pleased that Tyndale's convictions remained as fervent as his own. He must reach him in London, but for Marlon to travel with him was unwise. Marlon could be arrested as a supporter of Martin Luther.

"That is not all," Marlon hastened to say. "He went to see Bishop Tunstall about receiving authorization to translate."

Justin expected the worst. "And what did the bishop say?"

"He failed to get the bishop's support. Tunstall believes the time is not wise to begin such an endeavor."

"Nor will it ever be if left to the religious and political blessing of England. We cannot wait. Where in London is he?"

"He serves in the home of Humphrey Monmouth in Barking."

Justin turned to him in surprise.

"Do you know Humphrey Monmouth?"

"If he is the same man, my father has spoken of him. Is he a merchant, do you know?"

"He is. His house is in the parish of All Hallows."

They hurried on.

"Returning to London is dangerous, Justin, if that is what you have in mind."

"More so for you and Regina. I must know what William intends to do and whether he will risk a translation without the bishop's permission."

"If you will venture to England, then so shall I. If I dress as a merchant, I will not be recognized."

181

"The risk is too great, Marlon. If I go at all, it is better that I go alone."

But Marlon's dark eyes were determined. "If you will risk going to London, then I will join you. Our commitment to an English translation will bind us together. But why did you say 'if' you shall go? Is it because of Regina?"

"She is with child."

They entered the English House as dinner was being served. He smiled at Regina and wished to bend down and kiss her, but instead his eyes spoke his love, and he took his seat beside her.

She leaned toward him and whispered, "Did Marlon tell you of William?"

"He did. We must meet after supper to make our plans."

Captain Brice was talking to Thomas Poynitz, the man related to Lady Anne Walsh. It was from Poynitz that Justin had first learned of Tyndale's service at Sodbury.

Stewert sat beside their father. Now that Captain Ewan had taken interest in the work of Luther and was more interested in theological battles than in going to sea, the family rift had eased somewhat.

But it still had taken some getting used to for Stewert to accept Justin as a partner in the shipping business. Knowing this, their father wisely put an end to the reason for Stewert's suspicion. He divided all his worldly possessions between his two sons, making sure they inherited equally from his ships down to the last gold coin.

The prosperous merchants, some sporting richly ornate dress and expensive rings, ate heartily and discussed the work of Martin Luther. For the moment Justin's attention was diverted from Tyndale.

"Luther himself is no man of violence," declared one. "I have met him, and he deplores the use of anarchy, as some have propagated in Saxony."

"'Tis no surprise to be plagued with troubles," said Captain Brice. "In every movement there are fringe groups. Extremists who would turn the movement of God far right or far left."

Then they spoke of the peasant revolt.

"I spoke with the peasant farmers. They are quite upset that Luther did not support their revolt."

"What do you expect?" said another merchant. "The peasants heard him denounce the authority of the church and assert the authority of the Scriptures and the right of individuals to come directly to God through Christ. They then applied these arguments to social and economic problems."

"And it seems to me they had a right to do so," argued a third. "Feudal abuses can be demonstrated as being in error by Scripture, can they not? Why should they not have expected his support? Instead he but urged them to patience."

"He feared a greater danger than the abuse of the peasants' economic conditions," said one gravely, "and in my opinion rightly so. An uprising by the peasants might endanger the movement. Does not Scripture say to obey magistrates? And so he feared an uprising might endanger the orderly government in the Protestant provinces and do more damage in the end."

"So he urged the authorities to put the poor folk down at any cost," said still another in obvious disagreement.

"The authorities needed no urging."

"And one hundred thousand or more peasants were slaughtered!"

"'Twas not Luther's doing," Ewan Brice spoke up. "I have met the man. He is compelled to do only the will of God."

"Yea," said the merchant who had just returned from Wittenberg. "Luther has grieved deeply over this matter."

Everyone grew silent for a time. Then a merchant summed up the situation. "It may not have been of his making, and it is true that he has deplored violence on both sides. But there is little doubt now that the German peasants will remain in the Roman church. They feel betrayed."

There were other growing criticisms of Luther, for a man and a movement of such growing notoriety could not help but have others in disagreement, even among those who supported his primary beliefs on justification by faith and the authority of Scriptures. Luther's repudiation of monastic vows and his marriage to the former nun Katharina von Bora were seen by some as improper.

"Luther feels he has done the right thing. And his home is a happy one."

Justin spoke for the first time, his own marriage to Regina prompting him. "It is written that commanding to abstain from marriage and certain foods is doctrinally in error. I commend Martin Luther for recognizing his freedom in Christ and establishing a Christian home."

His father laughed heartily, as did the others. "With his lovely Regina, do you need to question my son's enthusiasm?"

"Putting aside such criticism of Luther," said another seriously to Justin, "hasn't your beloved Erasmus now turned against him?"

"Erasmus supported Luther's demands for reform," explained Justin. "But he stepped back from support when Luther broke with Rome. Like many, Erasmus wanted change within the church alone. But it seems to me that Luther has tried, and the church has no mind to hear just protest."

"And so they would rather issue bulls of arrest and have Reformers burned," said Marlon sharply.

The others followed his reasoning to the death of Lord Simon Redford and grew silent.

With events in Saxony as they were, Luther felt forced into the position of developing church organization and liturgy for the Protestants. He was convinced the common people had to be taught. Therefore he would develop a catechism for the parents and a shorter one for the children. A great lover of music, he wished praises to be sung by the congregations, not monkish chants in Latin but hymns of faith and worship in the language of the people.

After supper, as he usually did, Marlon joined Justin and Regina in their chamber in the English House.

"There is no one else in all England who feels the burning need to translate the Scriptures into English except William Tyndale," said Justin.

"As far as we know, there is no one," agreed Marlon. "That is, except for yourself."

Justin shook his head. Having left Cambridge, there

seemed no possible way to resume his study of the original languages. Time was not on his side.

"I am no longer the man. I have not the needed command of Greek and Hebrew. That would take several more years at least. We must rally to William Tyndale. Surely he is the man God has chosen for the task."

Regina mentioned that she felt guilt over being the one who had forced Justin to leave his studies. But he rejected her theory. He had made his own choice to leave Cambridge. She had tried to get him to enroll in the University at Wittenberg, but he had been too involved with the shipping business. And now a child was on the way. He seemed resigned to the fact that he would never translate the Scriptures.

"It is for us to stand with him," Justin said firmly.

"Without the bishop's authorization, Tyndale cannot work in London," said Regina. "What then can he do?"

"He must come to Antwerp."

"Indeed." Marlon leaned forward in his chair. "But will he come?"

"If he will not come to Antwerp, then he may go to Wittenberg to visit Martin Luther. At Cambridge, he expressed a high regard for the German's work."

"Then we will go to the house of Humphrey Monmouth," said Marlon.

Regina slowly rose to her feet. Justin guessed her thoughts. For Marlon to return to London was dangerous. But Justin himself could easily be arrested. By now Bishop Constantine would know who had rescued her from his custody.

Justin was silent. His mind was now on Regina. They shared a secret not yet known to the others, except for Marlon. *Now that she was with child, is it right to leave her and risk going to London? If something happened to me, what would become of her?*

His struggle heightened as he felt her intense gaze. Their eyes met.

She seemed to know exactly what he was thinking and how difficult it all was. She crossed to him and laid her hands on his arms. Her eyes looked directly into his. "I shall be quite all right. It is important we find William and do all we can to assist him. Hold nothing back if you are sure God is leading you in this matter."

Marlon quietly got up and left the chamber.

"Our lives were dedicated to serve Christ before we married," she whispered. "Should not our union also be dedicated to Him with the child as well? We must do what we know is right and leave all else to His care."

He held her close. "How is it that God has blessed me with a woman whose heart is devoted to Him? And yet to leave you at this time troubles me greatly."

"I know. But does it not help to know I wish you to go?"

"It does, though it makes leaving you no less difficult."

"I shall be perfectly safe and well. Felix is here and so are your father and brother. And I have met some very fine ladies recently."

"You are sure?" he pressed.

"Quite sure." She smiled, then held him tightly, her eyes closing. "I will be waiting for you."

He buried his face in her hair. "I am dedicated to you, Regina. My love for you is great. I need you desperately. If anything happens to you . . ."

"Nothing will happen, my love. You must go. And I must stay."

He raised her face to his. "Though we part, we are one in purpose and in love. We will do what we must and trust the Lord to bring us back together again."

"Yes," she whispered. "And if He has brought us together, then surely there is a future. But what will it be, Justin?"

"It is not for us to know all that He has planned. He will guide us a step at a time."

18

London

Justin sat with Lord Marlon in the pleasant surroundings of Humphrey Monmouth's ornately timbered house in Barking. Monmouth had greeted him warmly, having known his father. To the home of the cloth merchant had come many other businessmen and adventurers who sailed the trade routes of the world. They listened while Justin urged Tyndale to come to Saxony.

"It is true," said Tyndale. "Not only is there no room in My Lord of London's palace to translate the New Testament, but there is no place to do it in all England."

Justin produced for Tyndale a copy of Luther's German New Testament. He watched Tyndale's eyes light up as his lean hand reached for it.

"Luther was not idle during his enforced residence at Wartburg Castle. Using Erasmus's edition of the Greek New Testament, he completed the German version in less than a year," said Justin. The intimation that Tyndale also could do his work in Germany was not lost on William. Their eyes met and locked. A slight smile passed between them.

"Can you read German?" Monmouth asked Tyndale.

"Not well yet. But I am learning." He turned back to Justin. "Neither have I been idle these years."

"Nor have others," said Marlon Redford. He turned to the respected handful of merchant-adventurers who were friends and associates of those at the English House in Antwerp. "Do you bring news of the Reform elsewhere?"

The merchant-adventurers had sailed the world's ports and knew firsthand of political and religious movements. "Yes, indeed, the fire spreads. Denmark, Norway, and Iceland have rejected the teachings of Rome. And Gustavus Vasa is the first in his line to rule a free Sweden."

"Not to mention Zwingli in Zurich," murmured another, "and there is a very young man by the name of John Calvin who may one day stir the Protestant movement anew."

"We need reform," Justin agreed. "But without the Scriptures available to all in their own tongue, the church can easily lapse back into tradition and abuse. The light of the Word must always test every Christian. The best of godly men will fail or lag in their zeal. We dare put no final hope in leaders but in what is written."

Tyndale stood. "I am ready to translate into English," he stated quietly, "but I will need financial assistance."

Justin was on his feet. "You shall have it."

The other merchants were interested at once. Their travels had long ago enlightened them to the broader world. They not only measured ideas and church dogma but found the adventure of supporting a translation of the Bible in their own tongue both valuable and necessary if England was to know political freedom from Rome.

But Humphrey Monmouth was grave. "You are risking your life, William. And all those who assist you in any way also risk theirs." He fixed a sympathetic gaze on Justin and then on Marlon Redford.

"Yes, I know," breathed Tyndale.

"None need associate with you unless he is burdened to do so," said Justin. "All sacrifice must be given willingly."

"The printing cannot be done in England. You know what happened to Luther's other works. They were burned," warned Monmouth.

"And my father was executed," said Marlon firmly. "It is in his memory I seek to help light a spiritual fire in England that no book burning or executions can ever silence."

Monmouth shook his head. "Your father was a brave man, Lord Redford. And I shall do everything I can to help financially."

"So shall we all," said the other merchants.

"Are there printers in Germany who would aid us?" Tyndale inquired.

"I have friends in Antwerp at the English House," Justin said. "They will know the right printer."

"I would first go to Wittenberg," said William. "I will enroll at the university and meet Luther."

"Then to Wittenberg we shall go," said Justin.

All were on their feet now, and their enthusiasm was like sparks, lighting each other on to bravery.

Marlon gripped Tyndale's shoulder. "We have waited long for this moment, William."

"Too long," Justin said. "The hour is now."

"Then why do we tarry?" Tyndale asked. "Let us go."

Situated on a sandy hill, Wittenberg overlooked the Elbe River. The university, founded by Frederick, elector of Saxony, dominated the town. To Justin the atmosphere was as exuberant as its own Martin Luther, bursting with energy and changing moods. The Augustinian convent was now deserted, and here William Tyndale would be given a small chamber when he enrolled in the university.

Illustrating the diversity of God's gifted men, Philipp Melancthon, professor of Greek in the university and colleague of Luther in the Reformation, was the scholar of gentle reasonableness to supplement Luther's lionlike boldness and energy.

Philipp graciously received them into his chamber. Not yet thirty, articulate, tall and slim with deep eyes, he had already mastered the classical languages and Hebrew.

Like many others on the Wittenberg faculty, Melancthon was a friend to Luther and loyal to the truths he taught. His writing on the theology of the Wittenberg Reformers, *Loci Communes Rerum Theologicarum*, grew out of his studies of Romans and had been published in 1521. The work, in Latin, had established him as the theologian of the Lutheran movement. Luther himself had called Philipp's work "immortal."

"It is an attempt to make clear the most common topics of theological science," Philipp told Tyndale, his voice quiet and calm.

Tyndale leafed through the book. "You have accomplished much in a methodical fashion for a purpose, no doubt."

Philipp smiled easily. "To incite people to the Scriptures."

"That is also my ambition. If God permits, I shall translate the New Testament into the English language."

Philipp approved at once. "Then you must meet and converse with Martin Luther. He will see any visitor from England or elsewhere. Though his days are long and go well into the night, he shall be glad to see you."

Luther joined the group from England that night at supper.

As scholars, they conversed in Latin so that they might understand each other. Only Marlon, whose Latin was weak, sat with a scowl, discouraged that he was missing out.

Justin smiled at him and translated the more important parts of the discussion. "Luther and Tyndale agree on important doctrines. But on some, Tyndale deliberately has distanced himself," he explained quietly.

Marlon arched a brow. "On what then do they disagree?"

Justin leaned over his cup. "Tyndale believes the Lord's Supper is a commemoration of Christ's death, and Luther holds to Christ's actual presence in the wine and bread."

Luther and Tyndale's voices raised slightly, and Justin turned back to the vigorous debate. Luther's large fist came down on the table with a force that made the dishes rattle. Tyndale leaned toward him, his even gaze unwavering, and spoke firmly but quietly.

Philipp Melancthon caught Justin's eye, and his smile was disarming. Obviously used to Luther's stormy debates, apparently he was trying to assure his friends from England that the German priest's bluster meant nothing. Luther was enjoying himself, and he especially liked this William Tyndale.

Marlon leaned toward Justin. "What now do they argue about?"

"They do not argue. They discuss, with equal respect, their differences. Luther expresses his doubts about the authority of the book of James."

Marlon scowled again. "Why?"

"Luther believes it contradicts justification by faith apart from works."

"And Tyndale?"

"Tyndale declares that it assuredly belongs in the scriptural canon. He likens the works that James speaks of as a good tree bringing forth appropriate fruit—not for salvation but as evidence that it is a good tree with solid root in the foundation of salvation. Faith without works is dead."

"And what do you say?" Marlon whispered, although the voices of Luther and Tyndale were so strong he would not have been heard anyway.

"I agree," said Justin thoughtfully, "that James is part of Scripture. And that the works spoken of are evidence of new life, but not the *cause* of that life. They also differ about the use of music. Luther enjoys writing hymns and teaching congregations to sing. Tyndale says that music tends to distract too much from the importance of preaching the Word."

"What do you say to that?"

"I think," said Justin with a ghost of a smile, "that I would heartily enjoy singing with *Herr Doktor*. It promises to be an experience of enthusiasm and joy. As for William Tyndale, I think he will not be a mere translator of Luther but a servant of God with an independent mind. However, these two men have much in common. We have reason to thank God for raising such men up to light the path of reform."

Luther now jabbed a stubby finger against Tyndale's knapsack. In guttural Latin, he asked, "Friend Tyndale, what text will you use, then, in your translation?"

"The latest edition of the Greek text by Erasmus, friend Luther."

Luther was satisfied. He clapped his hands together. "Abide with us awhile. The university is at your disposal. Indeed, you and your friends will find Wittenberg a haven for your just and holy cause."

Tyndale settled at Wittenberg until about April 1525. Here he found in the learned environment all that was needed for his formidable work. Undisturbed, with lexicons and dictionaries at his disposal and the support of like-minded scholars who heartily approved of his zeal for translation, he set himself a goal of one year to complete the English version.

"The task before you is onerous. Won't you seek help?" Justin asked.

"I could ask you to check and countercheck each reference," said Tyndale. "But I realize the request would neither be fair to you nor to your dear Regina. So then! Return in peace to Antwerp."

Justin's travel arrangements were already made. He and Marlon were to leave that afternoon. "I feel a stranger to my own wife," said Justin. "Else I would be at your side from dawn to dusk."

"I know. And I surely understand your need to return to Antwerp. I have inquired for a clerk to aid me, and there is one named Will Roye, an Englishman. He seems a skilled copyist, knows Latin well, and is comfortable with Greek. And the work must proceed while it is day and God grants opportunity."

Tyndale opened the Greek New Testament to Matthew. His lips moved in silent prayer. With quill in hand he bent over the text, sucking in his breath with burning anticipation. Having labored first over the Greek, he began to translate into English. The pen hesitated, then with certainty moved across the paper.

"The book of the generation of Jesus Christ . . ."

Justin stood for a moment simply watching and hearing the scratch of the quill. No sound would fall as sweetly upon his ear as that of this one quill. And no other man, whether in drab scholar's robe or expensive velvet, would ever mean as much to his soul as this one scholar from Gloucestershire.

Justin's heart pounded, echoing the rhythm of Tyndale's pen. At long last, the Greek New Testament was beginning to find its way into the English language. A thousand prayers seemed to be uplifted in petition and thanksgiving to the throne of God. And there came to his memory a host of others, small and great—men such as John Wycliffe, Dean John Colet, Martin Luther, Erasmus, others, some martyred for their faith.

Their work appeared now to merge as one sublime task, coming together by the working of the Spirit until it hovered over a single man who sat diligently at work. One man, yet one completely yielded to the purpose of God. A humble man, a lone scholar, yet willing to give all and to face death by fire in order to complete the task.

A fragment of Scripture from 1 Corinthians flashed through Justin's mind. "I have planted, Apollos watered; but God gave the increase."

Indeed, God was at work in history. And whatever the cost to those involved, whether great or small, known or unknown by man, the result of Tyndale's work would be worth the price.

Justin stared at the candle on the translator's desk until his mind saw not the wavering, feeble flame but a brightly burning torch, growing until it enlightened all England, touching not only the palace of the king but vale and city, university and parish, and the light changed the direction of history and would touch the world.

Slowly he crossed to the door and quietly put his hand to the latch. Tyndale was too engrossed in his work to notice. Justin smiled at the sight, and moved with joy he thought, *William Tyndale, servant of God, may the sustaining grace and power of Jesus Christ enable you for so wondrous a task.*

In the spring, having completed his translation, Tyndale and Roye, his clerk, made the trip down the Elbe to Hamburg to receive the finances promised by the English merchants. When he reached the city, Justin and Marlon met him, anxiously eyeing the bundle containing the precious document.

"We must be cautious," said Justin and scrutinized the man Roye with an uneasiness he could not explain. He rebuked himself. *After all, hasn't this Englishman been with William serving faithfully for an entire year?*

It was Tyndale's turn to be cautious as he fingered his precious bundle and listened to their news.

"We know of a printer in Cologne."

Tyndale looked doubtful. "I have heard of the archbishop of Cologne. He is antagonistic toward Luther and all things concerning the new doctrine."

"He is that," agreed Justin. "But the printers we recommend are known by the merchants of the English House. As businessmen, they are not inclined to ask questions about what they print. I have already paid them a visit, and they have agreed to print all we can pay for."

"Not only that, they are craftsmen," said Marlon. "The work of Quentel and Bryckkmann is known throughout Germany."

"For the Lord's work, we should settle for nothing less than fine quality," Justin said. "We have arranged for our merchant ships to be docked in the harbor. From Cologne it will be easier to load the Testaments among the exchange cargoes and ship them down the Rhine to London. A Brice ship waits now to bring us to Cologne."

Tyndale smiled. "You have convinced me. Why do we tarry? To Cologne we shall go."

"Only one thing. As you have already intimated, in Cologne we shall be in enemy territory. We must watch our step at all times. Our business there must be kept in strictest confidence." He glanced again at the man named Roye.

"His labors have proven diligent thus far," Tyndale said.

Justin cared not for Roye. Then he rebuked himself again. *If you had stayed with Tyndale as you promised at Cambridge, he would not have needed Roye.*

Marlon too gave Roye an abrupt once-over. "It seems to me I have seen you somewhere before."

"No, good sir, you have seen me nowhere. Else I would have remembered you as well. I am lately come from England where I fled the Friars Observant at Greenwich. I came to Wittenberg in search of true freedom."

"Have you found this true freedom?" Justin inquired.

Roye quipped, with a bow to Tyndale, "And who might find freedom for even an hour when my master translates from dawn well past midnight? After so long an ordeal, it is a wonder my poor fingers have not been written down to the bone."

Justin said no more.

On board the Brice ship, Justin took Tyndale to the captain's cabin, and together they went over the handwritten copy of the New Testament.

"Not since I was a boy and came across the English version of Matthew have I looked upon anything as marvelous as this!"

Tyndale was pleased. "And yet my work is only half done. I will not be content until the Old Testament is also in English."

The dawn blazed with vermillion over the city of Cologne, stretching for some miles along the left bank of the Rhine. Justin greeted the morning with anticipation.

The spires of many churches thrust up from steep roofs, and the timber houses greeted them with the morning light. Wharves and warehouses clustered by the waterfront were already awake with sailors and merchants. In the distance the bells of the monasteries chimed, reminding Justin of his years in Rome, and in the far distance his eyes fell on the majestic cathedral, still unfinished after three hundred years of building.

Tyndale was wide awake and at his side. The New Testament was carefully wrapped in the baggage slung over his lean shoulder. Leaving Andrew in command of the ship, Justin and Marlon took Tyndale to the print shop in an alley behind the quarters of the leatherworkers.

Peter Quentel, recognizing them, came at once. "The manuscript, please," he said in low guttural German.

Tyndale produced the volume from his baggage, and Quentel's deft fingers turned the pages. When he looked up, his eyes pretended innocence. "I cannot read English," he said lightly. His eyes glinted. "Therefore I know not what I print. The price, you have it with you?"

Justin handed him a bag. "You will receive the rest when the manuscript is finished and it meets with Master Tyndale's approval."

Quentel nodded briskly and eyed Tyndale. "You may come as soon as the first sheets are printed to make changes."

"How soon until you have it finished?" Tyndale pressed.

Quentel stroked his chin thoughtfully and made low noises to himself. "Soon. I shall begin first thing in the morning."

Justin explored the hand-operated presses in the long, low building. The odor of ink, paper, and leather filled his nostrils. Quentel would use Roman type. Three thousand copies were to be printed at first, with copious notes, including marginal glosses.

When they left Quentel's shop, they went to an inn. A sprightly old man met them wearing leather breeches and a gaily colored stocking cap, from under which a splotch of thick white hair hung down across his tanned forehead. Under thick silver brows, pale blue eyes probed each visitor alertly, as Tyndale spoke quietly to him in German.

"*Gud, gud.*" The old man nodded and smiled suddenly. To show he understood perfectly, he placed a long bony finger to his mouth, and his eyes twinkled. "Shh, shh."

Around the white-tiled stove, wooden tankards were soon produced, also strong-tasting cheese and black bread. Night drew on, and the fellowship was warm and pleasant. They celebrated the success God had granted and dreamed together of the results in England.

Daily Tyndale left the inn by the back door, walked alone to Quentel's shop, and reentered by the back door. At night he corrected the printed sheets and returned them the next day. By summer's end, as September dawned with the promise of harvest, the work was nearing completion and Justin sensed his and William's hopes running high with the excitement they felt.

It was a warm fall day. The leaves were turning red and gold, and Regina sat on the steps of the house in Antwerp with her infant son, Seth, wiggling in her lap as she tried to read Justin's letter.

Above the baby's head she read aloud. "The work fast comes to an end. But I have a strange foreboding I cannot explain. Know that I love you very much and think of you and Seth with each hour. I wish you were beside me . . ."

Regina frowned. "What foreboding does he speak of?" she said to the small child, for she oft took to talking to him in the absence of others. "I wonder who this clerk Roye is? Surely he is trustworthy, or William would not be working with him."

Seth's plump little fingers snatched at the letter, and his large blue eyes stared up at her, wide and clear. He gurgled happily and broke into a delightful smile. She kissed his forehead. "If it were not for you, little man, I should not be missing out on this greatest of adventures."

Almost as if the baby understood, suddenly his features contorted into a cry. Regina laughed softly and hugged him against her breast. "No, I would not trade you for all the printer's ink in Quentel's shop. Besides, you will soon be big enough to travel."

Seth smiled, content again, and began to jump up and down on her lap so energetically that she cried aloud. In a second assault of gaiety he grasped a shining lock of her hair, and against all pleading for him to let go he held fast, gurgling and cooing, oblivious of her discomfort.

In Cologne, Justin slept little that night. He left the ship's cabin and went on deck to behold the stars. The September night was clear and chill. Restlessness hung over his spirit. His heart searched for a reason but found nothing.

At dawn, Marlon joined him.

Then, in the overhanging mist that had risen suddenly, a man who worked for Quentel came hurrying up the plank. Seeing Justin he swept off his cap and waved it frantically. "The work is known!"

Roye! thought Justin instantly. Or was it one of the young men working in the shop?

"Johann Dobneck—Cochlaeus—dean of the church at Frankfurt," said the German, panting. "He is a leading opponent of the Reformation, and he has learned of the translation."

"But how!"

"I know not, except Quentel is also printing a work for Dobneck, an edition of the works of a former abbot. But there is no time to waste. Dobneck has an injunction from the Senate to stop further printing."

Justin groaned. He bolted past the man and down the plank, with Marlon quick on his heels. They ran through the still dark street as the mist swirled about them.

A light burned in the print shop window. They burst through the door, and Quentel threw up his hands and rushed toward them.

"All your work is to be burned," he said. "And you and this Tyndale with it! *Go!*"

"The manuscript," Justin demanded, his spirit strained but calm. "Where is it?"

Quentel glanced over his shoulder at the door. He rushed then to the press, where he began grabbing stacks of paper and heaping them onto Justin's arms. Marlon grabbed several bags and stashed the sheets into them.

"Each sheet is lettered," Quentel said, still looking toward the door. "We got to K, but no further."

The printer was perspiring heavily, and his hands shook as he shoved the last stack at Justin.

"You must break up the type," Justin warned him. "Destroy the forms, else they will yet discover the work you did."

Quentel hurried to obey.

With the manuscript safely bagged, Marlon called out to Justin. "Be on your way! I will join you soon!" He sprang to Quentel's aid as Justin ran toward the back door carrying Tyndale's work, not daring to risk further delay.

The alley was still dark, but the sky was lightening in the east. He darted through the shadows, taking strange cobbled streets until he came to the inn. There he found Tyndale up and prepared to walk to the shop, but Roye was fast asleep.

"Let us hasten to the ship. We have been betrayed."

Tyndale stood momentarily frozen. "The work! I shall not leave without it!"

"I have it all here in the bags. Come! Or you will not live to see it printed."

"You are sure all of it is here?"

"All."

Justin grabbed his arm, but Tyndale turned toward the bed. *"Up!"* he shouted. "The Philistines are upon you, O Roye!"

Roye bolted upright and sat rubbing his eyes.

"Have you spoken to anyone of the work these past few days?" Tyndale asked.

"Do you take me for a traitor, Master Tyndale? I, who have labored as your clerk these long hard months, yes, even in the frozen winter of Wittenberg?"

Justin exchanged glances with Tyndale. "We may have been betrayed by a worker at the print shop."

Roye jumped out of bed and grabbed his clothes and shoes. "'Twas not I!"

Marlon was waiting on the Brice ship when the three of them boarded. The sun was coming up and beginning to burn away the mist. Andrew had the vessel ready to leave the harbor.

Tyndale took the bags and bent down, briefly searching through them to make sure all was there. He breathed a sigh of relief. "We have this to thank God for. Nothing is lost, and we have all escaped."

"What now?" Marlon whispered to Justin. "If we sail to Antwerp they may be expecting us and search the ship. It would be better if we sailed in the opposite direction."

Justin faced Tyndale. "The enemy is likely to write King Henry and Wolsey about the English New Testament. They will be on the lookout at printers and ports."

"If God means that the translation is to be printed and distributed," said Tyndale, "nothing shall ultimately destroy the work."

"There is another printer in Worms," Justin continued cautiously. "Although it will be more difficult to ship the Testaments into London from there since Worms lies inland. But the man may help."

"What is his name?"

"Schoeffer."

"Then by all means let us hasten to Worms. At least all is not lost." Tyndale breathed deeply with relief. "The darkened enemy of our souls may seek to trap us in his snare, but the Lord watches our steps. To Worms, then. But what of you, my friend? With each day your involvement deepens, and your life is put at risk. You must think also of your wife and son. Perhaps Roye and I should go on alone."

"I think of them much. But all three of us are in His hands and purpose. If God so wills, we shall come together again in peace. Has He delivered us all and the work for nothing? Surely He is with us. Let us now have peace and assurance and proceed ever toward the goal. Regina will always be ready to cheer us on."

"At least in Worms," said Marlon, "there is sympathy for the new ways of the Reformation. And a printer there is likely to befriend us."

In Worms Justin was reminded that it was here that Martin Luther had faced the Imperial Diet of Emperor Charles V, refusing to recant and taking his stand on the authority of Scripture. It was comforting to know that they bore in secret those precious words soon to spill over into England.

Since Luther's stand in Worms, many men had embraced the reformational ideas and could even openly attest to their faith. This was because Worms was in the Hesse region where the Landgrave Philipp the Magnanimous ruled. Philip was himself a supporter of Luther.

Schoeffer met them pleasantly enough, yet upon looking at Quentel's work he scratched his beard and shook his head with a sigh.

"I would do the work, but I cannot continue from where *Herr* Quentel has left off. My type, I fear, does not match nor do I possess comparable sheets. All must be done again from the beginning, from Matthew to Revelation. If you will agree to that, I can start at once. It is now October, and by winter's end you may set forth upon your journey."

Tyndale looked at Justin.

Justin was thinking of the long months he then must stay in Worms. "Begin at once, and you shall receive full pay."

Marlon later came to him in private. "I shall stay with William, Justin. Return to Antwerp."

Justin thought of Regina and Seth. By now the first winter winds would be blowing, and the storm clouds gathering. Yes, he must go home.

"Did not William make mention of a need for learning Hebrew before embarking on the Old Testament?" Justin inquired.

"He mentioned it, but here in Worms?"

"It so happens that I was speaking with Schoeffer. There is a large Jewish settlement here. Their synagogue, it is said, dates from the destruction of their temple by Babylon. He shall be well occupied studying Hebrew during the winter. And you . . ."

Marlon clapped a hand on his shoulder. "Never fear. I shall keep an eye on Roye. We shall expect you by spring."

When Justin entered the house in Antwerp it seemed somber and too silent. He was met by Felix in the great hall as he set down his bag and threw off his hat. One look at the servant's face and Justin tensed.

"'Tis the little one, Master Justin—there was no hope, so it seemed."

Seth! He tried to remain calm. "No hope? What happened?"

"He became ill. No physician could help him, nor all our prayers. 'Twas the Lord who took him home." He broke down in spite of himself.

Justin looked up the flight of darkened steps. "And Regina?"

"In her room."

"When did this happen?"

"Months ago, but she has not recovered her joy. Your return comes at a needed time, sir."

Justin left him and climbed the stairs. When he reached the door of their chamber he paused, hoping to bring his own emotions under control.

"The Lord gave, and the Lord has taken away," he kept repeating. "Blessed be the name of the Lord."

Regina sat in a chair reading. Hearing the door open, she looked up. She saw Justin and let out a little cry, dropping the book in her haste to reach him. The moment they embraced, her sobs came anew. He held her tightly, stroking her tumbling hair, and they wept together.

"He is gone," she finally choked. "The only other person I have ever truly wanted besides you—and he has slipped from my hands."

"No," he whispered, "we have not lost him. If he is taken from our hands, then he is in Christ's. Let us comfort ourselves with that."

"But why did He take him?" she wept. "Why?"

"I do not know."

"He was so young. Only a little baby."

He caressed her, kissing her softly as she sobbed. "I know, I know." He continued to simply hold her. "We are in a very dark place in our lives, Regina. Though we have no light at the moment, we have His Word. With it to uphold us, we can trust Him through the bewilderment of darkness."

"I do trust Him. Only—" Her voice broke.

"I know," he whispered again. "I understand."

The spring of 1526 arrived, and the weather was good for sailing. Justin and Regina embarked for Cologne.

Schoeffer had printed six thousand copies of the English New Testament, and these were bought by the English merchants and smuggled on board the Brice ship. The merchant-adventurers who bought them were adept at avoiding the censorship of certain books at the port of London.

Regina first marveled at their skill, then with unutterable joy threw herself with zeal into the battle. What a privilege God had entrusted to them! English merchants had banded together to smuggle into the darkness of England the forbidden light of the Word of God. Satan must tremble at the Sword they were about to unleash upon his spiritual garrison. He feared the Word as he feared nothing else. No human argument, no blade of steel, no human strength could make the impact that Tyndale's English New Testament would make against his forces of blindness, darkness, and superstition.

Tyndale joined them in hiding the Scriptures below in the hold. They concealed them in bales, stuffed them into crates, placed them between folded cloth, buried them in cheese, masked them with Rhine wine, or veiled them in leather and other commodities to be brought into the London docks.

When the labor was done, Justin and Regina looked at each other, dusty and perspiring but elated, and began to laugh. Marlon grasped Tyndale by the shoulder. It was done!

The hold of the rugged Brice ship became a cathedral of praise and joy for the victory God had wrought. For the time, all thoughts of possible future suffering were pushed from their minds. It was a time to celebrate, for the giant Goliath had been defeated by the sling of David. God had blessed humble men and women and empowered their feeble efforts to contest a king and a rigid religious establishment that stood against the purpose of God.

Yet the war was not over. Deep in his heart Justin knew

their spiritual enemy would rally his dark forces to oppose the entrance of the Scriptures by fear, threats, and death.

The moment passed into mellow contemplation, and he turned to Tyndale. "It is a great time for rejoicing, William. The lost Sword has been freed from its scabbard."

"Yes, truly, friend Justin! We have journeyed a long way since our youth in Cambridge. Yet there remains much still to be done. I wish you Godspeed."

"And you? Will you remain awhile in Worms among the Jewish settlement or go on to Marburg?"

In Marburg a new university was ready to open with the aid of Philip the Magnanimous. Tyndale had been invited by certain scholars to join them.

"I know not the leading of the Lord as yet. My intentions for the time are to remain here and pursue Hebrew with the rabbis. They have been kind to me and very helpful. I have high anticipations of completing the Old Testament within the next year."

"And your clerk, Will Roye?"

"Ah, he has grown weary of my long hours at the work. He has parted my company."

"Be cautious. Not even Worms will remain a safe haven once the New Testaments are distributed in England. When the king and Wolsey learn the name of the culprit, they will issue an edict for your arrest."

Justin and Marlon waited on deck. It was night over the Port of London, and the fog was thick. Soon their contact boarded in the company of a trusted merchant. His name was Thomas Garrett, and he would head the agency for distributing the New Testaments.

Justin was tense, but calm.

"Is William Tyndale with you?"

"No," said Justin, "he is in Worms."

"I would see the work."

They took him down the ladder into the hold, and in the light of a lantern Justin produced a copy of the English New Testament. Thomas Garrett anxiously looked through it. He was deeply moved. "I thought mine eyes would never behold such a sight as this. How many do you have?"

"Two thousand are here. Four thousand more on other ships."

"Reform-minded merchants will buy all six thousand copies. But they must be hidden until we can distribute them. When will the others arrive?"

"Captain Ewan Brice will arrive in ten days. Another ship, in a fortnight. We will do all we can to assist you," said Justin. "We will remain in London."

Thomas Garrett eyed the books thoughtfully. "If I cannot trust friends of Tyndale, who can I trust?" he said quietly. "There are tunnels in the London Bridge where other illegal books have been stored from time to time. We could use your help to get the Testaments there by small boats."

The fog seeped through Regina's hooded cloak as she stood on the wharf near the warehouse. It was late at night, and the quay was empty. When the last small boat was loaded for the trip to London Bridge, she joined Justin on board.

They manned the oars, dipping them silently as the small craft moved up the Thames. Water slapped softly against the sides, and the boat glided like a ghost through the gray mist. Marlon's boat would follow later and, one by one, the others.

London Bridge loomed ahead, and Regina's heart pounded. Then they passed through an arch and approached the landward side, where a cluster of ramshackle houses had been built on the extending wall. Steps led up to the houses, but in the wall were several small entrances leading into the secret tunnels that Thomas Garrett had described.

Regina's skin crawled with excitement as they docked. She stood in the darkness and swirling mist as Justin dragged the boat onto the sandbar.

Once in the tunnel, Justin lit a lantern and hung it on a peg. The air here was damp and stale. Working silently and swiftly, they stored the New Testaments in dry kegs. They had barely finished unloading when Marlon arrived.

Regina knew that as soon as the first New Testaments appeared on the London streets, the church would have agents out among the merchants seeking those involved. If Thomas

Garrett was discovered to be the agency for distribution, their own arrest would take place along with his.

Justin whispered to Marlon, "It is needful to remain in London. Thomas Garrett will need assistance in the distribution. Are you willing to risk further danger?"

"It has been five years since my father was executed for supporting Luther and possessing his writings. But he did not die for an empty dream. Tonight, with so many New Testaments, we have proof of that. We cannot turn back now."

19

Bridewell Palace, 1527

By 1527 Tyndale's English New Testaments, along with copies of the Cologne fragments from Quentel's print shop, had swept London. And today a conclave of angry bishops faced King Henry VIII and Cardinal Wolsey in the great hall of Bridewell.

A bishop produced a Testament and, with a bow, handed it to King Henry.

"Your Majesty, this is none other than a resurrection of the forbidden heresy of John Wycliffe. We urge you to issue a proclamation at once, prohibiting the importation of Tyndale's heretical work and ordering the arrest of those involved in the smuggling."

King Henry's face was somber. He leafed through the New Testament, then handed it to scarlet-robed Cardinal Wolsey.

"And just who is this William Tyndale?" King Henry inquired.

"An Oxford scholar, Your Majesty," Cardinal Wolsey replied. Unlike the bishops, his voice was calm. He had read the New Testament and commented privately that he found no glaring errors. He counseled tolerance.

But Wolsey would soon change his mind. In early 1528 he would become alarmed at the Testament's large-scale popularity among the common people. What stung Thomas Wolsey the most was the published satire against himself, written by Tyndale's former clerk, Roye. The poetic satire called "Rede Me and be nott wrothe' was attributed to William Tyndale, and it infuriated Wolsey. He moved to have Tyndale arrested.

King Henry stood and walked about the hall in thoughtful silence. The gold collar around his thick neck sported a diamond the size of a walnut, and suspended with it was a large pearl. He was a massive man who dressed to show off his size rather than to minimize it. He wore with flair a French-style cap of crimson velvet. Its brim was looped with gold-enameled tags, and his doublet was in the new Swiss fashion, having alternate stripes of white and crimson satin. As he paced, his hand rested on the gold pouch at his hip, which covered a dagger.

"He must be silenced, Your Majesty, for the good of all England," said another bishop. "He is a known supporter of the Lutheran heresy. Where have William Tyndale's New Testaments come from but Lutheran territory?"

King Henry stopped and scowled. He had received the conclave of bishops half-heartedly until the mention of Luther. Was not the whole of the European continent churning like the restless sea because of this pestilent German? If William Tyndale was a colleague of Luther, then he could not be a friend to Henry's throne.

Wherever Henry turned these days he heard talk of reform, and what he heard did not make him sleep securely. What of the peasant uprising in parts of Germany? Had the mobs there not been against the political rulers?

Luther might deny instigating these mass riots and bloodshed, but King Henry believed him responsible. Luther's works were forbidden books in England. The king saw the words *Lutheran* and *Reformation* as a rebellion against established authority, and he feared that it would spread throughout England and thereby unsettle his own plans and attack the foundation of his throne.

"Sire, surely William Tyndale is no friend to England. He is no less than a mouthpiece for Luther. Tyndale is a young rebel who serves his German idol's ideas of radical reform. The Lutheran menace must be silenced before it invades England."

The bishop had struck Henry in a vulnerable spot. The last thing Henry wanted was an uprising among his own peasants. And the conservative English bishops were among some of the most anti-reform leaders in Europe. They still supported a law passed a century before prohibiting an English Scripture translation on penalty of death.

"This is no time for toleration, Your Majesty," the archbishop of Canterbury protested. "If we do not move to condemn this work, all England will be ablaze with his teaching. Far better that the church denounce it now and set the books to flame."

Justin stood amid the large crowd gathered before London's Saint Paul's Cross. The October wind harbingered winter. It penetrated his rough clothing and whipped the bonfire's flame.

Before the assembly stood Bishop Tunstall in a heavily furred robe. Having once embraced certain reform ideas of Erasmus, Tunstall now lifted an English New Testament for everyone to see and announced, "Out of obedience to the church and the king, the work of heretics must face the wrath of fire."

He took a step forward and flung the New Testament into the fire. A somber hush fell over the crowd. Ceremoniously other clerics brought forward a large number of copies and flung them into the searing flames.

Justin's heart thudded within his chest as he watched the Scriptures being devoured. Time, energy, expense, the risk of life—all went up in the intense heat.

Tunstall, having issued his injunction against Tyndale's work, now urged, on pain of excommunication, the burning of every copy in London.

"Know assuredly," he threatened, "that any rebellious soul who persists in buying, selling, or possessing the heretical work of William Tyndale shall be excommunicated from the church. I urge all souls to humble themselves in subjection to the will of God. Accept the guidance of your shepherds with meekness of soul and turn from this heresy."

Several in the crowd now came forward and fed Tyndale's work to the fire. Justin was sure many of them had been deliberately planted in the gathering to add effect to the bishop's exhortation.

Later, in the quiet of Oxford's scholastic chamber, Thomas Garrett leaned across the table toward Justin. The November evening was chilly, and Regina warmed herself at the fire. The flickering firelight fell on Justin's face.

"The archbishop of Canterbury has issued a mandate similar to Tunstall's. He will also personally buy up as many copies as he can find throughout the Continent in order to destroy them."

Justin's eyes glinted. "The work of God shall not cease. If they burn these, we shall print more. The hunger is there, and the people risk arrest to buy the Scriptures. We must not hold back now."

"We will not," said Thomas. "The substantial moneys the archbishop spends to buy up the copies will be reinvested to print even more!"

Suddenly the door opened, and Marlon rushed in. "It's happened. The bishop and King Henry have released an edict for Tyndale's arrest. They know he is in Worms."

Justin was on his feet. "Then there is no time to lose. We must warn him."

"Go, and Regina with you. I will remain here to assist Thomas."

Tyndale was still located in the respected Jewish settlement at Worms, studying Hebrew. He greeted Justin and Regina with pleasure until he heard their news.

"The bloodhounds are fast on your trail," Justin warned.

Tyndale tossed his few personal belongings into a bag. But when it came to his books and precious parchments, he took care to pack them in an old worn satchel he wore slung across his back.

"It so happens I have received an invitation to take up residence among the scholars at Marburg," he told Justin. "Join me there—at least for a few months."

"Then we shall see you safely to Marburg."

The ancient city of Marburg had been a place of pilgrimage for the Teutonic knights during the era of the Crusades. Now the university, housed in a former Dominican monastery, was its focal point. As students arrived from England and all over Europe, it seemed to Justin that he was back at Cambridge.

Soon after their arrival he met a young man whose thesis on justification by faith captured his attention. The youth's name was Patrick Hamilton.

"I am lately come from the University of Saint Andrews," Hamilton said. "But I shall not be at Marburg for long. How can I be content when me own Scotland remains in spiritual bondage?" His dark eyes burned like coals, and his voice was impassioned. "I shall go and proclaim the new doctrines, whatever the cost. If I be not a servant to me own kin and me own blood, I ask you, who will? Aye, for too long has Scotland mourned in darkness."

Their eyes held, in a strange, binding silence. The Scottish Reformer broke the spell himself with a sudden smile. "Are you leaving Marburg soon?"

"Yes. It was good that our paths have crossed here, if only in passing. It is not often I meet a fellow Scot."

Patrick Hamilton was gone from Justin's life as quickly as he had come. But the brief exchange sealed an unforgettable message upon Justin's heart. When the news came later that year announcing Hamilton's death, Justin somehow was not surprised.

"The Scot Patrick Hamilton was burned as a heretic," Tyndale told him.

"At Saint Andrews?"

"Yes. By command of Cardinal Beaton, the archbishop."

Justin sat silently, unable to rid the ardent young face from his mind—or the dedication Patrick Hamilton had shown to the doctrine of the epistle of Romans.

Tyndale understood. He laid a hand on his shoulder. "He left his written thesis with me. I have not had time to translate it from the Latin. Much like my own *Parable of the Wicked Mammon,* the Scot wrote that faith alone in the work of Christ does justify. Perhaps you would like to translate it into English?"

"I would," said Justin softly, and then was taken with his own announcement. "One day I shall bring it to Scotland and preach it from Edinburgh to Inverness and to the farthest regions beyond."

While at Marburg, Tyndale settled into a brief but welcome reprieve and turned again to the work of translating the Pentateuch. To his joy, a young Oxford scholar arrived, John Frith, whom he had met while at Humphrey Monmouth's. Tyndale thought highly of the man's scholarship, and they became good friends.

But the news John Frith brought from Oxford was dark.

"The agency for the distribution of your New Testaments has been discovered by the bishop. Thomas Garrett was arrested."

Regina turned pale, and her eyes darted to Justin.

Justin's voice was tense but steady. "Did you also hear of a Lord Marlon Redford?"

"No," Frith hastened to say. "And yet I fear that many good men were also arrested."

"I must know," Regina told Justin. "Let us return to Antwerp."

The English House near the Antwerp harbor was of sober mood. Captain Ewan Brice and Felix sat at the table in the company of Thomas Poynitz and other merchants.

"At least Humphrey Monmouth was released," said one, obviously trying to bring a measure of encouragement to the room.

"Did he not recant?" declared Captain Brice somewhat shortly. "That is why he is free. He confessed his 'error' in housing William Tyndale."

"Or so he has said. Do you blame him so much? Who wishes to be burned?"

Captain Brice spoke quietly. "But with Thomas Garrett it is different." He pushed his chair back suddenly and stood, his broad shoulders squared. His gaze sought each man at the table. "I, for one, will die if need be, before I recant. I am proud to have associated meself with the likes of a man like Tyndale. And as long as God gives me strength, the Brice ships will be used to transport the Holy Scriptures to England."

"Hear, hear," echoed the firm voices.

"But what do we do about his young lordship Marlon?"

"'Tis nothing we can do. He is in the Tower like his brave father before him. And he too will likely die before Christmas. The lad is too strong in his convictions to recant," said Captain Brice.

A sense of grief fell heavily upon the room. Captain Brice walked to the window and gazed in the direction of the harbor. The sun was setting peacefully, sending a shimmer of golden rays over the water. "Even if he found his emotions overwrought and did recant, Marlon would soon loathe his decision and turn himself in again. The Redfords are stalwart folk. My daughter-in-law Regina is strong enough in her dependence upon Christ to face yet another sorrow added to Seth and to her father before that."

20

Marburg

Tyndale faced his friend John Frith. "How can I expect a scholar like yourself to become a common scribe to me?"

"I will most gladly be your scribe when the work needing my labor is the Word of God."

"Then what can I say? The Lord has sent you! Most of the Pentateuch translation is finished. With your able correction and transcription, the task will be done by the end of the year."

Tyndale's optimism proved well-founded. Now that the first five books of the Old Testament were in English, he was eager to set sail to Antwerp with the cherished work in hand. Although two other works had been printed in Marburg, Tyndale did not have the finances to print the Pentateuch there.

But John Frith was uneasy. "It is safer for you here in Marburg."

"The English merchants of Antwerp I can trust with my very life. And the work? Without their assistance I doubt if the New Testament would be in England this day. Besides," said Tyndale "they are too cautious with their finances to give me the money for printing before I show them the translation."

In March, William left John Frith to pursue his own work and set sail for Antwerp. He felt no uneasiness as he boarded the ship with the Pentateuch and his notes and comments, all carefully wrapped, in order to have his painstaking labors printed. He thought with satisfaction of the Old Testament in English being sold in London and throughout Europe.

But by nightfall the promise of spring weather suddenly and violently turned back to winter, and a great storm broke upon the vessel with the fury of unleashed demons.

Below, clinging to his work, a ceaseless prayer upon his lips, Tyndale heard the mast break like the crack of thunder. The ship reeled. The cargo crashed from one side to the other. Cold seawater poured in.

No! Tyndale wildly struggled to keep the Scriptures dry. But wind, water, and lurching ship mocked his feeble efforts. It seemed a thousand voices laughed at his desperate struggle. The lanterns went out with a serpent's hiss, leaving him in darkness.

A surge of water broke over him. *Lord! I ask not for myself—but the work, O Lord, what of the work?*

The ship yawed rudderless and without a mast, and the hatch cover tore loose. Passengers screamed in terror.

Madly Tyndale clung to his translation, arguing, pleading, bewildered. He felt the leather strap give way as the waters buffeted him again. He felt the bag slip through his clutching fingers. In a moment of utter despair he cried aloud, "My Lord! Why? Why?"

He was flung like a rag doll against the bulkhead, and he fell into darkness.

The Senate of Hamburg had authorized the reformational faith, and Tyndale found himself in the comfortable home of Mistress Margaret von Emmerson, a highly esteemed senator's widow. He had first met her kin in Wittenberg.

Here Tyndale was encouraged by the leader of the Hamburg Reformers and overcame his discouragement. Doggedly he began work on a retranslation and completed the first two books of the Old Testament by August.

He wrote the English merchants of his ordeal at sea, and a letter soon came from Justin Brice offering assistance. Anxious to continue the work, and needing funds, William packed up his meager belongings for the trip to English House.

"I hate to see you go now," Mistress von Emmerson said. She had soon developed a motherly concern for William. "Your visit to Antwerp will prove far more dangerous to your life than to stay in reform-minded Hamburg. Here we are evangelical, but Antwerp is now governed by the Queen of Hungary, regent for Charles the Fifth. And you know how he supports Rome. And the Senate has warned me that agents of Cardinal Wolsey and King Henry are searching for you in the Low Countries and in Germany."

"I must go to Antwerp, Mistress von Emmerson. There my friends await me. With their support the Pentateuch will be printed and shipped into London. Fear not." He ventured a kind but sad smile. "With the apostle Paul, I too believe that I shall yet finish my course."

Justin met William at the Antwerp harbor and embraced him heartily. "How goes the great work?"

"I have enough of the manuscript to show to your friends for approval of funds. Genesis is ready, and Exodus. The others will follow."

"They will be glad to hear that God is giving us success in spite of our misfortune. Where Satan has worked against you, God is working all things for good. You will stay with us at the English House. A room and all things you need will be given you—and any protection necessary."

"I am beholden to all."

"No, we are beholden to you."

The merchant-adventurers were eager to meet William Tyndale for the first time. They sat waiting with Thomas Poynitz and Captain Ewan Brice.

"This," said Justin quietly to the men who stood staring at the lean figure in the dark tunic, "is the man."

It was quiet. Then, all at once, they surged forward with smiles and strong hands outstretched. Tyndale was soon lost among them.

At the supper table they listened with intense concentration to his tale of the shipwreck and the loss of the manuscript.

"How much is again ready?" asked Poynitz.

"Hopefully enough," said Tyndale cautiously with a glance from face to face, "to receive your financial assistance. I have incurred debt in Hamburg and cannot go on alone."

"Tsk," boomed Captain Brice. "If need be, I shall sell a galleon to pay all."

Stewert shifted uneasily in his place but made no protest. Justin suspected he was hoping it wouldn't come to that.

"Let us see your work and how much is done," said Augustine Packington.

Tyndale hastened to his bag and spread out on the long table the books of Genesis and Exodus and his notes on the rest of the Pentateuch.

Justin marveled over the portion ready for the printer, and he and Regina exchanged smiles. The others assured William of support and that the Pentateuch could be printed in Antwerp.

"You will stay with us?" asked Poynitz.

"Yes," said Justin firmly. "He will."

Justin and Regina led Tyndale up the steps to the small chamber where he would stay.

Obviously weary, William set down his bag and sighed deeply.

Justin built a small fire in the fireplace, and Regina disappeared to soon return with a pot of hot cider, which she hung across the hearth. In kindred spirit the three sat for a while in silence.

A window faced the harbor and its anchored ships. A swallow's nest was built in the eaves above the window, and Tyndale watched the birds darting to and fro, feeding their young. "Yea, the sparrow hath found an house, and the swallow a nest for herself, where she may lay her young, even thine altars, O Lord of hosts, my King, and my God," he quoted.

"The vigilance of the authorities has increased against us," Justin told him. "Under threat of torture or burning fagots, some of our supporters have recanted. Humphrey Monmouth was arrested but was released after he vowed to meddle no more with heretics. Thomas Garrett was arrested and Lord Marlon."

Tyndale leaned forward anxiously. "Yes?"

"Marlon did not recant," Justin said. "He was burned at Smithfield."

Tyndale's breath eased from his lips, and he leaned back in silence. "Then what we do, we must do quickly. If they burn me, they will do no more than I expect." He looked at them squarely. "It is my friends I fear for."

"Long ago the consequences of involvement were

weighed and judged worthy of risk. The least we can do is to stand with you."

"I need add nothing," said Regina firmly. "I too have faced the cost and will not turn back. It is too late for that, Master Tyndale."

"Then we will see it through to the end," William said.

"And now," said Regina, "let us speak of more pleasant things. Your work in England is in more demand than ever. The *Obedience of a Christian Man* has even reached King Henry."

"Is that so indeed?"

"It was by the hand of Lady Anne Boleyn. It is whispered rather loudly that she will one day become queen. The king has told Cardinal Wolsey to convince the pope to grant his divorce from Catherine.

"It seems that Lady Anne's friend was reading *The Obedience of a Christian Man*. Her suitor begrudged her preoccupation and took it from her. Then he became so engrossed in it himself that he would not return it. It was discovered on him by the bishop and taken away. But when Lady Anne found out, she told the king, who demanded that it be returned to her at once. She then showed it to the king himself, who read it and was pleased."

"And what did King Henry say?" Tyndale asked, moved.

Regina smiled. "His exact words were, 'This book is for me and all kings to read'!"

By 1530 Tyndale's English translation of the Pentateuch appeared in London.

One morning while Tyndale was busy at his work, he heard footsteps running up the stairs. The door opened, and Justin rushed in. "Bishop Tunstall and Thomas More are in Antwerp!"

Tyndale stood, his hand still holding the quill. "They know I am here?"

"No, not yet. Venture not forth onto the street for any purpose. Trust no one. You must remain here in your chamber."

"I will indeed. But if they do not suspect I am here . . ."

"They have come as King Henry's commissioners. A peace treaty at Cambrai is being drawn up between King

Francis and the emperor. One of our own merchants, Augustine Packington, has received a message from Tunstall asking for an audience. I will go with him. And I have asked Felix to be on guard below."

"Let us hope they do not suspect the English House of keeping me."

When Bishop Tunstall arrived at the warehouse on the quay, his fine clothing and crimson velvet hat seemed out of place among the crates and barrels. His shrewd gaze drifted over the wares.

Packington hastened toward him with a discreet bow, then brought him into the small, cluttered office where Justin busied himself at a desk.

"And what might I do for you, good bishop?" asked Packington.

Tunstall took in Justin from head to toe. "Have not I seen your face somewhere before?"

"No doubt, my lord. My business often brings me into London, as well as other ports. But what business brings your lordship?"

"And you do not know?" Tunstall mocked, his lip twitching with an ironic smile. He turned back to Packington, who was a master of businesslike innocence. "My lord bishop?"

"I seek a multitude of heretical works by one outlaw named William Tyndale. I am sure you have heard of him. Such copies of the New Testament are wretchedly translated from Greek into English. They are full of errors and must, for the sake of honor to the church, be destroyed. Surely you know of those Dutchmen and strangers who have brought the books here to sell?"

"My lord, above all others I am sure I can assist you in your endeavor."

"But these foreign merchants shall never hand them over without good price, my lord," Justin pointed out.

"I am quite aware of the greed of merchants. Why else would they risk bringing in forbidden books?"

"Why else indeed? For the singular motive of covetousness, no doubt."

"Do your best to claim every work of Tyndale's, and I vow to pay whatsoever these greedy fish shall demand."

"I shall work most diligently, my lord."

When Tunstall had gone, Packington turned to Justin with a look of surprised pleasure. Then they burst into laughter. The books would be burned, but the high price paid for them would go directly back into Tyndale's purse.

Eventually the task was completed, and the bishop weighed out a bagful of gold guilders. "This is nothing less than robbery."

Packington bowed. "My humble apology, my lord. It was not I who set the price."

Tunstall looked at Justin.

Justin hoped his face was unreadable.

The bishop walked from the dock to where Sir Thomas More waited.

"You have committed a blunder, Bishop Tunstall. Surely the money will only pay for a better edition," said Sir Thomas with a hint of irony.

Tunstall heartily disagreed. "They shall be burned at Saint Paul's Cross. That in itself is a victory. The people, like frightened sheep, will think twice before buying any other copies."

More glanced back over his shoulder toward Packington's office. "I do believe that you underestimate the common man."

Tunstall's thoughts were elsewhere. "I am right glad, Sir Thomas, that you have been commissioned by the church to write against this William Tyndale's heretical works. If any wit can accomplish his ruin, it is yours, Sir Thomas More."

Tyndale now found himself at odds with a far more able opponent than Bishop Tunstall. More was not only a powerful and respected man in Henry's service, but he was also intelligent and a devout subscriber to the Roman church. Before Sir Thomas had finished his attack on William Tyndale, he would write nine books against him and his works, filling more than a thousand pages with arguments against heretics.

But for Tyndale, the "Pen and Ink War" carried on with Sir Thomas could wait until the work at hand was completed.

By 1530 the first five books of the Old Testament were printed in Antwerp and smuggled into England.

Arriving at the English House one day, Justin came to Tyndale's chamber and laid a book in front of him.

Tyndale set down his quill and looked up questioningly.

Justin arched a brow. "Surely you will answer the man?"

Tyndale picked up the book. *Dialogue Concerning Heresies,* by Sir Thomas More.

Justin explained. "He seeks to discredit you and attacks the other Reformers. We are called the 'pestilent sect of Luther and Tyndale.' We are the 'children of iniquity' who translate the Scripture into the common tongue and endanger the church by so doing."

Tyndale leafed through the book, reading snatches of arguments here and there.

"Yet what can I do?" he asked. "I am no match in wit with Sir Thomas More. And my ambition is not to debate theology but to translate the Scriptures. The truth, my friend, will survive such attacks as More makes. History shall be the judge of whether the Scriptures should have remained in Latin alone and the abuses retained in the system. When More and I both have gone from this world, the Word of the Lord will abide."

"What you say is true, but you must answer him," Justin pressed. "If you do not, your silence will be mistaken for defeat. And good men yet in doubt will be left floundering, believing Sir Thomas to have been correct."

"Perhaps, but if I answer him, I shall wax hot."

"Then ease your temper with prayer but answer him. Look at what he says!" Justin seized the book and turned pages. "He says the Roman church cannot err. Has it not already erred in setting aside the authority of Scripture? What More cannot defend on the side of tradition he simply excuses as of minor consequence—the abuses of the clergy, pilgrimages, relics, the veneration and worship of images, and more."

Tyndale scowled and tapped his quill.

Justin slammed the book shut, and his eyes glinted. "He has also attacked your scholarship. The English New Testament is 'corrupted,' so says More. And 'above a thousand texts are wrong and falsely translated, turning wholesome doctrine of Christ to devilish heresies.'"

Tyndale stood abruptly, his face tense. "It seems that Sir Thomas More, keeper of the king's conscience, is so dedicated to upholding the present erroneous traditions that he sees a thousand errors where none exist."

The so-called Pen-and-Ink War—Tyndale versus More —was argued by two capable men but from two separate and distinct premises. Thomas More asserted the supreme authority of the Roman church. William Tyndale appealed to Scripture as final authority. Agreement was impossible.

"When the last jot and tittle of our arguments have been written," said Tyndale, "the Scripture alone will remain as the final judge."

It was a pleasant surprise one day when Tyndale's friend scholar John Frith arrived from Marburg. He had with him a lovely young lady, who hastened to bow to Tyndale.

"And who is this?" William pretended confusion. "Your sister perhaps?"

John Frith smiled and cleared his throat. "My bride, sir."

Tyndale hastened to congratulate them both. They were so obviously in love that he dare not show his sobriety. "You will live here in Antwerp then?"

"Not far away," said Frith. "At least close enough to continue our work together."

Tyndale had always been in danger, but now that Sir Thomas More and the bishop had vehemently attacked both him and his work, efforts to capture him had mounted. The king had spies everywhere, and men had been sent out in disguise hoping to learn his whereabouts in order to bring him to trial in London. In Tyndale's mind he could see nothing but the glowing of kindled fagots.

But he tried to smile. "So fair a bride deserves more than my claim upon your scholarship, John. Go then and enjoy the spring and summer while it shines so pleasantly."

"We will go," said Frith, "but I will return to the work. I have already discussed the danger with her. She understands."

With the coming year the situation changed in England. Cardinal Wolsey, in spite of efforts to please King Henry and thereby maintain his own luxuries and lands, had failed to gain papal permission for the king's divorce from Catherine as quickly as Henry wanted. The cardinal was accused of treason and sentenced to death, but Wolsey's fear was so great that he had died of heart failure on the way to his beheading.

It now seemed beneficial to King Henry to separate England from Rome. By doing so he no longer needed the pope's authority to divorce Catherine and marry Anne Boleyn. But while some in England celebrated the break with Rome, others did not.

Thomas Cromwell replaced More as the king's privy counselor. Protestant in theology, Cromwell supported Tyndale and thought the man would be of benefit to Henry in the court.

One morning he asked the king, "Have you read Tyndale's *Obedience of a Christian Man*"?

King Henry was ready to listen to any suggestion that might help convince dissenters that the break with Rome was right. "I have read it and think the work excellent. What do you suggest?"

"That, Your Majesty, we seek to make amends to Tyndale, who is quite popular with your subjects. We could use a man in touch with the common folk. He might be a powerful force to aid you."

"Then send an envoy to find him. Offer him safe conduct back to England."

"The envoy, Sire, is already at Antwerp."

One night in April 1531, Justin accompanied Tyndale to meet secretly with King Henry's agent, a man named Vaughan.

"And if I return as you ask, what does King Henry expect of me?"

"He offers you the honor of serving in his court."

Justin and William exchanged wary glances.

"To serve the king? How so?"

"The king is much beholden to you for your work *The Obedience of a Christian Man*. Others in the court are also pleased. His new counselor, Thomas Cromwell, for example, and Anne Boleyn. The king wishes a writer and scholar of your merit to serve him at court."

"Does the king not have Thomas More?" Tyndale inquired dryly.

"Sir Thomas does not capture the religious popularity of the common man, who buys your work so readily. You, Master Tyndale, will advance the king's new cause of seeking to elevate his authority over the English church. He offers you a salary and safety."

After the meeting with Vaughan, Justin and William walked back to English House.

"He would simply use you for propaganda purposes," Justin said. "No matter how much we love England and wish to be free men again, how can you compromise your character and the work of the Scriptures to associate yourself with Henry's ambitions? You know the main reason why he wants your service. It would lend credence to his protest cause, that he might then have authority to marry Anne Boleyn."

Tyndale laid a hand on his shoulder. "I know that right well. Yet if we could get the king to agree to an authorized printing of the Bible . . ."

But when two more secret meetings between Tyndale and the king's agent failed to produce an agreement, King Henry sent Vaughan a note rebuking him for "overcompliance" and stating, "I order you to make no further attempt to bring Tyndale to England."

"We must be more cautious now," Justin warned. "The king will surely take a more hostile attitude toward you."

The news was not long in coming that validated Justin's warning. Frustrated, King Henry in typical fashion now reached out to ruin the translator. William's works were widely read and heeded. Since they could not be destroyed, and Tyndale himself would not cooperate and serve the ambitions of the king, little was left but to destroy the man himself.

Henry sent word to the emperor, "I demand Tyndale's surrender on the charge of spreading sedition in England," but the emperor refused to cooperate for reasons of his own. (Catherine, whom the king had divorced, was the emperor's aunt.) However, the new bishop of London after Tunstall's death was Stokesley, one of the strongest opponents of Protestantism in England. And Bishop Stokesley hired a man to search out Tyndale at any cost and betray him.

It was not the news of Tyndale's arrest that reached Justin one morning in 1533 but that of the arrest of the young and brilliant scholar John Frith. His wife sought out Regina.

"They will burn him," she wept.

As she sobbed in Regina's arms, Justin turned away. *How will he break the news about John Frith to Tyndale?* Regina wondered.

"They enticed him to England," Frith's wife said brokenly. "And the bishops deceived him. They sent a feigned supporter of our beliefs as if they would inquire of him something more carefully. He begged John to write it down for him that he might cherish it always. Then this wretched Judas took it straight to Sir Thomas More."

"Thomas More! But he has retired to private life," cried Regina indignantly.

"Yes," said Mrs. Frith, "but Thomas More is privately against Tyndale as much now as he was during his service to King Henry. Sir Thomas then gave evidence of John's faith to the bishops."

Regina sought to comfort her, to stroke her damp brow, to assure her that God Himself would stand with John even as He had with the martyrs before him.

But Regina was ever aware of how she would feel if it were Justin in the Tower, Justin who would face the conclave of bishops on charges of heresy. Justin would not recant any more than Marlon had, or her father, or the hundreds before them.

No words would come, only tears mingling with her friend's. Her whisper was a prayer for courage, strength, and peace.

"He will not recant," Mrs. Frith said at long last. "How can he?" Her eyes sought Regina's.

Regina shook her head, her eyes dimming. No, he would not. He could not.

And John Frith, for aiding William Tyndale in the translation of the first English Bible and for his doctrinal belief in justification by faith in Christ apart from human effort, was burned at the stake for refusing to recant. He endured to the end by the sweet grace of the Spirit of God who indwelled him.

"The persecution in England has reached a new level of intensity," Justin told Tyndale, who sat head in hand, thinking of his martyred friend. "A dozen more beside John Frith died. One recanted, but then in shame turned back to his accusers, and with your New Testament in hand—" Justin halted for fear his voice would break "—and *The Obedience of a Christian Man* in his tunic, recanted of his first denial."

William's hands clenched into fists. After a moment he banged them upon his desk where the revised translation of the New Testament lay. "It is worth our sacrifice. We must always remember that we light the path for others to follow. One day the Word of God will be available for all Christians to own and to read."

He looked up, his eyes moist. "We shall, by God's grace, see that they have it."

21

The wind was soft against her face, and the fragrance of blossoms and the sweet trill of birds mingled with the early morning light. He came to her and kissed her softly.

"Are you sure?" Justin whispered. "Are you sure this is what you want, Regina?"

"I will follow you anywhere. Then why not to Scotland? The Brice castle is yours, the lands, and the title. Felix already said he wishes to come with us. But you, Justin, are you willing to give up the merchant business to Stewert?"

"And why not? The trade between us is fair enough. His half of the castle for my half of the fleet. And as for my galleon, Andrew will be a worthy captain. Did I tell you? He and the Nubian are leaving for the New World."

"It suits Andrew and the Nubian well. Sometimes I think you would also like to join them."

He smiled. "Nay, I have another calling," he said thoughtfully. "We will identify with the spiritual struggle in Scotland. Our friend Patrick Hamilton did not die in vain. There will be others to carry on the reform, and why not us? Already a man named John Knox is teaching the Scriptures there."

"Then we will go—with God's blessing and guidance."

"We will go. But we cannot leave as long as we are needed here," he said. "If God continues to use us here, we must stay, whatever the cost."

"Yes, but I fear for William's life. I do not trust the new man from the university at Louvain—that Henry Philips. He may be an Englishman, and he may have made friends with the merchants, but I find something in his attitude which savors of self-seeking. Why does he ask so many questions of William?"

Justin too was bothered by Henry Philips. The man had fled Flanders after robbing his father but was said to have repented and now wanted nothing more than to learn as much as he could about the teaching of the Reformed faith. He had won Tyndale's compassion by claiming great zeal for the Scriptures.

"And why has he sought out Thomas Poynitz for friendship?" Regina continued. "Master Poynitz took him on a tour of Antwerp, and the man kept asking questions about the leaders of the town and of the buildings and alleys."

"I will certainly speak to William again about him," Justin said. "But William is not a man to be harsh with a new convert. You know how patient he was with Roye. And Henry Philips is eloquent. The fact that he enrolled in Oxford a few years ago only makes him more favorable in William's eyes. Not to mention that he comes from a wealthy family and is therefore assumed to be a gentleman."

"I do not trust him," Regina declared. "I have had no peace recently."

The next day Justin managed to get William away from his desk long enough for a walk along the harbor. The May morning was pleasant with promise and the walk among the ships refreshing. The shrill call of sea gulls pierced the morning haze, and the water slapped the sleeping hulls.

"You may be right, my friend, yet what do you really have against Henry Philips?"

"In truth, I do not know. Yet he is too inquisitive of your work and your habits. He could be an agent of Bishop Stokesley. With agents hunting for you all over Europe, we cannot be too cautious of strangers. If a Judas comes, he will not appear with a drawn sword but with a kiss."

Tyndale seemed hardly able to imagine that the easy manner of Henry Philips was a masquerade. Perhaps he missed John Frith too much to believe the gracious and mild Henry to be an enemy.

"With King Henry having set forth the Act of Supremacy, putting an end to Rome's authority in England, I think he does not work for the throne," William said. "If he serves anyone, it would be the bishop."

"Perhaps he serves no one but himself, but you must be careful."

Tyndale took Justin's words to heart. Yet his attention wavered from Henry Philips to the changes in England.

King Henry had moved to establish himself as head of the Church of England. Would this not mean a lessening of the stringent laws against heretics? Thomas More, who resisted the break with the pope, was now himself in the Tower and about to lose his head.

And Queen Anne Boleyn had within her keeping a gilded copy of the Scriptures printed in Antwerp. Would King Henry now move to authorize the Scriptures in the common tongue and permit them in the churches?

"Cromwell is in firm favor of such a move," Justin told him. "But the king has made no such change in his policy. It was not for personal conviction of the truth that he broke with Rome but to secure his own ambitions."

"True, yet God may use this to His own purpose. That which has recently transpired in the court of London may prove to be a crack in the walls of Jericho."

"It may be," said Justin. "Yet matters here in Antwerp have grown worse."

Tyndale grew silent. That was true indeed. They knew of two Reformers who had been burned in Antwerp. The emperor had ordered the queen regent of the Netherlands to put an end to heresy at any cost, and the bishops were authorized to do whatever they deemed necessary to crush the Protestant movement. Even possessing certain books sanctioned by doctors teaching at Louvain University was now against the law.

"I am not the only one concerned for your safety in Antwerp," pressed Justin. "Poyntz has spoken to me of this same matter. He will be gone from the city for some time. He has urged me to warn you to take no chances, not even with those who say they favor our beliefs. There are now many spies who have infiltrated the movement."

"Fear not, I shall be on guard."

Justin said suddenly, "Regina and I are soon to try our hand in Scotland. Will you come with us?"

Tyndale smiled. "I wish your witness in Scotland to flourish as the heather itself in spring. Yet I cannot follow. I will remain here. I am safe until my work is done."

Still troubled, Justin walked back with William to his chamber at the English House. Tyndale at once resumed his work on his new edition of the New Testament. Justin stood watching for a moment, then turned as a servant appeared on the steps.

"It is your father, sir. I fear that he has taken ill. He is on board Captain Stewert Brice's ship."

Justin found Regina and Stewert in the cabin and his father lying on the small bed. Felix too was there, and Andrew.

Justin knelt, taking his father's hand.

"'Tis only a little pain in me chest," Captain Ewan said with difficulty, pale and perspiring. "'Twill go away. What did you feed me?" he tried to jest with Stewert.

Stewert drew near and knelt beside Justin. For the first time in his life Stewert broke down. His heavy shoulders shook as he buried his face in his father's neck. "You must not leave us, my father. 'Tis only now we began to know each other."

Ewan Brice sighed heavily, his breathing labored.

Justin saw him try to solace Stewert with a weak squeeze of his hand.

"How can we aid you?" Justin asked. "Has a doctor been sent for?"

"He has," said Regina. "It happened so quickly . . ."

"Tsk," whispered the old captain. "'Twas a long time in coming. A very long time. Weep not for me, my sons. I go to a far fairer abode than ever we have found here."

He reached out now to Justin, who clasped his hand in both of his. The blue eyes grew moist as they rested on his younger son's face. "Yea . . . your precious mother was right in naming you so . . . a better son I could not have been blessed with. It is for you to be strong . . . the work is only beginning . . . you must carry it to Scotland, lad . . . she languishes."

"Yes," whispered Justin, "to Scotland."

Ewan Brice turned his eyes to Stewert. "And you, my troubled lion . . . you must find peace."

"I have peace, Father, but regrets as well."

Captain Ewan tried to shake his head but failed.

Stewert leaned his ear close to his father's mouth as the old man whispered, "Forgetting . . . those things which are behind . . . reaching forth . . . unto those things which are before . . . let us . . . press on to Christ."

"I had hoped we might have lunch together, Master Tyndale," said Henry Philips in his gracious manner. "But the fine dame of the House assures me you were going out this afternoon to dine elsewhere. A pity! For I wished to speak to you about a friend, a priest by the name of Gabrielle Donne. He is likely to be appointed the new abbot of Buckfastleigh in Devon. He seems inclined toward the need of reform, and I thought you might set him to the right path with your fair works."

Again, as he had in the past, the tall and handsome Henry Philips moved about Tyndale's chamber, admiring his small library and speaking zealously of his work. "The light has dawned upon England, Master Tyndale, and who shall be able to put it out?"

"Yes, but it has not shone brightly enough, Henry. I shall not be content until the king authorizes the usage of the Scriptures in churches and homes."

"May God grant it to be so." Henry Philips sighed.

William stood and smiled. "I would not think of sending you away without a hearty discourse over lunch. Surely Mistress Poynitz will be right glad to have you at her table."

"I fear not, sir. With Mr. Poynitz out of town these weeks, I would not wish to impose. I would ask you to be my guest in town, but to my embarrassment I left my purse in my room." He shook his head and threw up his hands as if disgusted with himself. "I suppose I was only anxious to tell you of my friend."

"You shall be my guest," said Tyndale suddenly. "I will be most interested to hear of the priest."

Henry Philips hastened to grab Tyndale's cloak from its hook, and he smiled. "You are truly a fair man, William Tyndale. I shall not forget this kindness."

The cramped, cobbled streets of Antwerp twisted and turned in many directions. Some of the passages Henry Philips led him down were so narrow that the men had to walk single file. The buildings overhead cast dark shadows upon their path.

Henry Philips lapsed into silence, which Tyndale found unusual. Walking beside him now, William's mind turned to Justin's warning. He looked sideways at the young man, who hurried along. His breathing seemed rapid and his jaw tense. Tiny beads of moisture glistened on his smooth forehead.

Tyndale then became aware of several soldiers ahead, holding drawn swords. Suddenly he stopped and understood. The street narrowed further, affording no escape. A sigh escaped his lips, and he drew his worn cloak more tightly about his thin shoulders.

Henry Philips stepped behind him, and the soldiers came running.

Tyndale made no move to turn and flee. The rope cut into his flesh as they hurriedly bound him.

"Let me return for my books and papers," he pleaded.

But without a word they ushered him off to the attorney's home, some twenty-four miles away, and then on horseback to the somber castle of Vilvoorde, six miles from Brussels.

Justin knocked on William's door and waited. When there was no answer he lifted the latch and looked in. The chamber had been ransacked.

In two strides he was at his friend's desk. The books and papers were gone! In a moment of hopeless wrath against his own simplicity, he slammed his fist against the table with a cry. Then he ran to the stairs and shouted for the servant.

"I have been out this afternoon, Sir Brice," he said, "but earlier Master Tyndale left with Henry Philips."

Regina rushed to Justin's side. Apparently one look at his face told her what had happened. "Henry Philips."

At his wife's urgent message, Thomas Poynitz returned to Antwerp. Having gathered with Walter Marsh, the leader of the English House, and other merchant friends, he paced the floor in anguish. The others sat stunned, shaking their heads in anger or grief.

Regina stood in the background, listening.

"It is my error. I should have known better than to trust him," Poynitz said.

"We are all to blame. We should have guarded William more carefully," lamented Augustine Packington in disbelief.

"This is an unheard of breach of privilege of the English merchants. They had no right to enter this house nor to search his chamber. We shall protest to the court in Brussels."

"And write to John also," said Mrs. Poynitz—her husband's brother was lord of the manor of North Ockenden in Essex. "Perhaps he can appeal to King Henry."

"We will all write and work tirelessly to do what we can," said another sadly, "but I fear our strength is too small to aid William now that he is out of our authority here."

"Yes, I fear the same," said Poynitz. "Charles the Fifth is turning upon the Protestants with swift wrath since King Henry tore England asunder from Rome. He wishes to convince Rome he is a loyal son. Yet I am determined to fight this with all my strength. The death of Tyndale will be a great hindrance to the gospel and to the enemies of it one of the highest pleasures."

Throughout the meeting, Justin had remained silent. He stood now staring out the window as the last rays of daylight flickered over the harbor. He knew—and Regina knew—that William Tyndale was in a dungeon in Vilvoorde Castle, and fifty armed men could not get him out, much less the protests of Thomas Poynitz and the merchants.

Regina came up beside him and silently slipped her cold trembling hand into his. He put his arm about her waist and drew her close.

Good to his word, Thomas Poynitz labored tirelessly to have Tyndale released. He pled unsuccessfully with King Henry and Cromwell for their intervention. "You have never had a more loyal subject than in the translator nor a man of higher character," he wrote.

Justin and Regina, in company with the other English merchants, appealed to the queen regent, Mary of Hungary. Their efforts proved fruitless as well.

Finally Justin told Regina, "I must go to Vilvoorde to try to see him."

Regina's heart seemed to lurch. "If something ill befalls you," she pleaded, "I do not know if I can bear it."

His voice was calm and steady, and she did not like the implication of quiet resolve nor the look of gravity in his eyes. "I will return to you," he insisted.

"If not . . ." Her voice broke.

"By the grace of God, Regina, I will. Then we will go to Scotland as we planned. Stewert has offered to take us there."

But she was not listening. "If you must go to Vilvoorde, I too shall go." Her hands clutched at his arms. "If something happens . . ."

He kissed her gently. "No, Regina, not this time." His determination silenced the protest on her tongue. "This time you must stay. Andrew and Felix have promised to guard you. I shall be back in a fortnight. I promise."

He embraced her, and she clung to him. He kissed her, then turned and left. She watched until he was out of sight.

Felix then spoke to her. "Have peace, my lady. Master Justin will return. He wishes to go alone because he knows that Master Tyndale shall die, and he wishes you not to see it. Yet his own allegiance to all that William Tyndale dies for demands that he be there with him."

22

Brussels, 1535–1536

William Tyndale rubbed his cold, stiff hands together to regain some feeling before picking up his quill. He glanced toward the dim light of the tiny window that still gave him a precious few hours to write. The frigid cell was dank and foul, and the sound of the lapping water of the moat drifted to his ears. The quill scratched as in Latin he began in thoughtful deliberation.

I believe, right Worshipful, that you are not ignorant of what has been determined concerning me by the Council of Brabant; therefore I entreat your Lordship, and that by the Lord Jesus, that if I am to remain here during the winter, you will request the Procurer to be kind enough to send me from my goods, which he has in his possession, a warmer cap, for I suffer extremely from cold in the head, being afflicted with perpetual catarrh, which is considerable in the cell.

A warmer coat also, for that which I have is very thin; also a piece of cloth to patch my leggings; my overcoat has been worn out. He has a woolen shirt of mine, if he will be kind enough to send it. I have also with him leggings of thicker cloth for the putting on above; he also has warmer caps for wearing at night. I wish also his permission to have a candle in the evening, for it is wearisome to sit alone in the dark.

But above all, I entreat and beseech your clemency to be urgent with the Procurer that he may kindly permit me to have my Hebrew Bible, Hebrew Grammar, and Hebrew Dictionary, that I may spend my time with that study. And in return, may you obtain your dearest wish, provided always it be consistent with the salvation of your soul. But if any other resolutions have been come to concerning me, before the conclusion of the winter, I shall be patient, abiding the will of

God to the glory of the grace of my Lord Jesus Christ, whose spirit, I pray, may ever direct your heart. Amen.

W. Tyndale

The end, Tyndale had thought, would come swiftly, but he was wrong. For fifteen months in this dank dungeon, cold and infested with rats, he waited for the decision. The commission that was to judge him was appointed in the autumn by the queen regent in service to Emperor Charles V. Tyndale had one small satisfaction—for those who could not speak English, his accusers had to translate his works from English into Latin. As they labored over his writings he hoped the light might begin to dawn upon their own minds.

The wet winter was over before the trial proceeded. Tyndale was sure what the outcome would be. But the delay gave him opportunity to continue work on the translation of the Old Testament. Late into the night he translated by candlelight, and his quill scratched boldly on the theme of the believer's justification by faith. His soul burned with the flame of that profound truth even though his body shivered with cold and rheumatism.

One supreme conviction held his desire captive—the need for King Henry VIII to permit the bare text of the English translation to be placed in the churches throughout England. To that end he prayed, to that end he continued to labor, knowing his time was short.

For more than six months he was questioned. The prosecuting ecclesiastics visited him in his cell or had him brought by the guard to the great hall, where the judges sat at a long ornate table, robed grandly in religious garb or severely in civic robes. The oral examination was conducted in Latin and centered primarily on theological disputes.

In early August 1536 the commission rendered its judgment.

Torches blazed down upon the gathering as the procurer general stood holding a long scroll of accusations. He fixed his gaze upon William, standing silent before them. As the procurer's ponderous voice distinctly articulated the charges, the words echoed in the stone hall.

"William Tyndale, you do stand before this authorized

commission as one hereby found guilty of the charges of heresy. By such evidence as we have before us in written form in your own hand, which you have also confessed as true by your own tongue, you are branded by your superiors as a wretched man, guilty of unlawfully translating the Scripture from Latin into English.

"And secondly, you are accused of doctrinal heresy in propagating the belief that faith in Jesus Christ alone justifies the sinner. At the same time you are adamant in clinging to your belief that tradition has no divine authority to bind the Christian's conscience to supreme obedience to the teachings of the church at Rome but have set such divine traditions aside as secondary to the teaching of the Scriptures.

"In so doing you are in disobedience to the true head of the Church, even His Holiness as Saint Peter's successor, and thereby your lord and master. In so propagating these heresies in favor of the heretical beliefs of the reformational faith, you have denied the teaching of the church by setting aside the doctrine of purgatory, the intercession of the virgin and saints on our behalf, and that they should not be evoked by the Christian in his soul's deliverance.

"This commission, in the month of August and in the year of our Lord 1536, finds you, William Tyndale, supremely guilty according to the imperial laws against heresy. Thereby you are found to be worthy of the sentence of degradation and death. Amen."

Justin rode his horse in view of Vilvoorde, which stood sullenly against the bleak fall sky. The castle had been built in 1374 by a duke of Brabant, and it was comparable to the Bastille, constructed in Paris about the same time. Surrounded by a moat and having seven high towers and three drawbridges, the thick walls made Vilvoorde an impregnable fortress. The castle was now being used as the state prison for the Low Countries.

He crossed the wooden drawbridge, and the horse's hoofs echoed. The gate was open, and he rode through. A number of rugged soldiers were on duty, and an officer stopped him abruptly.

Justin handed him the letter he had received from the

procurer in reply to his own. The officer handed it back and ushered him across the courtyard to an inner bailey. Rough-hewn steps led him up into a keep where the procurer's guard met him.

"You are permitted a brief visit. I myself shall accompany you."

The stone passage to the dungeons was lit with torches. Another flight of steps led down below the castle. Justin felt the cold dampness penetrate his woolen cloak.

He walked to the barred cell, and Tyndale looked up. At first William squinted to see who it was. Perhaps he thought it might be the soldiers of the imperial guard come to take him away.

Then, recognizing his visitor, Tyndale was on his feet and quickly to the bars. They grasped each other's arms in mutual affection.

"I thought I would never see a friendly face again, least of all yours," said William. "The Lord has granted me a kindness indeed!"

"We have interceded before King Henry and Cromwell, but the matter goes ill. If England is no longer bent on your destruction, it has done little to intercede. Cromwell did write to the governor of Vilvoorde but without success. It seems that since Charles the Fifth of Spain has failed to burn Luther, he will be satisfied to have you."

William was silent for a moment. "I have expected no better, my friend. If they shall burn me, they shall do none other thing than I looked for. There is none other way into the kingdom of life than through persecution and suffering and of very death after the example of Christ. But our enemy is not flesh and blood. It is the archenemy of Christ Himself, who bestirs men's minds to wrath and rejection of His Truth."

"You have said it well. If ever the light is to dawn, it will come through spiritual warfare and will mean the sacrifice of many," Justin said. "The enemy fears nothing more than the light of the Scriptures spreading throughout the world. And so I shall go on to Edinburgh."

Tyndale seemed to consider his statement. He was quiet, then slowly nodded. "You have chosen a rocky path to tread, yet worth the momentary sacrifice."

"Thomas Poynitz was arrested but is now free."

"Praise God for that. I should be loath to die knowing I have brought such a good friend to death with me."

"They speak of his banishment from the Low Countries and the loss of his business, but he and certain of the English merchants are determined to go on. Your arrest has kindled their zeal even further. I bring you their hearty affection, their deep gratitude for your work, Master Tyndale, and their unceasing prayers for your strength and courage."

"Being of like mind, Justin, the fellowship of your own convictions is an encouragement to me now. With the fairest of apostles I can say, 'My departure is at hand.'"

The guard motioned that his time was up.

Justin took off his woolen cloak. Then he looked to the guard for permission to give it to the prisoner.

The soldier stepped forward and examined every inch of cloth before nodding. Tyndale took the garment gratefully.

"Then it is here we part," Justin said.

There was a shared moment of deep silence. Then Justin gripped Tyndale's forearm through the bars. "As a lesser soldier I dare to leave you these words—the grace of Christ will be with you, and His nearness shall consume your heart with peace. And when in that moment you stand alone before those who are the lions of your flesh, remember to lean hard upon His breast for all that your soul shall tremble to face, and you will, according to His faithfulness, find it not wanting.

"For it is written that the death of His saints is precious in His sight. How much more a man who has labored to suffer any price and bear any burden these many years to bring His Word to the people of England. Yes, Master William Tyndale, your labors by the Spirit of God will not be in vain. Generations will arise to pronounce your name good. And the names of those who once stood so mighty in position to oppose you in translating the Holy Scriptures into English will be remembered for ill, as fighting not you but God."

Clearly Tyndale was moved. "Your words of solace are accepted in humble gratitude. Go and be at peace as well. I face the future with eternal confidence. I should rather be a doorkeeper in the house of the Lord than to dwell in the tents of wickedness, however comfortable they may be. No, not all their fair robes nor their momentary glory will be worth one glimpse of His face. And I? By His finished work of redemption I shall see it forever! Farewell. Go and be faithful in the place God has put you to serve Him."

On August 10 the ritual of degradation began—that of casting William Tyndale out of the church as a heretic.

Escorted by the imperial guard, Tyndale was led to the town square where a crowd had gathered. His eyes flickered over the curious faces of peasants and wealthier townsfolk. How many of them truly understood the reason for his ordeal? There was a din of voices, then silence, as the pageant of ecclesiastical and civil dignitaries assembled on the raised platform. As his eyes moved, they fell on Justin below in the crowd.

Tyndale was wearing a priest's robe. To acquire that robe he had first entered Magdalen College in 1508 as a young boy. For eight tedious years at Oxford he had excelled in theology, the arts, and especially in the original languages, to receive his Master of Arts, then on to Cambridge for extensive studies in Greek.

But now the painful ritual in reverse began. They forced him to kneel, and the knife in the agent's hand symbolically scraped away the oil of priestly consecration from his hands and bowed head.

Then they hauled him to his feet. Across the platform came a priest bringing the bread and wine of the Lord's Supper. As requested, Tyndale accepted the bread and the cup. But as he took them, the agent abruptly struck both from his hands, and they scattered across the platform.

A groan from the crowd was drowned out by a somber Latin chant, uttering condemnation, denying him the right to partake of the sacrament the church leaders thought was necessary for eternal life.

The priest's vesture was then ripped from his body. The bishop's fulminations could be heard over the echo of tolling bells.

It was now October, and the sun was crimson on the horizon of Vilvoorde as Tyndale was led for the last time across the square to his place of death. The chill wind pierced his worn clothes and rustled the woolen cloak Justin had given him.

239

A crowd was already in position behind a barricade of stakes, which had been hastily thrown up the night before in order to keep back what the authorities knew would be a large gathering. In that crowd mingled friend, foe, and the merely curious.

In the center of the square was a large wooden pole, his place of execution. A long chain hung from the post, and a noose of hemp was laced through it.

For the second time the ecclesiastical pageantry took place. Clerics assumed their elevated positions, their faces grave.

Justin interceded silently in prayer as William Tyndale raised his hands to be tied. He watched the executioner place the chain about Tyndale's throat, then wait silently for the command.

The steadfast look of conviction on Tyndale's haggard face brought a flash of unutterable emotion to Justin's heart. The purpose for which Tyndale would die was, as it had always been, firm and irrevocable. Neither the feel of the harsh rope nor the restriction of the tightening chain unnerved the soul the indwelling Christ was sustaining. In heaven, Christ the great High Priest made intercession for His servant, and Tyndale knew the faithfulness of the One he had served.

William Tyndale's accuser now shouted, "You wretched soul, recant! Consider your destiny, O heretic. Recant now! Save yourself from the flame."

But it was as if another voice—from heaven and from within Tyndale himself—silenced the earthly din. Like the sound of a trumpet, and as sweetly as a dove, the voice told Tyndale, "I am with you . . . be faithful unto death, and I will give you a crown of life . . . you shall walk with Me in white . . . I will never leave you, nor forsake you."

William Tyndale took a deep breath and lifted his voice in passionate prayer, "Lord, open the king of England's eyes!"

The fagots, brush, and wood were piled about his feet. The executioner moved at signal, and Tyndale was strangled. The attorney stepped forward then and with a torch set the brush to leaping flame.

23

London, 1537

Thomas Cromwell waited before King Henry VIII, who sat considering the gravity of the document in his hand. The king read its appointed and assigned injunctions.

> Given by the authority of the King's Highness to the Clergy of this his Realm, designed for the reformation of the Church. . . .
>
> I, Thomas Cromwell, knight, keeper of the privy seal of our said sovereign lord the king . . . have appointed that any person or proprietary of any parish church within this realm . . . provide a book of the Bible in . . . English, and lay the same in the choir for every man that wills to look and read thereon, and shall discourage no man from reading of any part of the Bible, in Latin or English, but rather to comfort, exhort, and admonish every man to read the same, as the very Word of God.

King Henry hesitated. Then, instead of tossing the document aside in rejection, he gestured his approval to Cromwell, who hastened to bow and place it with others that the king had approved and merely awaited his signature.

The king had just approved publication of a new English Bible published by Matthew Coverdale, a friend of William Tyndale's. Little did Henry know that the new Bible was nearly 70 percent Tyndale's work.

Assured that the edition was free of heresy, Henry VIII proclaimed, "Well, if there be no heresies in it, then let it be spread abroad among all the people!"

And in 1611 a new king from Scotland, James I, would authorize the King James Version, which would contain some 90 percent of Tyndale's wording.

* * *

The galleon of Captain Stewert Brice moved silently from the harbor of Antwerp and out into the broader waters of the North Sea toward Edinburgh.

The wind was fresh on her face as Regina stood on deck with Justin. He drew her into his arms, and she smiled, returning his embrace.

"Do you have any reservations, Regina?"

She wrinkled her nose at him. "What a baiting question! My reservations alter with the winds of persecution," she confessed wryly. "As you know very well. But my convictions are anchored to the Scriptures. And so, to Scotland," she declared firmly with a little smile. "It is onward, ever onward, knowing in whom we trust as guide."

He gave her an enthusiastic hug. "Since the death of Patrick Hamilton, there has arisen one John Knox at the University of Saint Andrews. By the distribution of William Tyndale's New Testaments we shall soon light a torch for the Scottish Reformation."

Below in the hold was a shipment of Testaments, packed in crates.

Regina smiled up at him and softly touched his cheek with her hand. Her mind wandered to the future and what it would bring.

Justin was talking now, intensely, of the Scriptures and justification by faith. His voice came with a compelling cadence that reminded her of those who had gone before, and her eyes clung to his as the wind blew and the ship moved forward.

Then Justin lifted her chin and kissed her softly. "Regina, Regina, we could, if you wish, go back to London. It is safer there now."

When she spoke after a moment, her voice was steady. "No. At this time we must count the cost and go forward. We now hold in our hands the Word of God. We will not forget the cost so many paid that we may have it." She looked up at him. "How shall we ever forget William Tyndale?"

"We will not," Justin said firmly. "Now that the fire is kindled, we will work to make it burn even brighter by a commitment to teach the Scriptures. We will follow those who went before us, that God might use us to multiply their labors."

He suddenly swung her off her feet. "Come. For this moment we have each other. And tomorrow? It is enough that Christ and His Word will be there to sustain."

He set her down firmly, and she grabbed his hand. "I feel like singing one of Martin Luther's new hymns—'A Mighty Fortress Is Our God.'"

They began, but their voices soon lapsed from singing to simply speaking the words ever so softly as they held each other. The night was sinking about them, and the stars appeared silver in the sky.

> And tho' this world, with devils filled,
> Should threaten to undo us;
> We will not fear, for God hath willed
> His truth to triumph through us.
> The Prince of Darkness grim,
> We tremble not for him;
> His rage we can endure,
> For lo! his doom is sure!
> One little word shall fell him.
>
> Let goods and kindred go,
> This mortal life also;
> The body they may kill:
> God's truth abideth still.
> His kingdom is forever.

EPILOGUE

I think it meet that every Christian man not only know [Romans] by rote and without the book, but also exercise himself therein evermore continually, as with the daily bread of the soul. No man verily can read it too oft or study it too well; for the more it is studied the easier it is, the more it is chewed the pleasanter it is, and the more roundly it is searched the preciouser things are found in it, so great treasure of spiritual things lieth hid therein. . . .

Now go to, Reader, and according to the order of Paul's writing, even so do thou.

First, behold thyself diligently in the law of God, and see there thy just damnation. Secondarily turn thy eye to Christ, and see there the exceeding mercy of thy most kind and loving Father. Thirdly remember that Christ made not this atonement that thou shouldst anger God again: neither died he for thy sins, that thou shouldst live still in them: neither cleansed he thee, that thou shouldst return (as a swine) unto thine own puddle again: but that thou shouldst be a new creature and live a new life after the will of God.

William Tyndale
Prologue to the Epistle of Romans, 1534 edition